ON THE EDGE

"Murray, I'm going to catch him and I'm going to kill him."

"Of course you are," said Murray.

"I've got an edge, Murray," he said. "Sometimes, when I look inside myself, I can picture what he looks like; what he wants to do; what makes him move. Sometimes I even know what he feels. I mean, it's nothing hard, but I can still use that. I can use it all to get him. That's my secret, Murray. That's my edge."

Murray paused, considering what Adam had said, then chose his words carefully. "Your kid disappeared," he said slowly, deliberately. "You're a father chasing after his daughter. Things may not be as clear as you think. Understand me? Can you follow that?"

Adam didn't answer.

"Adam?" Murray shouted. "Hey, will you please relax?"

But Adam glanced at his watch, hung up the phone, and walked quickly to the door. He was already ten minutes late.

BLOCKBUSTER FICTION FROM PINNACLE BOOKS!

THE FINAL VOYAGE OF THE S.S.N. SKATE   (17-157, $3.95)
by Stephen Cassell
The "leper" of the U.S. Pacific Fleet, SSN 578 nuclear attack sub SKATE, has one final mission to perform—an impossible act of piracy that will pit the underwater deathtrap and its inexperienced crew against the combined might of the Soviet Navy's finest!

QUEENS GATE RECKONING   (17-164, $3.95)
by Lewis Purdue
Only a wounded CIA operative and a defecting Soviet ballerina stand in the way of a vast consortium of treason that speeds toward the hour of mankind's ultimate reckoning! From the best-selling author of THE LINZ TESTAMENT.

FAREWELL TO RUSSIA   (17-165, $4.50)
by Richard Hugo
A KGB agent must race against time to infiltrate the confines of U.S. nuclear technology after a terrifying accident threatens to unleash unmitigated devastation!

THE NICODEMUS CODE   (17-133, $3.95)
by Graham N. Smith and Donna Smith
A two-thousand-year-old parchment has been unearthed, unleashing a terrifying conspiracy unlike any the world has previously known, one that threatens the life of the Pope himself, and the ultimate destruction of Christianity!

Available wherever paperbacks are sold, or order direct from the Publisher. Send cover price plus 50¢ per copy for mailing and handling to Pinnacle Books, Dept.17-488, 475 Park Avenue South, New York, N.Y. 10016. Residents of New York, New Jersey and Pennsylvania must include sales tax. DO NOT SEND CASH.

DISAPPEARANCE
JAMES COHEN

PINNACLE BOOKS
WINDSOR PUBLISHING CORP.

PINNACLE BOOKS

are published by

Windsor Publishing Corp.
475 Park Avenue South
New York, NY 10016

First Pinnacle Books printing: March, 1991

Printed in the United States of America

For everyone whom I've ever promised a dedication.

And my parents and brothers, who are, individually and together, wonderful.

And Lori E.C.C.—S.P., P.B, and A.A.G.G.

And Susie Maddox, with love from the whole family, north and south.

Chapter I

Fifty milligrams of pentobarbital, and the town of Calverton turned into a blur of concrete.

The sidewalks — sandy mixes of gravel and cement, cleanly carved and in long geometric rows — became one seamless strip of perfect city landscaping. The cracks and dirt, the litter and clumps of weeds — all the slight imperfections that show the age of a town — disappeared. It was all washed away by a sun that grew more powerful as the eyes dilated. Instead of a sewer grating, there was only a shadow. Nor were the trees visible, the leaves blending into a mass of color. There had been a summer shower, and the effect was blinding.

Should he reach for the sunglasses?

No; instead, he reached for the beaker. He put the lip of the container to his mouth and focused on his watch. Two ten in the afternoon. His usual late lunch just beginning, and the city disappearing for its designated hour. He stared out the side office window, guarding his eyes, trying to make sense of the passing people that interfered with his view. White people, black, yellow . . . If they moved close together, they were no different from the trees.

He took another sip from the beaker.

Seventy milligrams, and the people disappeared.

He rested against the counter, folding his arms and hiding his eyes in the sleeve of his white smock. His badge pressed into his chest: ADAM DRUIT, PHARMACIST. But to Adam, the badge and his body were as distant as the long row of bottles and pills. There was only the window, his imagination, and the beaker.

Still, that was more than all Calverton could boast. Calverton was a suburban town identified by exits, not landmarks. The few times Calverton had grown, it grew on top of itself, without regard for what once had been. Brick buildings pressed so close to sagging frame houses the buildings crushed them, splintering boards and nails into the front yards.

Downtown was the same, except for a handful of stores and, of course, the pharmacy, where Adam spent six days a week, nine hours a day. The Main Pharmacy, on Main Street—the one street Adam knew; thirty miles from Providence, and, more important, a hundred fifty miles from New York, a distance he made feel longer by keeping his car short on gas.

Calverton—as close as you could get to hiding in the fold of a map. Not only the perfect escape; it was also the perfect punishment. Now all he had to do was lose himself completely. He had to make the roads disappear, and the people, and himself. He needed the kind of peace some people found in death.

Instead of suicide, he found it in his favorite drugstore.

He looked over his shoulder and saw the store's owner, Murray Tuckerman, by the cash register. Murray was watching him, but Adam didn't care. What would Murray do—fire him? Fire the best damned pharmacist Murray would ever be lucky enough to find?

Christ, getting fired in Calverton?

Adam finished drinking from his beaker. One hundred milligrams of pentobarbital, and Murray disappeared.

It was nothing short of heaven. The hands on his watch wavered, and the minutes dripped away. He thought about the drug taking control of his body. What had been the lesson in school? Pentobarbital—a barbiturate, with deep sedative effects; almost hypnotic. Usual dosage: 120 to 200 milligrams. Result—an attack on the central nervous system. A deadening of the senses, particularly for pain. With an overdose, likely cause of death would be respiratory failure. No death today, though. If he overdosed from anything, it would be from the ringing of the cash register. A line of locals were hitting Murray's store for lottery tickets, pretending they had a chance to win, never thinking that if there was any luck in their lives, they'd be elsewhere. Instead, the customers kept repeating their lucky number, and Murray kept ringing in the dollars. "33-12-1-29. 30-23-14-6. 10-3-1-15 . . ."

Murray repeated the sequences to make sure he got them right. "34-40-6-35. That's one dollar."

"When can I get my film?" asked the customer.

Murray sighed and looked to a glass cabinet on the other side of the store. "You want it now?" he answered, his voice as tired and heavy as his body. Murray was in his fifties, and after working a lifetime, any trip from one side of the store to the other deserved a show of agony. But the man insisted, and

Murray took the receipt and went for the photos. "Number 03321," he said, reaching for the film packet. Sometimes it seemed half his life was spent reading numbers. "That's five dollars, fifty cents."

"Also my prescription," said the customer. "My Lomotil."

"Lomotil, Lomotil," Murray muttered. It was his pharmacy, but he wasn't the pharmacist, just the owner and manager. He returned to the drug counter, climbing the half step that gave him a clearer view of the store's three cramped aisles. From here he could see every person in the store, even when the store was crowded — like on lottery days, or during the Christmas season, when he sold the bulbs and the lights and the tinsel.

"You want me to shit on the floor?" the customer said. "Give me my prescription."

"I don't think it's been filled," said Murray.

"What's to fill?" said the customer. "Lomotil is Lomotil. Just take a bottle off the shelf and give it to me."

Murray wanted to say that would be against the law, but in a town without a good cop, what would be the point. "I don't know where he keeps the bottles."

"It's a small, plastic container," said the customer. "It says Lomotil on the outside and it helps my runs. Is that enough?"

Murray leaned back, glaring at his dozing pharmacist. Goddamn addict, he thought. Adam didn't know it, but Murray had seen him taking the pills out of the bottles and into his pockets. Murray now figured these losses into his prices and rescued his profit margin; still, it wasn't good business having someone in the shop who didn't keep his hands off

10

the merchandise. A soda jerk shouldn't eat ice cream, and a pharmacist shouldn't pop pills.

"I don't like to bother him on his lunch break," Murray told his customer.

The customer squinted hard, as if his bladder was going to give up on the spot and ruin Murray's linoleum. "Lomotil," he said painfully.

Murray sighed. "Let me take a look," he said, resigning himself to the shelves.

It was the one part of his store that had become a complete mystery to him. Aisles 1, 2, and 3 . . . no problem. But when he wandered into the land of antibiotics and histamines; of pills, powders, and elixirs . . . He picked up a liter vial that had been filled with a thick yellow liquid. Murray sniffed the liquid, then swirled it, watching the drug make a film about the glass.

The customer watched. "It's not yellow, and it don't come in bottles," he said. "It's in a tiny brown plastic container, and it's got my name on the side."

Murray kept looking through the rows of brown bottles. Ampicillin, tolbutamide, Metolazone.

"I don't see your name anywhere," said Murray.

"Well, it don't have to have my name on it," said the customer. "Just so long as it has my pills."

Murray glared at the man, then turned back to the impossible confusion of drugs.

"Lanotine," Murray murmured.

"Lomotil," the customer corrected.

Murray slapped his head, as if that had been the problem all along. He stopped by a shelf and reached for one of the brown bottles. He read the label, wondering what sort of drug had a name like allopurinol.

Adam grabbed his wrist.

11

Murray jumped like he was a shoplifter in his own store. "Look who's back from the dead," Murray said, still holding the allopurinol. In Murray's other hand was the prescription for Lomotil. Adam pulled free the slip of paper and held it close to his eyes. Murray watched. It was rare for Adam to wake from his midday "naps," and when he did, he was always a horrible sight. This time was no different.

"Front cabinet, by the register," said Adam.

"Front cabinet," Murray said, carrying out the mission. A moment later, he had unlocked the case and found almost ten bottles of Lomotil. Murray dropped the drug in a bag and rang up the charge, adding an extra fifty cents for the labor. The customer wasted no time taking the first of his pills.

Murray wagged a finger at him. "Remember. Only one every twelve hours."

The customer swallowed a second pill. "I'll be back Saturday."

Murray watched the man leave. "He lives on those things," he told no one in particular, then turned back to Adam and waved the bottle of allopurinol. "Hey, what's this stuff for, anyway?" He looked down the aisles, finding Adam again by the side window and dropping a pill into his mouth. Then Adam opened a second bottle and placed an extremely small tablet under his tongue.

"What's allopurinol?" Murray repeated, but this time in a whisper. Drugs terrified him, and watching someone take them—especially someone like Adam—turned Murray into a complete coward.

Adam rubbed his eyes, completing the transformation from Mr. Hyde to Dr. Jekyll. "Allopurinol," Adam said tiredly. "A blocking agent. Inhibits . . ." He struggled to free his memory—to focus on his profession. "Axanthine oxidase inhibitor," he finished. "It's for gout."

"Gout," repeated Murray. He tried grinning at his stupidity. "Won't do much for the shits."

"Might make them worse," Adam said. "Might have destroyed his liver."

Murray put the pills back on the counter, wishing he'd never seen them. What was the point of all these damn drugs? Poison, that was all. Feeling like a concerned fool, he pointed at the bottles near Adam. "What're those?"

Adam managed a smile. "Phenmetrazine hydrochloride," he said, enjoying Murray's predictable puzzlement. "With a side of metaproterenol."

"Mena—protol?" said Murray.

"Quickens the heartbeat," Adam explained. "Also opens the lungs."

"And phenme . . . ?"

"It's a diet pill."

"You're on a diet?"

Not exactly, Adam thought. Phenmetrazine hydrochloride was a stimulant, related to amphetamines. But along with the metaproterenol and a deep inhalation of Primatene, it helped wake him from his stupor. He was already growing bored with Murray, wondering when the day would end and he could go back to his house and really experiment.

"All these drugs are sick," Murray told him.

"It's money," said Adam. He knew the next question before Murray could ask it. "I'll write down what I use and you can take it out of my check."

Murray looked ready to give up. "I can't count all these fucking pills. I don't know what you use."

Adam walked away, sitting once more at his station, aware Murray was right and having already taken full advantage of this shortcoming. At home, Adam had stored away a nest of over forty pill bottles—most kept full, all stolen from Murray's shelf. True, Adam didn't intend to keep all of the bottles. There were people Adam treated outside the pharmacy, people who didn't have prescriptions. Still, the pills were stolen, and the cost came out of Murray's pocket.

People outside the pharmacy . . . The thought was a reminder, and he wondered if Ben had called. It was about time for Adam to dig him up a fresh supply. He swallowed a last pill to help clear his head, then dialed home to hear the answering machine.

A beep indicated five messages. Two were wrong numbers. The third was from his lawyer—a man who, for a fee, was single-handedly trying to save Adam's career, and who, again single-handedly, was now ensnaring Adam in a portfolio of lawsuits, all of which Adam expected to lose. "Adam, it's Brian. Call me when you get in. I need you in New York." There was a pause, then, "You can reach me at the office, or phone me at home if you want. My number's 675-36—" After thirty seconds, the message was automatically cut. Brian would never learn.

The fourth call was from his ex-wife. "Adam, it's me. Sherry's birthday's this week, and she wants to see you. Can you give me a call at Phillip's?"

Adam had been expecting this one. He knew his daughter's birthday. He had been thinking about it for months. And what made it so absurd was that Adam had spent the last year being everything but a father. Despite this, Casey was calling him. His ex-wife was daring to bring him back in the fold after Adam had worked so hard to slip free.

"I'll be home tonight," Casey continued. "You can

14

call me any time after dinner, but I want to—"

Casey was cut off, but it was only a temporary delay. She was also the fifth message.

"That's really annoying," she continued. "Look, give me a call as soon as you can. I want to make reservations. Do this for me, Adam, all right? I think it's very important Sherry sees you."

Casey hung up, and Adam did the same.

Sherry's birthday. His one and only Sherry. It was almost cruel of Casey to remind Adam, but Adam had done plenty of his own reminding. Now, it was just a question of phoning back, or letting his wife—*ex*-wife—try calling another year.

How much easier to wait. How much easier to turn off the answering machine, and let Sherry grow, and let Casey remarry, and let himself fade into Calverton.

"Excuse me, Mr. Druit?"

Adam turned and faced the woman, staring until he remembered her name. Mrs. Myers. She had been visiting the pharmacy twice a month, coming to Adam as if he were her doctor.

"Mr. Druit, I was hoping you could mix me up another vial of your special joint medicine," she asked.

"Are you sure you need it, Mrs. Myers?" he asked. "I was hoping the last treatment would take care of the problem."

"Oh, I'm certain," she said. "It just does such wonders."

Adam didn't have the stamina for a discussion. He agreed and went back to his counter for the medication. It was really nothing more than petroleum jelly, but he used the jelly as a placebo, spooning some into a small, plastic vial. When he handed it to Mrs. Myers, complete with an instructive label, for her, it

15

was a miracle painkiller.

"Remember, you use this with aspirin," Adam reminded her. "Just a dab on your joints."

"I'll remember," she said. "You know, you really should market this. It's remarkable."

"I'll think about it," Adam said.

"At least let me pay you," she insisted, but Adam, as always, refused. He dropped the vial in a white paper bag and pushed it on her. Mrs. Myers was now free to leave, and she might have, if not for her small boy. She turned to find him staring at her, not only certain of doing something wrong, but the evidence still in his hands—an open box of candy. She rushed across the store, grabbed her son's wrist, and went through the motions of punishing him.

Adam couldn't stand the scene. "It's all right; I'll cover it," he said, a comment that would have made Murray laugh.

It was all too much kindness for Mrs. Myers. "Oh, you're such a good man," she said, now smothering Adam with compliments, finally obliging him to seek sanctuary behind the pharmacy shelves.

Finally alone, he was almost amused at what she had said. "Good man"? It wasn't a term he normally used for himself. But then again, neither was "father"—at least not anymore.

He stared at the telephone, knowing he should call his ex-wife, instead wishing the phone would sprout legs, walk to the toilet, and flush itself down. And he wondered if he should make it happen. Because he could. If he really wanted to, he could make the phone dance, the chairs climb the walls, the sun disappear. . . . He could make himself do the same and more, with the right prescription. The thought made him laugh; a laugh that only got Murray angrier,

16

who was still trying to figure out Adam's inventory.

"What's funny?" Murray shouted. "That I can't count this shit and you're eating me out of my business?"

Adam couldn't answer. He tightened his white smock and ended the lunch break. Murray left to take up his post for the after-school raid on the comic books.

Adam thought again about what Murray had said—how Murray had no idea what pills he popped or serums he drank. Adam wondered if Murray had considered injections. What would Murray say if he saw the disposables in the trash bin? Had Murray already seen them? Was Murray that curious about Adam's habits—to go rummaging through the garbage?

"I don't know what you use," Murray had said.

Funny. Very funny.

If Adam ever gave him the list, Murray would be reading for a week.

Chapter 2

Casey took the aspirin, then looked at herself in the mirror as if she had broken a sacred trust.

It was how she had conditioned herself—to hate any type of pill, no matter how innocuous. A mental scar left after a year of pill popping.

Her favorite had been typical for housewives—diazepam, otherwise known as Valium. But Casey was also a working woman—a special projects supervisor for the city—and a working woman deserved more than a housewife, so she tried topping the diazepam with a chaser of clorazepate dipotassium. Taking the pills seemed so natural at the time, especially with a husband who brought them home with the groceries. During the evenings, if Adam was working late, she would invite over a few friends and have a pill party. An evening of quiet experimentation, with Casey as hostess. Only after Adam got suspended did she discover he was prepared to be her partner.

And that was their life. Before leaving the clinic, Adam had cleverly stocked their clothes bureau with medications. Who knew how many warning signs they should have heeded? All Casey knew was that, for her, life didn't turn around until she went to sleep on the sofa and didn't wake for five days. When she finally did, it was in the community hospital. A year later, she would still remember her almost numbing love for her daughter when Casey's sister brought Sherry to the hospital, as if heaven had granted her one last chance at life, and Sherry was her reward.

Then there was Adam's visit.

Two weeks passed before Adam came to her room. In that time, Casey had volunteered for therapy and begun withdrawal. She knew what it was like to be near death and was ready to fight her way back from the edge. It was a painful trial, but one she had to take, if only to save her daughter.

Not Adam. He came to her bedside higher than ever.

He was simply too smart with his drugs. Or perhaps the drugs had become too much a part of his body—indeed, perhaps he had transformed into a creature out of one of Sherry's comic books: a chemical man, with golden eyes, mercury blood, and urine clear as crystal.

Whatever the answer, Adam had evaded the danger. Indeed, it hadn't even crossed his line of vision. And now Casey could only wonder whether the drugs had also poisoned Adam's love for Sherry or merely blurred it. It was one or the other, because if there was one thing about Adam that Casey firmly believed, it was that drugs had destroyed, and were still destroying, his life. They were why he had left his wife, his child, his job. . . . Would Adam ever shake free?

Could Sherry ever again have back her father?

And as long as she was asking questions, what about herself? She stared in the mirror, wondering when her own body would hide the bruises left from her own abuse. Odd how a bad sickness never quite leaves the skin. In her case, an otherwise fair-skinned face was still tinged by thin veins about the sacks of her eyes. Her skin had also lost the clean, childlike softness she had somehow kept through the addiction. Now her skin was pocketed—a deep, flushed roughness, purple about the cheeks. Even her hair had been tainted. While it had once been dirty blond, to Casey it had simply become dirty. The blond was gone, replaced by strands of white.

She walked by the telephone, thinking again of calling Adam, but she had left her message. Instead she turned into the living room, where Phillip worked on their bills. Thank God for Phillip. He had cared for her during the recuperation, and then after her separation. Now they were live-in lovers, a cautious first step toward marriage, and even in the close quarters, they remained so right for each other. Since her recovery, Casey had grown intolerant of all vices, especially those which depended on an altered state of awareness, such as drinking. Phillip, meanwhile, was a macrobiotic health food junkie whose life was regimented between morning and evening jogs—a slim and trim man, relaxed yet carefully clean, whose most daring experiment with drugs had been taking three aspirins for a headache instead of the recommended two. Together, they competed not only to be the most physically fit, but the perfect mates.

Phillip looked up from the bills and saw Casey staring at him. "You all right?" he asked.

"Fine," she said, smiling until, satisfied, he returned to his work.

20

But things weren't fine, and they wouldn't be until Adam returned to his daughter the love he had taken away. That was why Casey had called him—not for Adam's sake, but Sherry's. How could Sherry even begin celebrating her birthday when every time she opened a present, she would be missing her father? And Casey *knew* this would happen. For years, there had been a special bond between Adam and Sherry—so close, in fact, that Casey had been jealous. And birthdays had been the worst. Birthdays were when Adam would steal Sherry away and spoil her nonstop until bedtime.

For the last thirteen months, Casey, and later Phillip, had tried filling the gap—at first struggling with a poor imitation of Adam's magic, then later settling for a reasonable distraction. But it had taken until this birthday to realize her mistake.

No; Phillip and she should never have tried competing with Adam. Casey had only one responsibility: to pull Adam out of his self-pity long enough to spend time with his daughter. Damn it, he was only a few hours away.

Except it wasn't just a few hours' distance, was it? It was three hours of travel and a year of time.

And how many pounds of pills? she thought. A dozen? Two dozen?

"Are you sure you're all right?" Phillip called.

Phillip. He was one more thing to feel guilty about, in part because she was thinking so much about the past, but mostly since she hadn't told him about the calls to her ex-husband. Rather than risk complicating the deception, she avoided him by turning down the hallway and knocking on an open bedroom door. "Sherry?" she called.

The girl looked up at her mother. She had been

reading a book, and not an easy one at that. At six years old, she was already proving to be exceptionally astute. Casey wondered if, under the circumstances, it wasn't more of a handicap than gift.

"Sherry, have you thought about your birthday?"

Sherry shrugged, and Casey bent down to be near her.

"I'm not sure what we'll do," Casey said. "I was thinking we'd take a trip, but would you prefer a party like the one at Patty's house?"

"I don't think I want a party," Sherry said, not at all convincing.

"It's a little late, but you can make a list of who you want, and we can go to the store for some games," she said. "We'll do it together—you, me, and Phillip. Think you'd like that?"

Then, to pump her up, Casey lifted her off the ground, swinging and playing with Sherry until the girl couldn't help but shriek from the sudden excitement. Casey mimicked her, and soon Phillip was also in the room.

"I thought a riot was going on," he said, grinning. He appeared ready to join in when the phone rang.

Phillip, the closest, left the room to answer it.

If there is a God, Adam thought, he must live on psychedelics.

How else to explain the slick rainbows of dirt and oil that greased the streets; the iridescent blue of car exhaust that tinted in the sun; the electric glow of neon above every liquor store?

Adam saw these things every day. No doubt about it; God was tripping. It was almost pointless taking drugs.

22

But then again, Adam had discovered a few colors even God hadn't imagined.

He left the pharmacy, put on sunglasses, and turned off Main Street, walking to a small Chinese market. The owner—Yu Ling—was Adam's only friend in Calverton, in part because Yu Ling couldn't speak English. Adam and Yu Ling communicated by smiling, with occasional help from Yu Ling's son, Michael.

Michael always took a keen interest in Adam. Michael was premed at Rhode Island University. He didn't strike Adam as someone who thought beyond his studies, but Michael had taken an interest in the neighborhood pharmacist, wondering why Adam sought out an old Chinaman to taste ancient herbal recipes.

Yu Ling was the first to see Adam. He sat on a plastic milk crate, near an open shelf of ginger root and garlic. He was dressed in dirty white slacks and a black, collared shirt. His face showed the kind of age that came from working fourteen-hour days for sixty years. Michael would never look anything like his father, even after his hospital residency. Yu Ling was not just first-generation American—he was last-generation Chinese laborer.

Yu Ling waved to Adam. His yellowed teeth showed broadly, his smile sinking into his wrinkles. Adam smiled back, never removing his sunglasses. He could see Michael returning from the basement, and he didn't want a premed student checking his pupils.

"Mr. Druit," said Michael.

Michael sat behind the cash register and turned a book for Adam to read.

"I got this question," Michael said. "Chapter six,

23

immunology."

"What about it?" said Adam.

" 'Identify a globulin solution effective for the prevention of measles, rubella, poliomyelitis, and infectious hepatitis.' "

Adam read alongside Michael, then picked up the book to see the cover. *"Advanced Pharmacology."* Adam looked at him. "They gave you this in premed?"

"I picked it up at the bookstore."

Adam studied Michael. Somewhere between being a kid and a college student, he had picked up some of the smarts a teenager needs to waste time while growing up. Michael was digging at Adam — had been digging since day one, certain there was more to the pharmacist than Adam let on. But Adam simply grinned back, knowing precisely what was happening and refusing to give Michael the pleasure of an answer. They stared at each other until a fly buzzed Michael and he brushed it toward his father. The fly flew almost in a line to Yu Ling, where it stayed on the old man's shoulder like a pet parrot. Finally, Yu Ling laughed, and Michael and Adam looked at him, surprised, because they knew Yu Ling couldn't understand what they said — or in this case, what they hadn't said. Michael shouted something in Chinese, but Yu Ling waved for Adam and Adam joined him.

Yu Ling leaned forward, almost dropping off the crate, and Adam caught his arm. Yu Ling looked up at Adam, his face less than an inch away, his mouth sliding about like a cow chewing cud. It took Adam a moment to notice Yu Ling's saliva was green. He said something to Adam, again nodded, then grabbed Adam's crotch.

Michael pulled Adam free. He yelled at his father, but Yu Ling simply laughed, pulling a mound of wet, mulched leaves out of his mouth.

"Damiana," said Michael. "Aphrodisiac."

Adam classified aphrodisiacs with stimulants, which explained the old man's good mood. But it didn't explain why Yu Ling wanted to build his interest in sex.

Michael could see the question in Adam's face. "He wants another son to take care of the store after I leave."

"You won't be leaving for years," said Adam.

"Eight years, including medical school," said Michael. "Father thinks that a seven-year-old boy will be the perfect age for breaking in a new grocer."

Adam smiled back at the old man. He reached in his pocket and found his list. Michael glanced it over. Skullcap, valerian root, nerve root, rosemary leaves, lemon balm, celery seed.

"New soup?" Michael grinned.

"Pulled it out of a book," said Adam. "Supposed to relax the nerves."

Michael read the list to his father, who nodded vigorously, as if understanding immediately the purpose of the mix and firmly approving. Yu Ling spat on the floor and disappeared into the back room.

"His parents should have taken him home," Michael said, meaning China.

Adam didn't answer.

"He could have been a doctor there," Michael said. "Instead, he chews leaves and laughs like an idiot."

"He's in control," Adam said.

Michael looked at him. "He's my father, not an idiot." He again opened his textbook. "A globulin so-

25

lution for rubella and measles."

"Immune serum globulin," Adam answered.

"Not Gamulin Rh?"

"Gamulin is RHo immune globulin."

Michael paused, considering the answer. He looked at Adam as if Adam had given away another dark secret.

"Right," said Michael. "Exactly."

"Any pharmacist would know that," Adam murmured.

"Any pharmacologist would."

He put the book under the counter as his father returned with the herbs. Yu Ling spread them across a cardboard top. As a present, Yu Ling added a small sandwich bag filled with a few choice damiana leaves. "Sex," Yu Ling managed, the one English word he could clearly say.

"I wouldn't know," Adam answered.

Michael looked embarrassed by both of them. He took ten dollars from Adam and gave back six. "I'm catching on to you," Michael said. "Just a few more chapters. That's all I need."

"Don't get yourself too excited," Adam answered, leaving the store.

Michael watched him from the door. "See you Tuesday," he said. "Next time, take off the sunglasses."

Adam watched another psychedelic sunset end, then turned up the walkway to his home. He lived in the ground-floor apartment of a three-story house — an anonymous brown-shingled structure with an exposed cinder-block basement and a porch that bent from the weight of rain and lumber.

It was an old building, as were all the houses on the block. In fact, it was hard telling them apart. This, however, was why he took the rental. He wanted a mirror image.

And inside the apartment, he wanted only a shell.

Like everyone else, he had his television, his sofa, his bed, his kitchen table. He also had a refrigerator and oven, as well as a downstairs basement for storage. But his corner of the basement was empty, and so were his closets.

Despite having spent a year in Calverton, Adam still lived from his suitcase, which had found permanence on top of the bureau. The apartment itself wasn't especially dirty; on the other hand, Adam did not spend a great deal of time cleaning. The sofa, television, and all the other furniture had come with the apartment. None was in great shape when Adam got there, and all looked the worse for his residence. The one pristine spot in the apartment was the kitchen, because he lived off frozen food wrapped in foil. There were no dirty dishes, because he rarely used dishes. Unless there were things other than food to prepare.

Adam unlocked the front door and rubbed his hand across the light switch. The main hall lit with the glare of three uncovered 100-watt bulbs. Out of a habit born from better days, he dropped his groceries on the couch, turned on the television, and went back to the door for his mail. There were no letters.

The television blared a food ad at him, but Adam had lost his appetite. Too many diet pills pepping him up and down. The good news was that he had lost fifteen pounds. The bad news—he was nine pounds underweight.

27

Well, there are also pills for that, he thought. And vitamins. Nutrition doesn't have to come from the major food groups; it can also come out of the bottle.

He carried the herbs into the kitchen and spread them on a counter. He filled a tea kettle with hot water and set it on the stove to boil. In a drawer was a tea ball. He unclasped it, then began measuring the herbs. Four parts skullcap, three parts celery seed, three parts lemon balm, two parts rosemary leaves, six parts nerve root, twelve parts valerian root. He shredded the roots, then crushed the leaves with a pestle. After mixing the herbs, he filled the tea ball and dropped it in the kettle, turning off the fire.

While the herbs brewed, he went into the bedroom, emptying his pockets of change, keys, and stolen pills. He was getting careless with the pills — stealing them far too freely. A look in the sock drawer told the story. Over forty pill bottles.

He made his selection, returned to the living room, and sat back down on the sofa. Was he ready? Could he do it now?

Without giving himself another chance to think, he lifted the receiver and dialed.

"Hi, Phillip."

Phillip needed a moment to recognize the voice. There was a lot of noise from Phillip's end of the line. Sherry screeching. Maybe Casey.

"Adam," Phillip said, his voice instantly cool. "It's been a while."

"A year," Adam said. He stared at the bottle of amphetamines and wished he had taken one before calling. Shit, what was he getting himself into? "Is Casey there? I'm returning her call."

This caught Phillip off guard. He excused himself,

and Adam listened as the laughter became muffled and then died altogether. Adam braced, embarrassed by himself, not at all surprised that his call had deadened Casey's household.

"Adam," Casey said. "Thanks for calling back finally."

"I would have called sooner, but things have been busy," Adam said.

"I've been busy, too," Casey said. "Sherry's birthday is in two days."

"I know, Adam said.

Casey moved the phone farther from Phillip and her daughter. When she cupped the mouthpiece, her voice seemed to deepen. "Her birthday's this weekend."

"I know," said Adam.

"She misses you. I thought it would be good for her to see you. I thought we'd come up for the weekend."

Adam popped open the top to his bottle and scrambled for a pill. He placed it on the back of his tongue and swallowed.

"I don't know, Casey. I'm not feeling so well."

"I know you're not feeling well," she said. "I know exactly what you're feeling."

"No, I mean I'm really sick."

"Christ, Adam," she said, getting angry. "If only you went to a rehab center."

"It's not that kind of problem."

"It's like dealing with a junkie—"

"I am not physically dependent on anything," Adam said. "Don't throw around terms you don't understand."

"I understand enough," she said flatly.

Adam tried keeping calm. "Let's get off it, all

29

right?" he said. "This has nothing to do with Sherry."

"Anything that has to do with you, has to do with her," she told him. "Why do you think I'm calling?"

Adam couldn't answer. He waited for his voice, hoping the words would find themselves.

"So what about the weekend?" Casey tried again. "Should I take your silence as a yes or no?"

"I don't think it's a good idea," Adam said.

"Look," she said. "Why don't we come, and you can make up your mind at the last minute?"

Casey could be like this . . . working as many angles as possible, finding a solution that no one wanted but no one could refuse. He still didn't know what to say. Finally, instead of saying anything, he slammed down the phone.

Wrong, he thought. Dead wrong. But she wasn't making sense. The idea was to forget his family and let them forget him; not to haunt each other, drumming back memories. God, he had tried so hard stifling them — to stop it all from mattering.

See his daughter? Could he do it? Should he?

Meanwhile, Casey stared at the telephone, absolutely hating Adam for what he was doing to himself. At the same time, she was overwhelmed by pity, because she also knew what at least *some* of the drugs were like. And for all the misery he caused, Adam had to be saving the worst for himself.

The phone rang again, and Casey picked it up.

"I'm sorry," he told her, his voice hoarse, his courage almost gone. "I swear to God, if I could see her, I would. But I can't. I can't handle it, Casey. I—"

"Calm down," she said. "You can think about it, all right?"

Casey could hear his voice trembling. She talked

quietly, sounding so soothing, wanting so much to help. "Just calm down. First, just calm down. . . ."

She talked this way for several minutes.

And then, just before hanging up, she heard what she wanted—he agreed.

Chapter 3

Friday, two hours after sunrise, and Murray was the only person on the block awake and getting ready for business.

That's what happens when a neighborhood goes to hell, he thought. It not only loses its enthusiasm, but the kind of people who can work full days.

He considered this thought while rolling the store's gate clear of the entrance. Next was the window fence and the three dead bolts. When he finally swung the door open, the store alarm began ringing, but after forty years of hearing it crying for the police, he was almost deaf to it now. It had never done any good; if it had, Murray wouldn't need the dead bolts and gates. But it was like a morning alarm clock. The bell went off, and Murray made his slow walk behind the counter to flip the switch.

He was behind the counter when a teenager entered the store.

Murray lowered his head so he could look over his reading glasses. The kid was maybe nineteen, in a dirty, torn sweatshirt and jeans that were marked with grease. Murray figured he had spent the night on the street, because the kid's face was filled with end-of-the-day exhaustion, not the early morning fatigue Murray felt. The kid's hair was also caked with dirt, made wet and thick because of the morning dew. He looked at Murray, shied away, then tried to lose himself in one of the aisles.

Murray used one of the store mirrors to follow him.

"Store's closed," Murray said loudly.

The kid didn't answer, and Murray left his post. He found the kid at the rear of the store, between aisles, mesmerized by the counter marked *Prescriptions Filled Here*.

"Store isn't open," Murray said again.

"I'm waiting for Mr. Druit," the teenager said quietly.

"Mr. Druit won't be here until nine."

The kid didn't answer. Murray touched his shoulder.

"I'm waiting for Mr. Druit," the kid repeated. "I'm sick."

"You're seeing a doctor?"

The kid shook his head.

"You got a prescription?"

"I don't need one," the kid answered.

Murray grabbed the boy's arm and led him toward the door. "First you see a doctor, then you bring in the prescription, and then Mr. Druit will see you. If you're really sick, call the fire department and have them take you to the hospital."

"But I need help," the kid said.

"Then get it," Murray answered.

Murray walked the boy outside and pointed him back toward the porn shops.

Almost eight thirty now. Some of his real customers began coming inside—people for the morning paper and other odds and ends. A few of the customers he knew by name, and almost all by face. Two people came in asking for their prescriptions. Murray checked a file box to see if they had been filled. Both had, and Murray charged the retail rate.

By the time Adam Druit came into the store, looking sicker than ever, Murray had already done $170 worth of business. A good start to the day.

"Good morning, Adam," Murray said too lightly.

Adam poured himself a cup of coffee, pulled on his smock, and went to the back of the store. The way their counters were positioned, they could spend the entire day in the store without ever coming face-to-face.

"A friend of yours came by earlier," Murray said. "A kid. Looked like he'd come out of a shit factory."

Adam still didn't answer. Murray got annoyed. Christ, was he pill popping this early in the morning? Murray went through the store and into the pharmacy, looking for Adam.

Murray found him sitting at a desk, conducting inventory, actually doing work.

"Did you hear me?" Murray said. "A kid came by looking for you earlier, and two prescriptions got picked up."

Adam nodded, then said, "Someone might be coming by in another hour looking for me. Just send him back."

"All right," Murray said.

"Another thing," Adam said. "I might take some time off today or tomorrow."

"Yeah?" Murray said, not arguing since Adam hadn't asked permission.

"I've got family visiting," Adam said. "My daughter."

"Your kid, huh?" said Murray. "Hey, that's great."

"Yeah," said Adam, less than convincing.

"Well, don't worry about the store," Murray told him. "I can handle everything."

Now Murray sounded less than convincing. But the front door opened and he returned to his cash register, watching the people drift in like so much cold weather seeping indoors. Occasionally, Murray made conversation, but in the morning at least, he preferred keeping to himself. Nor did he have to check storage or refill the shelves. He had a boy come after school to take care of the heavy lifting.

There was only one thing Murray needed to do in the morning, and that was his own inventory to see what needed to come out of the basement.

He was checking the shampoo when two things happened: the phone rang, and another customer came through the door.

"Adam Druit, please," the man on the phone said.

Murray knew the voice. He pushed the hold button.

"Call for you on my line," Murray shouted across the store.

Murray watched the blinking light above the hold button. When the blinking stopped, he pressed the button, lifted the phone and covered the mouthpiece.

". . . review next Wednesday. Allen said he'd be a character witness," said the lawyer. There was a moment of silence. Murray and the lawyer waited for Adam to say something. Murray wondered if Adam had heard Murray lift the receiver.

"I don't want your help," Adam finally said.

"That's not true," the lawyer said. "You're too busy thinking about your personal problems. This is a *professional* problem. We're not just talking about a license to work; if they get you on the license, that's the start of malpractice suits, and you can really say good-bye."

"But I'm guilty," Adam said.

"No, you're not. You only did the dispensing. Scott was responsible for the diagnosis, and Willis asked for the medication."

"I knew it was illegal," Adam said.

"What's illegal?" the lawyer said. "The drug was experimental."

"The drug was unclassified."

"But it's used in Europe."

"I knew what I was doing," Adam said a last time. "I had used it before. I would have done it again, except this time the patient died."

"The patient was already dying."

"Tell that to the relatives," said Adam.

"The goddamn patient *begged* for the antibiotic," said the lawyer.

Adam lost all patience. "Look, Brian. My kid's coming to town, all right? I'm cleaning out my system, I feel like shit, and I've got more on my mind than some fucking lawsuit."

With that, he hung up. Murray hung up after the lawyer, then he returned to his posture by the cash register and finished with a customer. Someone else was coming through the front door—an old man, on two brace canes, dressed in a suit and worn shoes.

"Good morning, Mr. Hufflin," Murray said.

Hufflin gave Murray a cursory glance, then continued to the rear of the store. Adam met him at the counter. He didn't wait for the receipt—Adam knew the order immediately, went into the box for filled prescriptions, then handed the old man his bottle.

"I'm also going to give you a salve," Adam said. "Rub the area about the genitals to sooth the itching. If you show any redness, stop using it and try a lubricating gel."

Hufflin nodded thanks, took the package, and left. Murray leaned back on his stool, grinned, then maneuvered closer to Adam. "Why does Hufflin need a gelatin for his balls?"

While Adam turned back to the shelves, Murray grabbed the receipt.

"Leave it alone," Adam said.

"This is mine," Murray said. "Anything that has to do with money has to do with the owner." Murray stared at the piece of paper. " 'Penicillin,' " he read aloud. "Jesus Christ, Hufflin has the clap?"

Adam walked away, but Murray was fascinated.

"He's in his eighties," said Murray. "In his eighties and he goes out and catches the bug?" Murray looked at Adam with clear admiration. "And to think that if you hadn't opened up a pharmacy, I never would have known."

"You shouldn't know now," Adam said.

Murray turned his attention to a wooden bureau where Adam stored the rest of the receipts. "We could blackmail half of this town."

Adam glared at Murray.

"Just a joke," Murray said.

Adam looked past Murray and toward the front door. Eddie Hearns waved a clipboard and came inside. Eddie was a stocky man, with a right arm that was always being stretched by a briefcase heavy with samples. He was a salesman whose district covered western Rhode Island and the northern edge of Connecticut. He belonged to a wholesale company — Continental Distributors, Inc. — that Adam had

37

relied upon while at the hospital. Now Adam relied on them for almost a third of his pharmacy's supplies: in part, because they didn't care about his licensing difficulties; mostly, however, because they undercut the prices of any other wholesale distributor by nearly 70 percent.

Continental Distributors was a drug diversion company. Most wholesalers bought their drugs directly from the manufacturer, at prices determined by the marketplace—usually dependent on the size of a purchase—and with a small margin of profit for the wholesaler and the pharmacist. Continental bought its drugs from secondary sources, including nonprofit hospitals and charitable organizations. These types of purchasers were allowed to buy drugs directly from the manufacturers at noncompetitive rates well below the market price—often 50 percent below. Continental, in turn, paid these organizations to buy above their needs, then sell the excess purchases to Continental. Continental sold the drugs to selected pharmacies at lower than usual wholesale prices, but not so low the pharmacists were aware of the circumvention.

Adam was the exception. While working at the hospital, he had also ordered excessive supplies, and he had sold them to Continental for an overhead of $19,000 a month—money that he routinely spent on laboratory supplies and the purchase of European drugs not yet legal in the United States. As a former conduit for Continental, he was well aware of how they bought their supplies. Now, as manager of a retail pharmacy, he knew what prices were fair.

Continental kept Adam well supplied, too. While the company did gain a smaller profit from him, they were spared the extra expenses necessary to keep

38

retail pharmacists from becoming suspicious. This meant they could sell him sample boxes without having to repackage the merchandise.

"Your lucky day." Eddie grinned to Murray. "I see, looking on your shelf, that Mr. Druit has run short on simethicone. So happens we have a special. One week only."

Eddie heaved his briefcase on the counter, snapped the clasps, and opened it. Inside were loosely packaged bottles cluttered inside plastic food sacks, a pocket calculator, several larger containers, and a folder. It wasn't how companies usually did business, but Continental was not a usual company, nor was Adam a usual customer.

Adam looked at the clipboard, which had a form on the top listing the month's available supplies. Adam checked it against his own list, then estimated prices.

"Harrison Community bought in last month," Eddie said. "And there's a hospital in Dade County that's getting us supplied with Biphetamine."

Murray tried understanding. "Biphet—"

"Appetite suppressant," Adam said, still checking the lists.

"Everybody's watching weight," Eddie said. "If you want, we'll get you five milligram tabs, six bucks per one hundred." He gave a list to Murray. "Over the counter, we got cosmetics, cleansers, Ex-Lax, Bufferin, Head and Shoulders, Contac. . . ."

The phone rang again and Murray answered it.

"Main Pharmacy," said Murray.

"I want to speak with the pharmacist," said the caller.

"May I ask who's calling, please?"

"This is Dr. Anson, Mrs. Williford's physician,"

the caller said. "Your pharmacist gave her the wrong prescription."

"Wrong prescription," Murray murmured. He looked at Adam, remembering the earlier phone call, imagining every type of lawsuit. He covered the mouthpiece and handed Adam the telephone. "Dr. Anson," Murray said. "He says you gave someone the wrong—"

"I know what he says," Adam said. He took the receiver and continued reviewing the list of drugs. "This is Druit. . . ." Adam went further down the list, checking allergy medications. Chlor-Trimeton. Ana-Kit. "No, I changed it because your prescription was inappropriate."

Murray watched Adam as if his store was in the balance.

"No, I don't see it that way," Adam said on the phone. "The way I see it, I saved your fucking ass, doctor." He hung up, regained his thoughts, and looked to Eddie. Eddie also looked on guard, but he always felt that way about Druit. Anyone who could fall from a top job to this didn't deserve the benefit of a doubt.

"We also got Prell shampoo, seventy cents on the bottle, sixty cents per case," Eddie said automatically. "And we can also throw in some medicated soap, if you want to stock up."

Adam shook his head and handed Eddie a clipboard. "Here's my sheet, except take another three percent off the top."

Eddie wasn't happy at the request. "This isn't a charity, Mr. Druit."

"But it came from one," said Adam, "and I'm giving you a twelve percent markup, just like my other orders."

"This comes out of my commission," Eddie protested.

Adam pushed the sheet on Eddie. "If your company has any problem with my order, let me know."

Eddie glared at the piece of paper, folded it, then dropped it in his briefcase. "I'll need fifteen down."

"No problem," said Adam. "Murray, write him a check for one hundred fifty."

Murray found the checkbook near the front cash register, hidden beneath a rack of throat lozenges. Eddie followed him through the store, lugging his briefcase alongside. He rested on a wood stool while Murray wrote the check. For Eddie, it was time to relax after a sale. It was the most enjoyable moment to the job. He reached for the rack of candies and, quietly, said, "Mr. Druit counts his pennies."

Murray opened the checkbook and found a pen.

"He should be more respectful of my position," Eddie said. "It's not easy selling merchandise. And with the markdown you guys get, it's not worth my while to come by for a piss."

"One hundred fifty?" asked Murray, already writing.

"Pay to the order of Continental," Eddie said, then whispered, "I just hope he pays for what he pops."

Murray tore the check out of the book and handed it to Eddie. Eddie, however, was comfortable on the stool. He chewed on a chocolate bar, winked at Murray, then leaned back, stretching to see the rear counter. Adam was finishing a drink of water. Eddie watched, grinned, and finally swayed forward, whispering, "I shouldn't do business with a junkie."

Murray didn't answer. Eddie, enjoying himself, faced him.

41

"What's his favorite. Amphetamines? Depressants? Probably mixes them all up. Got one eye open, one closed," Eddie said. "Hey, what are his eyes like? Have you checked his arms, or the inside of his fingers? Does he normally look tired? You tell me the symptoms, I'll tell you the drugs."

"Thirty-five cents," Murray said.

Eddie stopped talking. Murray pointed at the half-eaten candy bar.

"Thirty-five," he repeated.

"Of all the fucking shit . . ." Eddie dug fifty cents from his pocket, dropped it on the counter, grabbed his briefcase, and left the store. Murray wandered back to the pharmacy to tell Adam the deal had been closed. He found Adam frozen in mid-motion, pills spread on the counter, an empty bottle in his hand. For a moment, Murray wondered whether to interrupt him. "What?" Murray asked. "Forget what you're doing?"

But Adam was really staring at the bottle. Adam turned the container, changing the reflection, his eyes widening, then closing. . . . It was the actions of a man studying himself, staring, perplexed, into a fun house mirror.

"How do I look?" Adam asked Murray. "Am I okay?"

Murray wasn't sure what to say. It wasn't just a matter of lying; Adam had never before asked a personal question. "Sure," he answered.

"I don't feel okay," Adam said.

"You're okay," Murray insisted, then feeling compelled to be somewhat truthful, added, "I mean, it's not like you take care of yourself."

It was too truthful. Adam glanced at Murray, then turned his attention to the telephone.

42

"I can't do it," Adam said.

Murray came close enough to rest a hand on Adam's shoulder. "If something's not right," he said solemnly, "you don't do it. But when something is right—when that something's for someone you love, like your kid—you damn well better."

Adam stared hard at Murray. Murray had not only crossed a line by getting too personal; he had also revealed a degree of knowledge that Adam hadn't confessed—which only made sense, since Murray's information mostly came from overheard conversations. Murray knew immediately he had dropped too many cards. After giving his advice, he turned and walked quickly back to his post by the cash register.

Adam let him go. It was the smartest thing to do. Regardless of what Murray might advise, Adam knew what he must do.

Already Casey was regretting her idea.

First, it had pissed off Phillip—not so much because he felt threatened by Adam, but because Casey hadn't first discussed it with him. After spending all this time building a relationship, Phillip suddenly felt like some peripheral part of Casey's life.

Second, there was Sherry. Casey had expected her to be tentative with the news, but Sherry's response had been deadening. After all this time, the girl was completely on guard—uncommitted to the idea, only vaguely curious about her father. Maybe it was better for Adam to drift off and let the bond die. In fact, this was already happening. Maybe Sherry and Adam both knew better than she did.

But the wheels were in motion. While Phillip and Sherry packed, Casey made their reservations at the

43

motel, then called to see if Adam could join them for dinner. "It's about a three-hour drive," she said. "If you like, we can eat at seven."

"Sure," Adam answered, guarded and aloof—like father, like daughter.

"Good," Casey said. "I'm proud of you, Adam. You know that."

"I know."

"It's good for you to see Sherry," she said. "Let me put her on the phone. She wants to say hi."

And then came the first sign of trouble. It came when Sherry reached for the phone—"Go ahead, sweetie, I have a surprise for you," Casey had said—and waited almost half a minute for someone to talk. Finally, she looked up at her mother and handed back the receiver.

When Casey listened, all she heard was a dial tone.

Adam had hung up. And when she tried phoning back, all she got was the answering machine. It would be the same story all weekend. When they reached the motel, the front desk passed a message saying Adam would miss dinner. Saturday morning, Adam left another message that he wouldn't be available until the evening. In the evening, there was a note saying he would be out until Sunday noon.

Of course Casey phoned, but all she ever heard was the tape—at least for the first few calls. After that, the phone simply rang. Adam didn't even give her the small pleasure of leaving messages.

Casey felt like such a fool. Instead of fixing every-thing—instead of making her daughter happy and coaxing Adam back into the fold—she had obliged Sherry to endure another rejection. Casey wanted to go home right away, except Phillip insisted they take

44

Sherry to Adam's apartment.

"Come on," Phillip said. "We didn't travel all this way to see Calverton."

What an ironic reversal. Before, Phillip was the one fighting the trip; now, as if to prove his own strength, Phillip insisted on it.

"He's not worth it," Casey argued. "Dragging us all the way here . . . Doing this to his daughter . . ."

"He doesn't know what he's doing," Phillip said.

"He's probably passed out on the floor."

"All the more reason to go there," said Phillip.

"That's *enough,* Phillip," Casey shouted. "She's *my* daughter, and this is *my* decision."

It was the wrong thing to say. Casey had struggled hard to make certain Sherry was guided by *their* decisions, not simply hers. Casey wanted Phillip acting as Sherry's father, regardless of whatever relationship Sherry developed with Adam.

So their fight ended with apologies and a trip to Adam's apartment. Phillip and Sherry waited in the car while Casey rang the doorbell. Casey expected to catch him with his hands once again in the cookie jar. It wasn't what she wanted to see, but she prepared herself for the worst.

Adam didn't disappoint. He arrived at the door a wreck — hair tangled, face unshaven, shirt out, slumped as if his spine had been left in the closet. His apartment was a shadow of the person. Casey took a step forward, looked about and stepped back into the sunlight.

"Adam?" she said.

"Sorry, Casey," he said. "I'm not feeling well."

"I can see," she said.

Now, Adam saw his daughter. He stepped deeper into his apartment. "Look, I'm not going to be able to do anything. I'd like to, but I've got other things planned."

Casey went by the sofa and turned on the light. Adam winced. Near the sofa, on a small coffee table, was Adam's weekend supply of pills—the bottles in a neat row, waiting to be opened. Most of the pills looked new to Casey. She wondered what plateaus they promised.

Casey looked at one of the shaded windows. "I suppose it was unreasonable," she said, "to think that for one weekend—for your daughter's birthday . . ."

"I'm not high," Adam said.

Casey didn't answer. Adam moved beside her.

"All right," he said. "I'm a little high. But I was fine until today."

"Fine for how long?"

"Since I knew Sherry was coming." He tried straightening his hair. "I just took a little herbal tea."

"Sherry's *birthday*," she said.

"I'm sorry. I didn't know you'd be coming here, all right?"

"No, not all right."

Adam walked to a bookshelf where he had left his drink. He cradled the cup and sniffed its vapors. "I wanted to see Sherry, but I changed my mind. It seemed like the only fair thing to de—let her go on with her life and forget me."

"That would be hard to do. You're the family nightmare."

Adam didn't answer.

"You could at least have said good-bye to her."

"I'm not much on good-byes."

"You're not much for anything. Except maybe these," Casey said, shaking a bottle of pills.

"I'm not hooked," Adam said. "I told you I've been clean for days."

"And you look like shit."

"I've got my own business here. It doesn't matter what I look like." He went to the window and pulled back the edge of the curtain. Sherry was sitting tight in the backseat, her head tilted toward the house but not daring to look at it. Phillip, in his own way, had assumed the same position. "I can't be her father."

Casey came up behind him, resting her hands against his back. "Let's at least get you outside."

"I don't think so."

"Just say hello. If you want, we can eat lunch together."

"This isn't right," Adam said.

"Worry about it later," Casey said. "Go change clothes."

Adam walked slowly toward his bedroom. "You wait in the car," he told her.

"Adam . . ."

"I'll see you in five minutes," he promised. "I've just got to change. You said so yourself."

Casey looked doubtfully at him and tried to smile. "Outside in five minutes?"

He nodded.

Casey went to the front door. "All right. I'm trusting you," she said. "And the only reason I'm trusting you is that I love you. Sherry does, too."

"I know. And I swear to God, I love her too."

She opened the door. The brightness caught her off guard. "Jesus, it's sunny outside."

Casey blew him a kiss and left the house, closing the door. She went back to the car and climbed into the front seat.

"Is he coming out?" Sherry asked.

47

"He wants to, sweetheart," Casey told her. "He's just not feeling very well."

"Should we get a doctor?" Phillip asked. "Does he need any medication?"

Casey laughed bitterly, then she gave her daughter a brush and a small mirror and told her to make herself neat. Sherry brushed her hair, her eyes focusing past the mirror and toward the front door. It had been a long time since she had seen her father. Her mother liked to say he lived too far for visits, but this didn't seem so far. Well, Sherry had never believed that anyway. The one or two times she had talked to her father on the phone, his voice had always sounded closer than her aunt's, who really did live far away and whom they could only see by traveling on a plane. Her mother had also said that a year wasn't that long not to see someone, but for Sherry it seemed long.

Sherry sat still, staring in her purse, where she kept a picture of her father and mother. It was a picture that dated back to the month she was born. She had sneaked it from a photo album her mother kept hidden in the bottom of a sewing basket.

"He's not coming out," Phillip told Casey.

Casey didn't answer. Sherry kept her eyes on the purse. She knew where her father was—by the window, staring at her. She inched closer to the window. Maybe if he had a better view; if he could see her looking in her pocketbook and knew she was thinking about the picture.

"Damn it," Casey said, leaving the car and walking up to the house. She knocked on the door, waited, knocked again, then tried the back. Sherry heard her mother shouting, but couldn't hear anyone answer. The front window, Sherry thought. That's where he is; watching me.

Casey returned, climbed in the front seat, and slammed shut the door. Phillip looked at her, but neither said a word. Phillip seemed to understand. He turned the ignition while Casey faced Sherry.

"Is he coming out?" Sherry asked.

"Your father . . ." Casey stopped herself. She so wanted to say the truth. "He's just not feeling up to it, sweetheart. He'll give us a call."

"I don't want a phone call."

"That's all he's up for right now, Sherry. There's nothing we can do about it."

"But I want to see him."

"I'm sorry," Casey said too sternly. She again caught herself and reached back to give her daughter a kiss. "He wants to see you too, but he just can't."

Sherry pulled away and pressed against the window, so her father could see her fully. Phillip turned the car around, and Sherry slid across the seat so her father could see her again. She finally turned to catch a glimpse of her father.

All she saw was a curtain dropping against a window.

It was early evening when the phone rang. Adam let it ring a full minute before cursing the answering machine and lifting the receiver.

"Mr. Druit, it's me," the caller said.

Adam rubbed his eyes, barely comprehending what he heard.

"I'm running low, Mr. Druit. I stopped by the store, but that old guy chased me off. I need your help."

"Ben," Adam finally managed, focusing his mind,

49

willing to do anything to forget the day.

"Can I see you?" Ben asked. "Can I see you now?"

"This isn't a good time."

"But I *need* to, Mr. Druit," Ben said. "Please, I swear I'll never bother you again."

"Ben . . ."

"Please, Mr. Druit. *Please.*"

He met Ben at their usual place—a pub not far from the pharmacy. Ben was at a corner stall, a pitcher between himself and a friend, uncertain whether to watch the door or stare at his drink. His friend huddled in a coat, as if the pub's air conditioner had turned the small bar into a meat locker.

Adam had met Ben a month after starting work at the pharmacy. The boy had stumbled inside asking for something to calm his nerves. He talked quickly while his face sweated and his arms itched like crazy. Adam knew immediately that he was dealing with heroin addiction. He took Ben in back, gave him methadone, then let the boy sleep in the basement.

That was the beginning of Adam's volunteer work—his own private rehab program, for the addicts that couldn't make it in the centers. Not a bad way for Murray to share his profits, Adam thought. And who the hell cared about the personal risk? What he did was right. That was what mattered in New York, and that was what mattered here. Casey couldn't see it. Maybe the law couldn't see it, either. But fuck the law if it didn't make sense.

"Hi, Mr. Druit," Ben said—relieved, anxious and, as always, sweating. His lips were blistered from a fall and the inside of his thumb was stained from nicotine. "You don't look so good."

It was not what one wanted to hear from a heroin junkie.

"How are you?" Adam asked.

"I had a rough day," Ben answered. He smiled, and Adam could see that one of his teeth had been chipped. "So you got some painkiller?"

"You should have told me about your tooth. That must hurt."

"It's okay," Ben said. Adam looked to his friend. Ben tried laughing and shook his friend's arm. "Petey," Ben whispered. To Adam, he said, "Petey's feeling sick in the stomach."

"Is he—"

"He's not on *anything*," Ben said. He wiped his mouth and dropped an open hand, waiting for Adam to fill it. Adam caught the boy's wrist and pulled back the sleeve. Ben's arm was marked, but not bad.

"I can't give you this forever," Adam said.

"I know it," Ben said automatically.

"I wish you did." Adam put the bottle in Ben's palm, and the boy's fingers clamped about it. Adam also dropped a package of clean syringes on the tabletop.

"Excuse me for a moment," Ben said nervously, going to the bathroom. Adam took a long breath, bought a Scotch at the bar, and returned to the table. Ben's friend still hadn't moved. Adam slid alongside him and shook his arm.

"What's your problem?" Adam asked.

Petey took another sip from his beer. It took Adam a moment to see the swirl of blood in Petey's mug. He opened the boy's mouth and found his gums bleeding. When Ben came back, Adam was rubbing a piece of ice against them.

"Sorry I took so long," Ben said. He was calmer— almost sedated. "I really needed it bad."

51

"Your friend has a cut that isn't clotting and he has no color," Adam said. "Go on home. I'm taking him to the hospital."

Ben smiled agreeably. With the sedatives, he could carry himself slowly and easily. A wonderful thing, drugs. "Thanks for your help again, Dr. Druit."

"I'll see you next week," Adam said.

"Next week," Ben repeated. "And if you see my dad . . ."

"Don't worry," he said, and Adam led Ben's friend out of the bar and to an emergency room. The boy Ben had called Petey had no identification, no money. Within the hour, he also had no life.

Adam had sensed the boy's death. His heart had been weak and his veins collapsed. It had nothing to do with Ben. Petey wasn't an addict; he was an alcoholic — a teenager with more alcohol in him than blood. Adam figured the boy must have been drinking at least since he was twelve. Imagine . . . twelve years old, sneaking into the liquor. Seven years later, and he comes to Calverton to die.

Christ, Adam thought, the day sinking in.

One more tablet, and the bedroom ceiling turned bloodshot red.

Adam swallowed deeply, then rested the empty water glass on his stomach. He was lying on top of his bed, the curtains to his apartment still closed. But it didn't matter anymore. Now it was nighttime, and there was no need to hide from the sunlight. Just as there was no need to hide from his family.

He was no longer a father. He was just a walking hallucination.

The glass slipped out of his hand, rolled off the

52

bed, and shattered. Adam moved to sit up, but his fingers sank through the bed sheets and into the floor. He pulled back quickly, but not before his fingers were covered by ants.

"Shit," he said, trying to shake them off. He sat up quickly, his foot stepping on the glass—a very real cut, bleeding from a gash in his right heel. The pain washed away his hallucination and he stumbled toward the bathroom, falling on the toilet and rubbing his hurt foot. The heel was throbbing. He could see it throb, like the beat of his heart, and could feel the glass under his skin. He tried pulling it out with his fingers, but his heel was rippling now, the skin slipping through his fingers.

"Stop it," he ordered.

The skin kept rippling. When he touched it, it was like touching the bed sheets—his fingers seemed to sink through his body until he could feel the bone.

"No."

He ran his fingers through his foot until he reached the piece of glass. The glass was molten heat. His fingers caught fire the moment he touched it. The pain was unbearable. He could see his fingertips dissolving—smell the incineration. There would be nothing left of his hand. There would be nothing left of him.

"Oh, God!" he screamed.

The glass was out.

Adam fell on his knees, sinking over the toilet and vomiting. He was empty now—empty of blood, life, and love. His tears came out all at once, and he wiped them aside.

Then he went back to the bed and fell face down, smothering himself in dreams of his daughter.

He dreamed of the good times—when Sherry was

still a baby, feeding her milk, lifting her in the air; cradling Sherry, caring for her. . . .

Then the memories changed. Suddenly nothing came easy. Not his marriage, not Sherry, and certainly not his job. Once, he had been the world's golden boy. Now, even with his own child . . . *especially* with her; the one person on earth he completely loved . . . Now, he couldn't even look her in the face.

How could he let it happen? Why couldn't he control his life? And why the hell was everyone always trying to drag him back home?

Fine fucking father. Fine fucking human being.

Then he fell asleep, letting the memories of his daughter take complete control. Nor would they let him go until the morning . . .

No matter how hard he cried, or how many times the telephone rang.

Chapter 4

Adam woke at ten in the morning, his foot swollen and inflamed. Someone was knocking at the front door, but he kept absolutely still, wishing the person away and getting his wish. Finally, Adam found his way to the bathroom and washed out the wound.

After the cut had been bandaged, he plodded into the kitchen, ran faucet water into a cup, and stirred in some instant coffee. He also turned on a light—a major achievement for someone who had spent the last day behind closed curtains, hiding from the sun like a vampire.

It was hard to make sense of the weekend. Casey and Sherry had come to town—that he knew. And Phillip. Adam had decided not to see his daughter. He had also decided to enjoy his liberation with a celebration. It was the sort of celebration that could easily have led to his death. Adam suspected that was his intention, only now he couldn't remember. Regardless, it had led to another workday.

When the telephone rang, Adam unplugged it. He would no longer be Adam Druit; instead, he was just the neighborhood pharmacist. If the drugs didn't kill him, then he'd let the years do it. But no more phone calls, no more explanations, no more history. He would move out of the apartment if he had to or out of Calverton. There were towns like this everywhere in the country and people like Murray looking for a good deal. For that matter, there were plenty of people like Adam, who enjoyed being paid less in cash than privacy.

Adam Druit? Don't know the man. Never existed. Or if he did exist, he wasn't worth remembering.

Adam showered, changed clothes, and drove to work.

It was the most peaceful drive Adam could remember having. He had done something good for a change—kept his daughter from seeing him. Now Sherry could forget and Phillip could be her new father. Adam certainly didn't deserve the privilege or the responsibility. He drove down Main Street, pleased with himself, certain that he had made the last sacrifice necessary before forever blending into the town's cement. He parked near a corner and walked the last block to the pharmacy, enjoying a deep breath of morning air before beginning what was, for him, the start of his true citizenry in Calverton.

"Sorry I'm late," he said loudly. His message was as much for his pharmaceuticals as for Murray. He would never be late again. A promise. He would never—

"Jesus Christ, I've been phoning all over for you," Murray said.

Adam faced Murray. Murray was heaving, and his white shirt was damp with sweat. His face showed nothing but pity.

"You look awful," Murray said.

"That's what I've been hearing all weekend,"

Adam answered.

"So you heard? Casey reached you?"

"Casey?"

"About your kid," Murray said.

Adam waited. Murray stared at him and realized his mistake.

"Shit, Adam. I stopped by your house, but you weren't in. And the cops were calling—"

"Murray, what the hell are you talking about?"

"Your kid," Murray said. "She's missing."

Casey and Phillip were at the police precinct, alone on a bench, Casey's head tucked protectively between her legs. Phillip was rubbing her back. Earlier, it had been meant to comfort her; now, it was just a motion.

It had happened shortly before nine the previous night. After leaving Adam's house, Casey and Phillip had tried rescuing the day by driving to the shore. Casey wanted to smother Sherry's memories of Adam, and she did this with an all-out attack on the seaside town of West Bay. They played on the beach, bought souvenirs, ate cookies and ice cream, dashed in and out of stores. . . . They overdid everything until, by the evening, Sherry lay on the backseat, her head buried in a rolled coat, drifting asleep. Phillip, meanwhile, was all set for heading to the interstate and driving home.

But first they stopped for gas.

These details would be pressed forever in her memory. Phillip, driving, saying they should top off the tank before getting on the highway. Casey arguing briefly, but not wanting a fight—the day had gone well, and Phillip had been a fine substitute father. So

57

they pulled into the Arco station—Phillip leaving to pump the gas, Casey in the front passenger seat, Sherry in the back. Phillip tapped on the window. Casey rolled it down, and he asked if she wanted a soda.

Casey said yes; Sherry, sleepy, didn't say a word. Phillip gave a playful salute and ran toward the building. She couldn't see him go to the machine, because a tanker truck blocked her view. She could, however, see his wallet in the front seat of the car. Without it, he couldn't pay for the gas.

"One minute, honey," Casey whispered to her daughter, kissing her head. Now the words were an epitaph.

Sherry never answered—curling tighter, her mouth slightly open, her hands pressed between her legs. She wore a pair of brand-new blue jeans, red sneakers, a white and gold football jersey, and plastic bead bracelets. Her hair was pulled back by barrettes. The straps of her purse were wrapped about her wrists.

"One minute, honey."

Casey pressed down the locks and left the car. Thinking back, she hadn't rolled up the side window that she had unrolled for Phillip. *Damn* Phillip.

Casey gave Phillip his wallet; he paid for the gas and got change for the soda machine. Two sodas—both colas. Meaningless details. The first quarter jammed—Phillip forced the coin return and tried again.

Twenty seconds.

Phillip tried another quarter without any problem, then a second, and pushed the button.

Thirty-five seconds.

Casey's turn. In went the quarters, out fell the soda, and the clock kept running.

58

A minute ten.

Casey walked around the oil tanker and to the car. "Sherry?" Casey called.

The backseat was empty, the left side door open. "Sherry," calling a bit louder.

Phillip hadn't noticed a thing; not yet. He counted his money and sat in the driver's seat. Casey looked about, then returned to the building. Sherry had gone to the bathroom, that was all. Casey went to the side of the building and checked the women's room. The door was locked. Casey knocked on the door, then got the key from an attendant.

The toilet was empty.

"Sherry?"

She returned the key and asked the attendant if he had seen her daughter. No—he hadn't seen anyone. He had been in the garage. It's what he told Casey then, and what he told the police later.

"Goddamn it, Sherry!"

Phillip still hadn't caught on. He honked the car horn and got out of the car. Casey could have slapped him. She talked quickly, telling him to check the road while she again walked about the building. Together, they searched the high grass of a nearby marsh.

By the time they called the police, thirty minutes had passed.

Now Adam stood in the precinct house, staring at his ex-wife and her lover.

"Casey," Adam said softly.

Casey looked up at him—her eyelids swollen, her face blanched from shock. He expected her to hug him; to seek support from her former husband.

"Go to the desk sergeant," she said. "Tell me who you are and everything you know." With that, she again covered her face. Phillip left his seat and walked Adam to the sergeant. Briefly, Phillip explained what had happened at the gas station. Through it all, Adam said nothing.

"We tried calling you all night," he finished.

"I took something to help me sleep."

"It worked," Phillip said.

The desk sergeant saw them coming. "Mr. Druit?" said the officer. "If you'll sit at the table, Bill Wyler will be with you in a moment. He's writing the report on your daughter."

"Of course," Adam answered. He sat down and looked about the room. It was clean, open, and quietly efficient — everything he didn't expect from a police precinct. Then again, he had only seen the ones in New York City. Out here, appearance mattered.

Bill Wyler was a product of his office. Immaculate, handsome, his suit creaseless . . . When he greeted Adam, he leaned forward and looked deep into his eyes. "We've already checked the neighborhood near the gas station," he said, getting to the point. "I don't think she went into the marsh, but we won't know absolutely until we've done a complete search."

"Certainly," Adam said.

"It's still too soon for anyone to panic. Odds are she wandered off and got lost. We don't get any missing children out here that don't turn up."

Adam covered his eyes, scared for his daughter, embarrassed for himself.

"Your wife has given me a picture of your daughter. I thought you might like to add your own thoughts to help us. Fathers know different things about their children."

"I didn't see my daughter very often," Adam said.

60

"You must know something about the kind of clothes she liked, places she liked. Did she enjoy movies or games? Was she scared of anything particular? Does she have a favorite kind of food? A favorite friend?"

"I haven't seen my daughter in over a year."

Wyler listened, thought a moment, then sat back.

"Family problems," Adam felt obliged to add.

"Were you close to your daughter?" Wyler asked.

"We were once close," he said. "I don't know." He shook his head, confused, looking to Wyler for help.

"I'm asking so we can figure out where she went," Wyler said. "We're contacting all the places your wife can remember taking your daughter up until the moment she was lost. It's possible she ran off to one of those places."

"Of course," Adam said.

"It's also possible she ran away to see you. That means she may turn up at your door or be lost somewhere in Calverton. It's a possibility."

"I understand."

"We've already talked to the police in Calverton. They'll be keeping their eyes open. But you might want to contact any friends or relatives in the area and let them know what's going on. You never know who might see something."

"I'll get the word out," Adam promised.

Wyler smiled and shook his hand. "Your wife has been here for over twelve hours. Either you or her boyfriend should get her to a motel."

Adam left the detective. Casey was sitting alone at the bench, her body slumped against an armrest. At first, Adam thought she was asleep, but when he was almost by her side, she looked up at him.

Adam had never before seen such pain; not even

61

the day Casey and he separated.

"Where's Phillip?" Adam asked.

"Getting coffee," she said. "What did the detective say?"

Adam sat beside her. "He thought I should go back to Calverton, in case Sherry tried running off to see me," Adam told her.

"That makes sense."

"He doesn't think it's anything serious; he thinks she just got lost."

Casey stared at him. "Doesn't that sound serious to you?"

"You know what I mean," he said softly.

He tried to put an arm about her, but Casey twisted until he let go.

"You want a motel?" he asked.

"No," Casey said. "Thanks."

"The detective said there wasn't much point in hanging around his office."

"Phillip is getting me coffee."

"Casey—"

"Stop bullshitting me with your attention, all right?" she said. "I don't need this right now."

He left the bench. "I know how you feel," he said. "She's my daughter too."

Casey glared at him.

"I'll phone the moment I get home," he told her.

"Thanks," she answered.

Adam left the precinct and drove slowly home. He took the side roads back to Calverton, thinking the police would have the highway covered. Besides, Sherry had always liked the countryside. She loved playing in the grass and hiking in the woods, or getting herself lost in a pile of leaves. When he passed a farmhouse, he stopped. Sherry also loved animals. If

62

she saw a horse, or sheep, or cows . . .

Adam closed his eyes, haunted by memories.

Over an hour later, he reached his apartment. He went there first, just in case Sherry had shown up. Although the door was locked, he walked through all the rooms, calling her name, just making certain. Before leaving to search the streets, he wrote her a note. "Stay here," the note read. "I'll be back soon. I love you. Daddy."

After one more walk through the house, he left, leaving the door unlocked. He went straight to his car, sat in the front seat, and collected his thoughts. It wasn't enough to roam the streets. He needed a plan of action. Of course, the first stop was the police, to make his presence known; but then he would need to get the word out that his daughter was missing. Everyone had to be looking. He would have Murray put up a notice in the store, and of course Michael Ling. And . . .

Adam sat back.

There was no "and." Calverton was not his town. He knew no one; he had made a point of it. No favors, no friends. He had dug himself a grave, and now his daughter had slipped into it.

Sherry, he thought. Where would you go? How would you get lost?

The police, of course, assured him that all of the patrol cars had been informed of his daughter's disappearance. They suggested he stay at home, where they could reach him. They also told him the odds were nothing had happened—that Sherry got lost somewhere in West Bay and would be found in a matter of hours.

Adam left, certain the police couldn't find Sherry even if she was standing in front of the precinct. He returned to his car, turned the ignition, and began searching the town.

He saw a number of houses that day. He saw the sameness in the life-styles and learned how to tell people apart, from the type of house owned to the number of cars kept in the garage. One house, for instance, belonged to a family of four—a set of parents, a teenage son, and a baby girl, Adam guessed. He knew immediately there was a family, because the garage was for two cars and one of the cars was a station wagon. Through one window was a nursery—the walls decorated with pink wallpaper—and a boy's ten-speed rested in the yard.

Adam observed these things in a matter of seconds, recording them in his memory, then traveled to the next house. He checked all the main routes his daughter could have taken from the freeway to Calverton. Then he checked Calverton proper.

Calverton had its own "natural" town line—a set of railroad tracks, with a depot that had been neglected since its construction. On either side of the tracks were fields of overgrown, dead grass, sprinkled with cans and litter that never made it to the dump. Once Adam drove across the tracks and into town, the curl of front yards disappeared, along with the finished homes. In their place were the remnants of a town—an abandoned warehouse; a vacant gasoline station, its windows boarded by warped, broken plywood boards. At some time in its history, Calverton had overextended itself—reached for the railroad tracks and then contracted. These were the relics left behind. Alongside the relics, a bit closer to town, was the area's poorest neighborhood. It had no formal name, but most people referred to the area as Willow Street.

It was hard for Adam to read the neighborhood. It was as if the homes were so small that everything—sofas, bedsprings, toys, footballs, brooms, old televisions—had been forced outside. Laundry lines extended not only behind people's houses, but between them.

Things became worse when he entered downtown Calverton. Adam parked and checked the district store by store—always looking for his daughter and asking the store managers to keep an eye open. Maybe they listened.

Finally, it was time to return home. His note was by the front door, unread. He crushed it and went inside, heading straight to a bottle of depressants. Then he called the police in West Bay. He wanted to check in, tell them about his progress, and find out if there was any new information. The desk sergeant put Wyler on the phone.

"We have some more information, Mr. Druit," the detective said. "Someone came in who was buying gas at the time your wife visited the station."

"Does he know where my daughter is?" Adam asked.

"He may have seen your daughter," said Wyler. "He says he saw a man and a small girl enter a car and drive away in a blue station wagon."

Adam tried answering, but couldn't.

"It may or may not have been your daughter," Wyler continued, "but until she shows up, we're assuming it was."

"What . . ." Adam couldn't make sense of his own thoughts. The tranquilizer, he thought. Or was it the news?

The detective seemed to know what Adam wanted. "He doesn't remember anything about the man, or

65

much about the car, other than it was large. He did remember the man and the girl. But he only remembered that," said the detective, "because the girl was crying."

Chapter 5

Anthony Pecco lived three miles from the West Bay gas station. He was eighty-one years old, and until three years ago had owned a fruit and nut shop in lower Manhattan, New York City. He had since retired, selling his business to a Korean family.

He needed glasses for driving but didn't wear them, which was part of the reason he didn't remember a lot of details about the disappearance. But he also hadn't paid much attention to the incident. As a father of five children, he was more than familiar with family fights, which was all it seemed at the time.

Detective Wyler directed Pecco to an office, then returned to Adam and Casey.

"We'll go over the details with Mr. Pecco a few more times," said Wyler. "He's agreed to be hypnotized, but that won't be until tomorrow, so I don't think there's any reason for either of you to hang around. Mrs. Druit, you're staying at the Quality Inn on Route 83?"

She nodded.

"Do yourself a favor and get plenty of rest." Wyler smiled at her—a smile of sympathy, meant to hide his thoughts. "When we get your daughter back, she's going to need you in good shape." He turned to Adam.

"Mr. Druit, expect a police officer to visit you at your home later today."

"All right," Adam said.

"While this isn't taking off in that direction, as the parent without custody of the child, you have to be a suspect."

"I understand."

"In the meantime, let's not give up on your daughter simply getting lost. That's still a possibility."

"Of course," said Adam, wanting to believe it.

Wyler patted Adam's shoulder and returned to Pecco. Adam walked Casey out of the station house. She was almost carried by his grip—as if weightless. Outside, Phillip sat on the hood of his car, watching the highway.

"Anything new?" Phillip asked.

Casey stood absolutely still, her eyes focused on the ground. For a moment, Adam thought she was in shock, but Casey rested against Phillip and buried her face in his neck. Phillip led Casey away, and Adam went across the parking lot to his own car. He drove back to his house, where he thought more about his daughter and collected his drugs before the arrival of police. Finally, he sat cross-legged on his sofa, staring at a white wall, the curtains drawn, reeling through his daughter's life as if he were watching a movie.

"Sherry," he whispered, his daughter again secure in his arms, enjoying one of his favorite memories— Sherry resting against his chest, almost asleep, with one of her hands twisting his hair. She had been only two at the time. It was Adam's prime as a father, well before the crisis at the hospital; well before a lot of things.

He pushed aside these thoughts, wanting to focus more on his daughter and her kidnapper. What sort of man would abduct a little girl? And why was the man in West Bay? Was he driving his own car, or was that also stolen? Was he going to harm Sherry? Where was he going? What did he do to survive?

Then the real thought . . .

How could Adam catch him?

There was a knock on the door. Adam just now heard it, but it could have been going on for minutes. He answered, expecting the police officer.

"I want to look around, Adam."

Phillip pushed past him, scanned the living room, then turned into the bedroom. Adam followed. He found Phillip opening the closet doors, then turning and staring at the pile of clothes that had collected on his dresser.

"Why are the closets empty?" Phillip said. "What are you doing? Packing?"

"I never needed the closets."

Phillip shook his head, disgusted, not about to be put off. He got on his knees and looked under Adam's bed. "You've got big problems, Adam. Tremendous ones. But I'll be damned if I let you make Sherry part of them."

"I didn't kidnap Sherry," Adam said.

"That's not good enough," Phillip said, reaching for the suitcases. "You're a goddamn addict. You don't know what you are or where you are. You don't give a shit about anyone and you sure as hell don't give a shit about your daughter."

"Don't talk to me—"

"Except," Phillip continued, "except if you could use her to hurt Casey. Then you might do something, wouldn't you?"

Adam tried pulling Phillip out of the closet and out of the house. Phillip spun about, waving a wood hanger like a club.

"Don't even think about it," Phillip said.

Adam stopped and Phillip returned to his search.

"We wouldn't have come over here if it hadn't been for me," Phillip said, returning to his own thoughts. "Casey was ready to drive home Sunday morning. I talked her out of it. I talked her into giving you one more chance."

"I didn't touch Sherry," Adam said quietly.

Phillip didn't hear. He was talking more to himself than Adam. Adam reached for a jacket and went outside, passing two police officers at the door. "Make yourself at home," he told them, leaving.

He went to his car and once again began driving the streets, searching for his daughter.

It wasn't a good time of day to see Calverton. A clear, early evening sunset had colored the streets with a deep red. It was as if the town had been stained with his daughter's blood.

Phillip loves Sherry, he thought. Well, why is that surprising? Who couldn't love Sherry?

He drove through downtown Calverton and made a right onto Bishop Avenue. Like Willow, the name of the street had little to do with the neighborhood; there were no churches, and certainly no bishops. There were liquor stores, one or two groceries, and a pawnshop. All the stores were protected by wire fences. The biggest liquor store had its cashier behind a Plexiglas window. Outside, the poorest residents of Calverton—those without homes, and some that had merely drifted into the town, somehow straying off the freeway and never quite making it to either Providence or Boston—made a home of the street corners and doorways.

Adam left his car and entered the pawnshop. Wire mesh fences wrapped into the store, keeping the owner and his son in a secure, isolated prison beyond the reach of customers. The owner—finishing a sale—didn't look at Adam. There was no need to—the pawnshop was protected from crime. The owner's son, though, not only looked up; he waved Adam outside. Adam obliged, and in another moment, Ben left the store, joining him in the sunset.

"You promised not to come here," Ben said.

"I don't want to get you in trouble," Adam said, "but my daughter's missing."

"You *promised*."

"Look, you see lots of people in this store. I thought you might—"

"If anyone sees us talking. . ." He looked toward the store, his face in agony. "Shit, he's watching. He's going to see you."

"My daughter. She'd be alone with a man. They'd be traveling in a station wagon."

"If my dad—"

"Will you stop that?" Adam shouted. "Your father doesn't know who I am."

But Ben didn't hear. He rubbed his arms and walked nervously in place, desperately wanting Adam to leave.

"Shit, shit, shit . . ." Ben murmured.

Adam calmed down. Ben could never be of help. Ben also had every reason to be nervous; Adam had broken a trust.

"All right, I'll see you Tuesday," Adam said. He started to walk away, but turned back. "Incidentally, I got some bad news about your friend."

Ben looked confused. "Friend?"

"Your friend Petey. At the bar?"

"Petey?"

Ben's confusion was real. Adam supposed most of Ben's friends were disposable. He shook his head. "Never mind," he said.

Adam continued walking the neighborhood. The

71

sunlight was nearly gone, and the few working street lamps were flickering to life. Light also shined from the passing headlights of cars and the neon signs on the stores. Still, if his daughter was here, she'd be lost to the night.

His last stop was across the railroad tracks, beyond the gas station, just shy of where Calverton's "safe" neighborhood took root. This was the truest center of the town. Indeed, when the town was designed, this—not the courthouse or downtown Calverton—was meant to be its heart.

Adam parked the car and entered the Calverton library.

"Where's a pay phone?" he whispered to the evening librarian.

She pointed toward the rest room. Adam found the booth, entered, and closed the door. He had two phone calls to make: one to Casey, one to the police. He called Casey first.

"Hello?"

"Hi," Casey answered, sounding tired, but also familiar; more accepting. "I'm sorry about Phillip."

"It's all right."

"He thought maybe you wanted to hurt me. Revenge, I guess."

"That's what he told me."

"Phillip cares a lot about Sherry. There's nothing wrong with that."

"It's okay," Adam assured her. "I didn't call about Phillip. I just want you to repeat everything you know about the—disappearance." He had almost said kidnapping. Was he ready to admit that?

"You've heard everything," Casey said. "Sherry was in the backseat. I went to give Phillip his wallet. I came back, the door was open and Sherry was gone. I checked the gas station, I talked to the attendant—"

"Was Sherry holding anything valuable?"

"What are you talking about?"

"Did she take anything with her when she went out the door? She had her purse, didn't she?"

"It was filled with junk," Casey said.

"Are you sure?" Adam asked. "There wasn't anything someone might sell?"

"I don't know." He could sense Casey's confusion—her struggle for an answer. "Let me look through her things. Maybe I can remember something."

"Call me at home," Adam said. "Try calling me late, after eleven."

He hung up, wondering what Casey would tell Phillip, hoping she didn't dismiss his request. He didn't think she would. Casey was desperate, too.

He called the police station and asked for Wyler. Out, the clerk told Adam, but a Detective Shirley would be taking care of things while Wyler was gone. Yes, Shirley could call Adam in the morning. Yes, pictures of his daughter had been distributed. No, there was nothing more to do, except wait and see if anyone recognized her or the car. "If it's any consolation, Mr. Druit, we have more information than we normally do for an incident like this."

Adam thanked the clerk and hung up. " 'Incident like this.' " What was this kind of incident? Why couldn't anyone say the word?

Adam closed his eyes, again imagining the blue station wagon, trying to put himself in the mind of its driver. New questions came to him. Which direction was the car pointed—north toward New England or south? A man like this didn't get lost in West Bay—he looked for these small towns. Drifted in and out of them, attacking quickly, then continuing. Never a clue, never a fear of discovery, because there wasn't anyone to recognize him. Most times, word of the

73

crime never got past the state line. A psychopath, perhaps, intent on following a ragged path that led nowhere, except away.

He'd never return. Too dangerous. Maybe a snake-like path, zigzagging through the state, but never back to the scene of the crime.

In a blue station wagon, he thought. A dirty station wagon? Did the man camp in the woods? Or was it a city car? Maybe a trailer hitch was on the rear bumper. Could Anthony Pecco remember that? Had the police asked him?

Adam walked to the information desk of the library. "Where can I find the newspapers?" he asked.

The woman pointed to a distant wall with a long rack of newspapers. Next to the newspapers was a world atlas.

Adam took off his coat, claimed a desk, and carried off the atlas. Then he went back to the papers, not at all certain where he should start. Providence? Boston? New York?

He picked the Providence paper, flattened it on the desk, and began turning the pages.

Chapter 6

Michael Ling should have been at the front of his father's grocery store keeping an eye on the tangerines, apples, and green peppers and guarding the cash register. If he wasn't going to watch the produce, he could at least be studying.

Instead, he was on the telephone—long distance—interfering, as his father once told him, with other people's lives.

"Yes, I'm still waiting to speak with Mr. Fischer," Michael told the secretary, all too conscious of the expense of calling New York City. "I can keep holding, yes," he answered.

"Excuse me," a customer said, shaking a plastic bag filled with leeks. Michael looked to his father for help, but Yu Ling would not share Michael's responsibilities; not under these circumstances. Yu Ling remained on a crate, drinking his tea, staring into the lap of his pants. Michael glanced at the customer, his telephone, then again at the customer, knowing the cord couldn't stretch the distance.

"Put your money on the counter," Michael shouted.

"I need change," the customer said.

Fuck, Michael thought. He glared at his father,

dropped the phone, and ran to the register. With a motion he had mastered after years in the store, he weighed the leeks, slid the ten-dollar bill under the cashbox, counted the change, shoved it at the customer, and was back at the phone in less than a half minute.

"Hello?" he said into the mouthpiece.

"I said this is Barry Fischer," the person answered.

"Yes, Mr. Fischer," said Michael. "Dr. Barnes said I should give you a call. I'm phoning about Adam Druit. He said you could answer a few questions for me."

"How do you know Adam?" Fischer asked.

Michael had already invented his story. He told Fischer he was a personnel administrator at Rhode Island University. He explained that, after some preliminary talks with "the Board," they were considering Adam Druit as an undergraduate instructor. Unfortunately, Adam was reluctant to accept the position because of difficult circumstances surrounding his last job. At Adam's suggestion, Michael was calling several of his former colleagues to find out "the full story."

"I really don't think I should be going into any details," Fischer said. "The person you should be talking to is the director."

"I will be," Michael assured, but Dr. Barnes thought you could give me a fuller picture."

"Well, I knew Druit," Fischer said. "He was in charge of the pharmacology department."

"Excuse me," Michael said. "Did you say pharmacology or pharmacy?"

"I said pharmacology, but he was in charge of both really," Fischer said. "Pharmacology is responsible for pharmacy. The pharmacy is for dispensing drugs, while the pharmacology department also examines

76

the effects of drugs, their uses . . ."

"I know what the departments are for, Mr. Fischer; I just didn't hear you clearly," Michael said.

"Certainly."

"And you would recommend him?"

Fischer hesitated. "A qualified recommendation."

"Do you mind if I ask why?" Michael said.

That was all Michael had to say. Fischer began explaining the fall of Adam Druit, which was becoming something of a myth at the hospital—a reminder of just how far down a ladder someone could fall. Not that Adam had meant anyone harm, aside for perhaps himself. Nonetheless, it had been charged that Adam illegally arranged for the transport of a new antibiotic into the United States, although the drug hadn't received experimental approval from the Food and Drug Administration, and administered the drug to a patient. After the patient had died, Adam had been suspended by the hospital, and later, when the relatives of the patient sued, he was also fired and had his license suspended. The matter had since been taken to a review board and the courts, where Adam's attorney was appealing the judgments. The appeal, as Fischer understood it, was based on the drug's established use in Great Britain and the clear consent on the part of the patient. The attorney also claimed Adam didn't profit from the drug's use. As for the patient, he had been critically ill and beyond conventional therapy.

Michael asked if Adam Druit had himself experimented with drugs.

"That's not something I'll comment on," said Fischer.

Michael grinned, thinking of the exchanges between Adam and his father, wondering how much proof the lawyers would need to drive the last nail into Adam's coffin.

Michael finished the conversation by mentioning Adam was presently employed at the Main Pharmacy.

"No, that couldn't be right," Fischer said. "Adam can't be working. Not with his license on hold."

Michael retreated, saying Adam Druit only worked behind the cash register, adding receipts and stocking shelves. Fischer was shocked. "Jeez, that's too bad," he said, as if nothing could be worse than working the counter of a corner store.

Michael hung up, took care of another customer, then joined his father.

"I got the whole story," he told Yu Ling.

Yu Ling ignored him. His son, for all his promise, was forever searching for enemies. In school, it had meant fights with classmates and suspensions from teachers; in the store, Michael tested Yu Ling.

"He shouldn't even be working," Michael said. "He doesn't have a license. They took it away."

Yu Ling enjoyed his tea. He thought of earlier years—before Michael, before Calverton, back to his childhood in San Francisco's Chinatown. In those days, Chinatown was more a forgotten country than a neighborhood. That was in 1927. If not for his father, it would have been the only world Yu Ling knew. But his father was a laborer for a railway company. His job was to transport explosives. His father was often gone for months at a time. Once, he kissed Yu Ling's mother good-bye and didn't return for a year.

The job would eventually wear his father out, but while he worked, it meant Yu Ling, his mother, and three brothers had an apartment. Perhaps it spoiled Yu Ling. When he was nine, his father took him to the railway camp. His father thought Yu Ling could take advantage of the opportunity—either to find work, or to learn his father's practice.

Yu Ling for the first time saw a world that extended beyond the San Francisco Bay. His father's team worked across deserts, over mountains. . . . All the pieces of track fit perfectly together, becoming joints to one long finger that pointed east. Soon Yu Ling always looked east, even when the track turned in a different direction, because the morning sun also called him, rising gloriously and full of promises. One of those promises was that people were wiser in the east. People went west for adventure and east for culture. He hoped that in the east there wouldn't be the China-towns and ghettos that had mastered his family.

"A fraud," said Michael. "He comes in here telling me about medicines, when he drugged some old woman to death."

I came with the clouds, Yu Ling thought. His path was so determined that rarely did he bother with roads, and only once did he land in the company of railroad bums. There, he met another Chinaman, and they traveled two weeks together, before the clouds led Yu Ling in a different direction. His companion translated briefly for him the words of the hoboes. Yu Ling learned they considered him a crafty, goddamned Chink drifter. Yu Ling had heard it all before, except the word "drifter." Drifting, as in drifting across water? That was not at all what he did. Sooner or later, there would come the eastern shore, which he would call home. How could that be similar to a piece of wood floating lost on a lake or sea?

Beautiful expectations. If only the east had kept its promise.

But Yu Ling reached the east coast, and then the sun rose above the ocean, still calling him forward. And the clouds drifted past the shore and over the water.

Yu Ling was left on the shore, short of the horizon.

So he found new Chinatowns. Chinatown, Washington, D.C. Chinatown, New York. Chinatown, Boston.

And always, the clouds turned out to sea, and the sun made a glittering path across the ocean, creating a road Yu Ling couldn't walk.

Yu Ling instead turned west again. With his wife and baby, he found his home in Calverton.

"I should call the police," said Michael.

Michael pulled the tea out of his father's hand, hoping to force the old man to look at him. Yu Ling kept staring as if the cup were in his grasp. The tea was Yu Ling's retreat, and while Michael could take away the cup, he couldn't steal the dreams in Yu Ling's mind — clouds that had come from the tea and again promised Yu Ling a way to happiness, away from a son who punished him.

"*You* should be at the cash register," Michael ordered. "I already do all the work around here."

"I need a new son," Yu Ling said in Chinese.

"I need my own apartment," Michael answered in Chinese.

The grocery door opened and Michael turned. His anger slipped behind a guarded expression. "Mr. Druit," he said.

Adam looked worse than usual. His skin was pale, his eyes red, his shoulders hunched. He looked as if, instead of sleeping, he had made it the responsibility of his muscles and nerves to find time for their own rest.

He wore a jacket, but it was unbuttoned. Underneath, he had on a white shirt stained with several days' sweat. It was four days since he had first stepped into the library to search the newspapers. In that time, he had rarely bothered to go home, never showered, and only tasted food.

80

He had, however, found what he needed.

Yu Ling finally looked up and saw Adam. He waved Adam closer and gave him a small shopping bag. Adam looked inside it and saw a new mix of herbs. Finally, Yu Ling's expression changed to one of deep sorrow. He covered one of Adam's hands with his own, then kissed it.

"I told him about your kid," Michael said.

Yu Ling slumped in his chair with the sadness of generations.

Adam could have tried talking with Yu Ling, but he didn't have the time. Instead, Adam turned again to Michael. "I need to speak with you alone," he said.

Adam touched Michael to lead him outside, but Yu Ling refused to let go of Adam's hand.

"Sit down," Michael said. "Keep my dad company. He can't understand you anyway."

Adam did what he was told, and this satisfied Yu Ling, as if he could now protect Adam from Michael.

"I wanted to ask you a question, Michael," Adam said. "I wanted to know why you find me so interesting."

Michael stopped looking pleasant.

"Tell me the truth," Adam said. "What are you looking for?"

"I'm curious," he said. "I want to know why you're here. You're too smart for this place."

"So are you," said Adam.

"But at least I want to leave."

Adam considered the answer, then accepted it. "All right," he said. "And how much do you know about me?"

"Not much," Michael said.

"What does that mean?" Adam said.

Michael shrugged.

"Because if you know anything, then you should

81

know I've got nothing. Understand? That's why I'm in Calverton."

"So?"

"So," Adam said, "I've got nothing to lose."

Michael stared back, amazed. Adam was sending a message: I'm not worth blackmailing. But how did Adam know? Had someone told him about Michael's phone calls or was Michael simply that obvious?

"You shouldn't be dispensing medicine," Michael answered.

"You're right," Adam said.

Michael wondered what to say, uncertain, since he didn't know what to do. Not yet. "I should tell someone," he said.

"Will you?"

Michael thought a moment, then shook his head.

"Why not?" Adam asked.

"Because . . ." Michael considered his answer. He sensed a prize waiting if he gave the right one. "Because we trust each other."

It seemed the right answer. Adam leaned forward to confide with Michael. "It wouldn't matter anyway," Adam said. "I'm leaving Calverton."

Michael was stunned. Yu Ling noticed. From the corner of his eye, Michael could see his father give the slightest of smiles.

"I've got an idea about where my daughter is," Adam said. "I've spent the last few days going through different newspapers in about a five-hundred-mile circle. I've been collecting these." He reached in a coat pocket and pulled out a handful of copied newsclips. Michael fingered through them; there were no more than ten, some on the same stories. They were about the disappearances of small children—two boys, one girl.

"You're sure she's kidnapped?" Michael said.

"Almost," he answered.

Michael again examined the clips. The dates had been underlined, along with the descriptions of the children.

"Take a look at where I got these," Adam said. "East Brunswick, New Jersey. Mount Kisco, New York. Quaker Hill, Connecticut."

"I don't see the connection," Michael said.

Adam reached into his pocket and pulled out a map of the eastern shore. The three towns, in addition to Calverton, were circled in red. On the map, Michael could begin to see the relationship.

"It's almost a line."

"It's easier than that," Adam said. "The disappearances make a line heading north."

"It's too simple," Michael said. "Hundreds of kids disappear every day."

"The man who kidnapped my daughter just drifts from town to town," Adam said. "Maybe he goes into cities too. Who knows how much farther south he started—I didn't go any more down the map. If Sherry's alive, he's taken her north. That means I have to look for her there."

"You don't know if this is the same guy."

"I've got to tie up some loose ends, that's all," Adam said. "Call Casey. Go to the police. . . ."

"This doesn't make sense," Michael insisted. "If he kidnapped your kid, then where's the ransom note? Where's the blackmail?" Now Michael was excited. Adam had to stay in Calverton. Michael had just uncovered important secrets in Adam's life. Secrets that had to be worth something. "Who's going to run the pharmacy?"

Adam freed himself from Yu Ling's grip and insisted Michael follow him outside. Michael obeyed. His game was ruined. All the phone calls, his penetration into Adam's past . . ."There's someone I'd like you to meet," Adam said.

Adam looked over Michael's shoulder, toward the street corner. In Adam's car was Ben.

"That teenager is breaking off heroin, but hasn't been able to last in a program. A friend of mine has been keeping me supplied with methadone, which I've been passing along to Ben for three months. No profit in it. I swallow the cost. Like I said, a friend supplies me, so I don't pay a lot."

Michael stared at Ben. Ben stared back.

"Ben doesn't have any friends; at least who aren't in the same shape," Adam said. "I was hoping, since you're familiar with medicine, you could keep an eye on him while I'm gone."

"You mean be his supplier?" Michael said.

"No, I mean be there for him when he gets weak," Adam said. "You don't have to worry about the drugs. I've given him a prescription for an analgesic, which he'll pick up every week. It's already filled and waiting for him, except instead of an analgesic, the bottles have his methadone."

Michael grinned, starting to see the angle. "Come on," he said. "Who is it? His old man? Does he pay you for this?"

"No one pays me anything."

"You want me to do all the work while you collect the cash?"

"There's no money involved," Adam insisted.

Michael had to laugh. Christ, if only his father could hear this. Adam Druit—not only working without a license, but a drug peddler, too. What he found especially funny was how he had underestimated Adam. A man with this much on his hands wasn't going to jump if Michael came haunting him with ghosts. Adam was out of his league.

"I wouldn't have brought it up except Ben's been working hard," Adam said. "If you don't think you can handle the responsibility . . ."

"I can," Michael said.

"He may not even bother you. But if he has a problem, or if he needs a clinic—"

"I'll take care of him. No sweat. On one condition."

Adam waited.

"Nothing special," said Michael. "Just don't go killing yourself until I figure out how you can return the favor. All right?"

Michael reached out to shake on the agreement. Adam accepted his hand, then wrote down his supplier's name on the back of a card. "If you want to leave me a message, phone Detective Wyler in West Bay."

"You got the cops in on this?" Michael asked.

"Wyler's handling the investigation for Sherry," Adam said, again uneasy. But Michael put him at ease with a final assurance. Satisfied, Adam led Michael to the car and introduced him to Ben. Michael was professional, polite. Ben didn't respond. He looked once into Michael's eyes and saw everything but a friend.

"I've got to go," Adam said.

"No problem," Michael said.

"I hope you can handle this," Adam said. "I know I'm trusting you with a lot, but Ben's a good kid. If this goes well, I'll phone some friends about schools and maybe I can get you a recommendation. Maybe—"

"I said no problem," Michael repeated. "Just put this down as a favor."

Michael waved good-bye and went back to the store. Earlier, when Adam had said he was leaving, Michael had felt miserable; now, he never felt better. Yu Ling saw the difference. Michael made certain he did.

"Adam Druit is a smarter man than I realized," Michael told his father.

Michael waited for his father's reaction. Yu Ling didn't answer. He hadn't heard. His eyes were directed toward the window. Through the window, above the neighboring roof, Yu Ling could see the clouds, still traveling east. Away from Calverton.

Chapter 7

Adam rested on the sofa and remembered the night he'd abandoned his family.

It was the day Casey returned from the hospital. Rather than face his wife, he phoned a baby-sitter, then packed and left the apartment just an hour before Casey's arrival. Nor did he say good-bye to Sherry. Instead, he sneaked away while the little girl napped.

That was what fatherhood had been reduced to: Adam Druit, a man whose control of the world extended to his own metabolism, feeling endangered by the presence of everything he valued, including his own child. It was incredible. Someone trusted for his thinking and judgment—whose unorthodox experiments with drugs had enhanced his skills . . . made him sharper, more alert, more capable of seeing the endless subdivisions of an idea and then implementing the exact right choice. . . . A true wonder who had, for years, kept everyone in awe, including Casey . . .

Here was a man who prided himself on being on top of everyone and everything, and all of a sudden he wasn't just on top, but floating freely away.

Drugs. Thank God for them, at least. They were more than an escape; they transformed Adam—giving

him a chance to take himself or anyone else apart molecule by molecule, making whatever he wanted. The ultimate power. And for those who understood drugs
. . . for those blessed few . . . the world itself became
transformed. It became a union with life.

For a short time, Casey had understood. Then she
abandoned him, and Adam was not only left between
two worlds, but abandoned with their child.

An unbearable circumstance: his daughter, oblivious to her transformed father, turning to him for love,
trying to keep him from floating too far away; meanwhile, Adam floating farther and farther off. A safe
distance, where he couldn't see anyone. Not his dying
patients, not his family, not his child . . .

Adam opened his eyes.

Nearby was the telephone. He stared at it, knowing
he had to make his calls, but unable to stop the memories.

Sherry. What would have happened if he had stayed?
Would he have saved his daughter or hurt her? Christ;
what would he have done?

He sat straighter, forcing himself to focus on the
present, reaching for the phone and making three
calls—one to his lawyer, one to Casey, and one to the
police. His call to the lawyer was a return call; a chance
for Adam to excuse himself from life while he tried to
save his daughter. Adam didn't explain his trip, but he
made it perfectly clear that if anyone called him at
home, they would get only an answering machine.

His call to Casey was just as short. "I've got some
ideas about Sherry," he told her.

"Adam . . ."

"I don't have time to talk about it right now, all
right?" he said. "I'm leaving Calverton. I'll let you
know if anything turns up."

"If what turns up?" Casey asked.

88

"Anything," he answered. "Just some long shots. But if I don't do it now —"

"Adam, for Christ's sake, what are you talking about?" Casey said.

"I'm talking about finding Sherry," he said.

"You?" Casey said. "Finding Sherry?" She struggled with the concept, not sure whether to love Adam or hate him for even contemplating such a conceit. "Adam, you can't even find your way to a fucking clinic."

"I can do it, Casey," Adam said. "You can trust me."

Adam didn't know how absurd he sounded. The innocence of it all was too much for Casey, and she cried.

"And I didn't kidnap Sherry," he said. "I swear it."

"I wish you had," Casey whispered, hanging up.

Then Adam phoned the West Bay police. He talked to Wyler's assistant — had the police tape the conversation, so Adam wouldn't have to call back. Adam said he left his apartment door unlocked, just in case Sherry reappeared. At the same time, he didn't think Sherry was in West Bay or Calverton. Adam explained briefly his research in the library and said he was going north. He would phone every day; otherwise, if they had any messages for him, they should call Casey.

"I'm sure the detective would appreciate talking to you himself," the assistant said.

"Tell him I'm sorry," Adam answered, hanging up.

With his calls out of the way, he threw his bags in the car and went back to the apartment, just to be certain the door was unlocked. He also left a note on the mailbox telling Sherry to go inside, not giving a damn about thieves. He was ready to go, except for one thing — he was still missing the tools of his trade, the magic that had kept him alive for the past two years and would help keep him alive now. He drove downtown and parked in front of the pharmacy. It was seven in the evening, and Murray was getting ready to close early. Adam had been his company at night. Without a companion, Murray didn't feel safe.

Adam walked to the rear of the store, where he kept the prescription drugs. He reached in a desk drawer and found the keys to the cabinets. On a marble countertop was a black attaché case, with plastic bottles that fit securely between blocks of soft Styrofoam. He began replacing the empty bottles with ones from the cabinets.

Murray walked up behind him.

"Didn't you hear me?" Murray asked. "I said 'hello.' "

Adam didn't answer. He twisted the top off a brown bottle, reached in a drawer, and removed a box labeled "Isordil—Sublingual, 5 mg." Small gray pills, no more than five millimeters in diameter. He filled a bottle, then reached in another drawer. Capsules, part purple, part clear, filled with tiny red and white pellets. "Dexedrine," said the label. "5 mg." Then he reached for a tinted bottle. "Valproic acid," Adam scrawled on its side, filling it with the red syrup.

"Every customer that comes in, I ask about your daughter," Murray told him. He picked up one of the bottles and shook it. The pills clicked in the container. "You gonna be gone long?"

"Don't know," said Adam. He put another jar in the attaché case. "Chlorpromazine hydrochloride," he wrote.

"You want mc to close up the pharmacy?"

"You don't have a choice," Adam said.

Murray put the bottle back in the attaché. "That means you're not coming back, I suppose. You're leaving me here with all this garbage."

"I'll be back."

"Sure," Murray said, walking away. He watched

90

Adam snap shut the attaché case, then walk to the rear sink, lift his head, and take two deep swallows. Adam rubbed his eyes and faced Murray.

"Vitamins," he told Murray.

He went for the door. Murray watched, mystified. Despite the drugs, despite the trauma of a missing kid, Adam was carrying himself like a family doctor who had just snapped together his medical kit and was heading for the next sick household.

"I'll phone you in a week," Adam promised.

"I bet you don't know the phone number."

"I'll call information."

"Do that," Murray said.

"I will," he said. "And Murray, don't stop asking about my daughter, okay? I'd appreciate it."

Murray waved him out. "Take care of yourself," he said.

Adam nodded and left, only now seeing the picture of Sherry against the front window. It was good to see. Still, she wasn't in Calverton; Sherry was somewhere else. And Anthony Pecco was the first step to his daughter.

It was for Pecco that Adam had packed the hallucinogen.

Adam looked once at the sheet he had torn from a phone book directory, then headed south to West Bay.

The differences between Calverton and West Bay were especially noticeable at night. When the sun disappeared, Calverton virtually hid in the darkness, as if afraid of being seen. In West Bay, the bright yellow street lamps made their first appearance five miles outside of the town. It was like having an escort into the city, to assure everyone that West Bay was a good place to visit, to spend money and that nothing dangerous

91

could happen there.

West Bay was a resort town. Motels routinely said NO VACANCY, and the roads were dotted with ice cream stores, pizza counters, kite shops, T-shirt counters. . . . The city survived on throwaway items as cheap as the plastic syringes Adam stashed in his attaché case. Along the shore were the amusement arcades and nightclubs — speed limit 15 miles, just to make certain no one missed a chance to spend money. Adam drove a quarter mile, then escaped the traffic by heading inland. He parked opposite a two-story bungalow. Through the living room window, to the side of the porch, Adam could see the glow of a television set.

He took his car keys, pocketed two bottles from the attaché case, and walked to the front door. He knocked once, waited, then knocked again. After the second time, the volume lowered on the television. A curtain drew back, then dropped. Two bolts slid free. When the door finally opened, Adam forced a smile. "Mr. Pecco," he said.

"Mr. Druit?" Pecco answered. The indoor lights deepened the lines and shadows of Pecco's face. Adam studied him carefully, trying to judge Pecco's fitness, aware that Pecco was over eighty. He wondered how many milligrams Pecco could safely metabolize.

"I had some more questions about my daughter," Adam said. "Since I'm leaving town, I wanted to first try them on you."

Pecco welcomed Adam into his house. Adam entered quickly, giving only a cursory glance at Pecco's furnishings. It was a warm wood interior, with furniture that had aged and discolored. Pecco had moved into West Bay one year before it went tourist. Now he was the poorest person living this close to the boardwalk. Every real estate agent in the area was probably praying Pecco would die. Adam wanted to be sure he didn't accommodate them. He looked for a satisfactory work area and chose the living room couch.

"Would you like something to drink?" Pecco offered.

Adam watched how well Pecco walked into the room. Clear, careful footsteps. Normal breaths. No sweating.

"I've told the police everything I know," Pecco said. "They tried to hypnotize me."

"It didn't work?"

"Guess I don't hypnotize easily." Pecco turned off the television and settled in an armchair. Without television, Adam could hear music from a neighboring house; a rock record. Probably the whole neighborhood was two or three generations younger than Pecco. Pecco didn't mind. He didn't seem to hear the music. Adam wondered if he was hard of hearing.

"My daughter was kidnapped," Adam said. "From what you told the police and from what I've learned since, it's almost certain."

Pecco sank deeper in his seat. "Sorry to hear that."

"I wanted to talk with you and make sure I got everything." He put his hands in his pockets, his fingers resting on the bottles. "I'm a pharmacologist. Did you know that?"

"No, I didn't."

"A year ago I worked as director of a clinical pharmacy in a hospital. That's how I made my living—helping doctors decide what drugs to administer to their patients."

"Didn't know pharmacists did that," said Pecco.

"Pharmacologist," Adam corrected. "A lot of people think we just fill out prescriptions. That might be true for some pharmacologists or pharmacists, but others do the prescribing. A doctor comes to us for advice, and we tell them what the patient needs. We have to know our medicines before we give them out."

"I can appreciate that," Pecco said. "I owned a store in New York — "

"I'm telling you this because I want you to know I'm a professional," Adam said. "I wouldn't put you at any kind of serious risk."

Pecco just listened.

"My daughter . . ." For a moment, Adam had a perfect image of his daughter — imagined her sitting on Pecco's lap like a granddaughter. He could see Sherry resting her head in the creases of Pecco's shirt, her hands tucked between her legs.

The silence made Pecco uncomfortable. "I told the police everything I know," he said. "A man with a little girl in tow. He was wearing a windbreaker, think. A white man, with dark, short hair. Didn't see his face. Got inside a dark-colored station wagon."

"You don't remember anything else?"

"I wish to God I did, Mr. Druit," said Pecco. *"Dr.* Druit. I wish I had the man who kidnapped your daughter in this very room. I'd likely blow away his head. But that still doesn't mean I remember anything else."

"Even with the hypnosis?"

"Right, sir," said Pecco. "Didn't pull anything out of me."

"Did they give you any drugs when you submitted to the hypnosis?"

"No," said Pecco.

"Nothing to relax you?"

"They didn't think I needed it," Pecco answered.

"So you wouldn't have objected?"

"Hell, no," said Pecco. "I'm no stranger to medications."

"I'm asking, Mr. Pecco, because that's what I'd like to do," said Adam. "Do you have any heart trouble?"

"No heart attacks, if that's what you—"

"Are you presently on any medications?"

"Just something for the bowels. But—"

"Are you allergic to any medicines?"

"Not medicines," said Pecco. "Foods, maybe."

"Is anyone in your family—"

"I haven't got any family," Pecco said curtly.

Adam couldn't pretend sympathy. His thoughts were already on the next question. "Mr. Pecco, have you been in the hospital recently for any medical treatment? Is there anything in your past that I should know?"

"I don't mean to be rude," said Pecco, "but I don't see how that's any of your business."

Adam put one of the bottles on the coffee table.

"I want to give you a drug, Mr. Pecco," Adam said. "Something to make your memory more vivid."

Pecco frowned more deeply.

"I prescribed this in the hospital," Adam explained. "Its toxicity is extremely low, especially at the dosages I intend to administer. The hallucinogen is a sedative, usually for operations. But at certain levels, it can reproduce very vivid memories."

"Hallucinogen? You mean like LSD?"

"LSD is illegal," said Adam. "This is medicine."

Pecco nodded slowly, as if he appreciated the difference.

"Have you ever had any problems with medications? Has any member of your family—"

"I already answered that," Pecco said. He looked at Adam, studying his eyes, judging Adam's character. "I don't know if I like this idea." He hesitated, then said, "You're really a pharmacologist?"

Adam nodded.

"And this thing on the table. It's medicine?"

"Absolutely."

Pecco lifted the bottle, twisted off the cap, and smelled the inside. The odor made him pull back. "Do I need an injection?"

"We can mix it in a little juice, if you have any."

"In the refrigerator," Pecco answered, leaving the room, going to the kitchen, and pouring a cup of orange juice. Adam worked quickly, afraid Pecco would change his mind. He unscrewed the bottle, measured 10 milligrams into a small plastic cup, then set it aside. Pecco returned, putting the glass of juice near the cup. Adam poured the medicine into the juice.

"Please sit on the sofa and drink this," Adam said, handing him the glass.

Pecco sat and studied the glass. He held it up to a light and turned it slowly, looking for the drug. He saw nothing, and when he smelled the juice, he detected only the orange pulp.

"I know what I'm doing," Adam assured him.

"You already said that," Pecco answered, taking a long breath and a hesitant sip. When he tasted nothing, he took another one. Within a minute, the glass was emptied.

Adam, satisfied, took away the glass, then counted the man's pulse. An injection would have been the quicker method, but also more dangerous and less likely to be agreeable to Pecco. Instead, the drug would take the slower route into the blood system — through the intestinal walls. Adam guessed ten minutes before Pecco showed the effects. Adam suggested they turn on the television, and Pecco agreed, leaving his seat to turn on a late-night comedy show. Pecco watched the television while Adam watched Pecco. Adam left only momentarily, to pour himself a glass of water and prepare a solution of quinidine sulfate, just in case of any problems with Pecco's heart. Once Pecco slipped into a hallucinogenic state, Adam estimated he had fifteen minutes to get the information; then Pecco would fall quickly to sleep.

Adam reached in his pocket and opened a bottle of amphetamine tabs. He set one on the back of his tongue and sucked on it slowly, like a candy. He wanted to be wide awake for this—clear-headed, quick, ready.

When he returned, it took Adam a minute to see the change in Pecco. "You enjoying the show?" Adam asked.

"It's all right," Pecco answered.

Adam glanced at the screen. "You feel anything yet?"

"I suppose."

Adam finally noticed. Pecco wasn't watching the television; he stared off to the side. When Adam turned it off, Pecco's attention remained fixed to the open air. If anything, his concentration grew stronger, no longer bothered by the secondary image.

"Mr. Pecco, what do you see?"

Pecco shook his head. His expression was one of amazement.

"You should see lots of colors, Mr. Pecco," Adam said. "Don't be at all concerned. It's part of the experience."

Pecco looked at Adam and Adam tightened. For a moment Pecco's face had flushed and his eyes turned wet from tears. It had all the appearance of a heart attack, and Adam, alert to trouble, was set to jump forward. But then Pecco stopped crying; instead, he smiled broadly.

"That was wonderful," Pecco said. His hand trembled as he reached out to rub the wall. "I had a hallucination, I think." His fingers gently traced the outline of a face. "My wife."

Adam found Pecco's hand and held it. "It's the drug," Adam said.

Pecco looked about the room. He leaned back, as if unable to keep his balance. "Jesus Christ. You poisoned me."

"No," said Adam. "It's medicine." Adam felt the power of the amphetamine, noticing every detail of Pecco's face, thinking ahead to any actions Pecco might make. When Pecco started slipping off the sofa, Adam moved instantly to catch him and sit the man softly on the carpet. Adam loosened Pecco's shirt and again checked the pulse. They were in two different worlds—Pecco in a slow moving, sedated, dreamlike state, and Adam at a fever pitch, all too aware of the dangers for which he had volunteered Pecco.

"The house is moving," Pecco said. He struggled against Adam, trying to free himself.

"Hold still," Adam said. "Think of the gasoline station. Remember what happened to my daughter."

Pecco stopped fighting. He closed his eyes and nodded, talking to himself, remembering why he had taken the drug. "Yes," he murmured, ever so tired, imagining the details of that night. When he opened his eyes again, he was standing next to his car, pumping gas, his body frozen while the rest of the world moved. The islands of the gas station stretched forever. Indeed, the gas station could have been the world—its only purpose to serve Pecco's car. His car, and the tanker, and the silver Toyota, and the . . .

"Think of the station wagon, Mr. Pecco."

He remembered the car. A deep, dark blue. Not as dark as the night sky, but as mystical. In his dream, the car had an iridescence; and when the driver stepped out, the light from inside the car was blinding.

"I can't see," Pecco said. He was guarding his eyes, as if the light was real. "The car is glowing."

"What about the driver?"

Pecco strained for a view. Dark hair that had a wet

sheen and reflected the fluorescent coolness of a street lamp. His eyes . . . Pecco could see them now. Metal red. "God," Pecco groaned, hunching forward. A moment later, the demon was in the neighboring car, dragging out a little girl, tearing at her clothes and forcing the child into the station wagon. But it was no longer a station wagon—it had become a hearse. "A monster," Pecco said. He held tightly onto Adam. "Your child's been kidnapped by an awful creature." He looked to Adam for help.

The monster glared back at him.

"Oh, God," Pecco cried.

He slumped forward and Adam caught him. "It's just a nightmare," he told Pecco. Pecco didn't hear, his face tightening. "Forget the driver—think of my daughter."

Pecco grew less tense. The pain in his face became sadness. In a few minutes, he would be completely sedated. "Beautiful," he whispered. His fingers relaxed and slid off Adam's arm. "I've never seen a child so warm, so lovely." Pecco's vision took him into heaven. Adam shook Pecco to keep him awake.

"What does she look like?" Adam asked.

"Brown hair, soft face," he said. "She's holding something. A purse."

"What does the purse look like? Can you see it?"

Pecco turned his head slightly to get a better look. He nodded, excited. "Plastic purse," he said. "With pictures of mice."

"Is there anything special about the mice?"

"They're dressed, and they're in a circle, dancing."

Adam leaned away from Pecco, stunned by the accuracy. His daughter had carried that purse for years. If there had been any doubt of Sherry's having been kidnapped, Pecco had just taken it away. Pecco's smile disappeared. "She's going." His expression grew deadly serious—a man forced to watch something awful. "She's in the car. He's grabbing her. Hitting her."

"Tell me about the car," Adam said. "Can you see the license plate?"

"She's screaming," Pecco said. He crawled to the sofa, struggling to stand. Adam forced him to relax. "He's *killing* her."

"No, he's not," Adam said. "He wouldn't do that in the gas station."

"I can see it," Pecco insisted. "She's *screaming*. She's—"

"Read the license plate," Adam said.

Pecco closed his eyes and dropped back. "Blue sky," Pecco said. "Light blue sky."

"The license," Adam pleaded.

Pecco didn't answer. The anesthetic had taken full hold.

Adam checked Pecco's pulse and, satisfied, carried him to the bedroom. Adam sat beside Pecco until he was certain the drug had eased into little more than a sleeping tonic. Then, assured of Pecco's safety, Adam concentrated again on his clues, reaching into his back pocket for a map, knowing he had to hurry north. If only he knew how much of the hallucination was fantasy and how much was real. The purse had been real—Pecco couldn't have known the design otherwise. And it was possible the kidnapper had greased-back hair, slick and wet. That could be useful in an age of blow dryers.

Adam wiped his face. He could feel the ebb of his last pill and knew he needed another. At the same time, he realized that if he kept going at this pace, the pills would catch up on him. Still, there wasn't time for sleep. He had to find Sherry.

A few minutes later, he was back in the car. He slid the attaché case on the side seat, reached for a second bottle of amphetamines, then settled behind the steering wheel. His movements were quick and automatic — not daring to waste a second, anxious to keep close on the trail of Sherry's kidnapper. Only once did he pause, and this was after seeing himself in the rearview mirror. Adam stopped, staring into his own eyes, mesmerized.

Christ, he thought. What a sight.

It was enough to make him believe in the living dead.

Chapter 8

Wheeling, Massachusetts was a restored eighteenth-century village, styled after the more famous Old Sturbridge Village in the central part of the state. During July and August, Wheeling took particular pride in its summer stock theaters; however, after the summer, most of Wheeling's revenue came from tours of the town. To insure this money, all of the buildings on Wheeling's main street were registered historic landmarks.

The Wheeling Trading Post was one of these landmarks. In fact, Jack Kiley couldn't change the front of his store without an ordinance exemption from the township. That same ordinance required him to make his store available to tour groups twice a day. Crowds of families entered his pawnshop, most of them the sort of people who wouldn't otherwise be caught dead in such a place. They certainly weren't about to buy a second-hand watch or radio. So Jack tried making up for the business by selling souvenir pencils, glass ashtrays, and some remainder bicentennial flags. During the season, maybe a hundred tourists a day saw his store and bought his pencils.

So why did everyone suddenly expect Jack Kiley to remember some no-name who may have sold him a gold hairbrush?

Well, not *everyone,* Jack admitted. Just one person who wouldn't stop bothering him.

The question came long distance and over the telephone. Probably from a pay phone, too, because the operator made the connection.

"I've been calling stores looking for a woman's hairbrush," said the stranger.

"I have lots of brushes," Jack had said.

"The one I want would have been sold to you during the past week. A gold one."

Jack heard the voice straining; the sort of sound a customer made when he wanted something bad. Jack considered his answer carefully, sensing an easy dollar, and wondering just how many he could turn.

"I got a brush," he finally said. "Came in two days ago. Woman's brush, right? Nice finish?"

"Yes," the stranger said.

"Sure," Jack said. "But it's sold. Got a down payment."

"I'll pay you fifty dollars for the brush."

"Already got fifty," said Jack.

"I'll pay a hundred," said the stranger.

Jack, pleased with himself, looked to his cabinet and saw a half-dozen brushes.

"You're sure, though," the stranger said. "The brush I want would have come in last week."

"Sure I'm sure," said Jack. "But we close in three hours."

"I'll be there in two," the stranger said, hanging up.

Jack grinned, certain he had made the sweetest deal of the week. And to make the deal better, he'd done it to some roaming asshole who needed two hours to reach

103

Wheeling.

The next hour and a half passed easily, even with the tourists. Jack sat by his coffee machine, sipping a hot cup, watching as his store seemed to sell itself. A dozen flags, a violin, a low price on a quality camera . . . Good money coming in, good savings going out. It was enough to make him think of taking a three-day weekend — ride with the luck, leave right now, and enjoy the time.

"We talked on the phone?" the stranger said.

There were maybe four people in the store when the stranger arrived. Still, Jack knew the man instantly. It wasn't the stranger's appearance; the man was dressed like any of the rich pricks that had overrun Jack's town — a mock country look that should never be allowed outside a city. But he remembered the voice, plus the stranger had this stare. He looked through Jack, as if Jack was an obstacle to something else.

"Did we?" Jack said, feigning disinterest.

The stranger's attention shifted to the display case and he pressed a finger to the glass. "Is that the hairbrush?"

Jack followed the stranger's finger. There were five brushes on display. None was real gold, because Jack had almost all his valuables in a safe. Yet he unlocked the counter, put on a velvet glove, and held one of the brushes as if it was priceless. Very carefully, he rested it on the counter.

The stranger stared at the brush a long time. Meanwhile, Jack studied the stranger. A minute passed, and not once did the stranger blink.

"You bought it this week?" the stranger again asked. His voice was quiet — almost pleading. Weakening, Jack thought.

"What's so special about it anyway?" Jack said.

"It belonged to my daughter," the stranger confided.

"She's missing."

"Runaway?"

The stranger turned the brush in the light. "Is this really the brush?" the stranger again asked.

Jack shrugged. "You only asked if someone sold me a gold brush. I don't keep inventory like that. You wanted a brush, you got a brush."

"A *gold* brush?" the stranger asked.

Jack looked annoyed. "Hey, she's your daughter. Is it her brush? Can't you recognize it?"

The stranger shook his head. "I thought I could. I gave it to her mother five years ago. I thought I could recognize it, but I can't." The stranger moved closer, his eyes pleading. "Is this the brush?"

Jack wanted so much to say "yes," but he couldn't make the final lie. The stranger scared him. Jack sipped his coffee and hid behind his coffee mug. "Look," he finally said, "you promised me a hundred bucks for a brush. I can't tell you anything for certain. If you don't want the brush, don't buy it."

The stranger dropped the brush and turned away, his eyes now focused on a clothes rack. It was a long row of dresses, skirts, blouses, sweats. . . . Jack sold any item on the rack for five dollars.

Jack thought he was losing a customer. He wondered if he should bring out the real gold brushes. "Don't get so impatient," Jack said. "Wait a minute and I'll get something from the rear."

But the stranger ignored him, dipping into the clothes rack and carefully pulling free a child's sweatshirt. He held it up to the light with the same interest he had shown the brush.

"Sherry," he whispered.

"What?" Jack said.

"It belonged to my daughter," the stranger said.

Jack didn't like hearing that. He thought the stranger

was maneuvering, maybe to say the brush and shirt already belonged to him. "Hey, it's just a sweatshirt," Jack said. "You want it, it's five dollars."

The stranger reached into his coat for a curl of bills. The stranger stripped away ten dollars and dropped it on the counter. Jack took the money, finding some comfort from the exchange. It was something that put him back in control, and he went to the cash register. "We'll put the extra five toward the brush, right? That's a difference of ninety-five. Make it ninety even."

The stranger spread the sweatshirt on the counter and folded it carefully, as if handling a silk linen. Jack waited, impatient to finish the deal.

"He was here."

"Excuse me?" Jack said.

"The man who took my daughter," said the stranger. "He sold you the sweatshirt."

"Hey, friend, I don't know anything—"

"What about the brush?" the stranger said. "Do you have a ticket for that?"

Jack considered whether to answer. The stranger tried making it easier by dropping two hundred dollars on the counter.

Jack coughed in his fist, collected the money, and walked to the rear of the store. "You wait there," Jack ordered. He kept the pawn tickets above the safe, near his gun. He glanced back and saw the stranger slouched tiredly by the counter, running his face against the sweatshirt. Satisfied, Jack went to his file box.

There was, in fact, a possibility he had this mysterious brush. Between conversations, he had given the matter serious thought and remembered being sold a gold-plated brush five days ago. The sale had slipped out of Jack's memory, because Jack hadn't been in the best of minds at the time; he had, in fact, been drunk. But he had bought such a brush from a dark-haired man with a mustache. He looked like one of the tourists Jack saw coming in and out of his store every day. Wore a Nike windbreaker, if Jack remembered correctly. Jack considered passing this information to the stranger.

But then he couldn't find the right file card.

"Hell," Jack murmured.

He wanted card 466-G. G for "Gold," plus the item number. "465-G, Bracelet," said a preceding card. "Bamburger, Joseph." Behind it was "467-G, Chain; Hoefler, Donna."

No luck. Jack had two choices: he could forfeit the deal by telling the truth or he could do his best to keep the customer happy.

"I got it," he said, carrying the wrong card. "Joseph Bamburger. From Boston. Number's 465-G. Came in last week."

He scribbled the name on a notepad, then tore off the top sheet, folded it, and pressed the piece of paper into the stranger's hand.

The stranger kept his hand open. "I didn't think he'd be from Boston," he said. "He wasn't heading east."

"What can I say?" Jack said.

The stranger nodded, even smiled. "Thanks," he said. He reached in a pocket and pulled out another fifty dollars. "You don't know how important this is."

Jack offered a mild refusal, but the stranger pushed the money on him. A moment later, the stranger was out the door. Jack followed, watching the man weaken in the late sunlight and stagger toward his car. Hell, the stranger was no more than a shadow; when the sunlight faded, so would he.

Jack gave the deal a last thought, then locked the store, determined to give himself a three-day weekend. That required doing his inventory this evening, instead of Sunday. He turned off all the lights but a desk lamp and settled in his office. It was a dreadfully sleepy evening, made easier only by the extra cash in his pocket — money gained without having to sell a single piece of merchandise. His company was a small television set — one of many he had ticketed in his shop. He worked until eleven.

Then, just a few minutes past the hour, he heard a windowpane crack.

He flicked off the television and the desk lamp. He could hear the window clasp being turned and the frame forced up. Jack found his gun and moved quietly out of the office. He was surprisingly calm; but in a way, he had anticipated the break-in. He sat on a stool, waiting until the thief was completely in the store — until the thief had stumbled onto the floor and Jack could hear him moving past the clothes rack. Finally, Jack turned on the store lights.

It was the stranger. The man straightened himself, momentarily off guard, his face ashen. Bloodless, Jack thought. If the stranger had been weak earlier in the day, Jack imagined he was now near a state of collapse.

The stranger reached in a coat pocket — slowly, to assure Jack he wasn't reaching for a weapon. The stranger was returning the piece of paper Jack had sold him.

"You wrote down the wrong name," the stranger said. "Joseph Bamburger didn't take my daughter."

Jack said nothing, showed nothing. The stranger leaned forward to drop the paper on the counter.

"I want to know who sold you the gold brush."

Jack shook his head. "You got a lot of balls breaking into my store and asking me anything."

"I want what I paid for," the stranger said.

"I don't know what the hell you're talking about," said Jack. "Stop by in the morning if you got a complaint."

"There's no time," said the stranger.

"Bullshit," said Jack. "I don't even know what you're

108

talking about. You got a receipt? You got any proof you bought something here? You write me a check?"

"I don't care about the money," the stranger said. "My daughter's been kidnapped. The man who sold you the brush may be nearby."

Jack didn't believe a word. "Look," he said, "if you got a problem with a kidnapper, you phone the police. Hell, I'll phone them for you." He reached for the phone, expecting the stranger to stop him.

"Tell them my name is Adam Druit. Tell them to call the police in West Bay. Ask for Detective Wyler."

Jack stopped, now wondering if he was somehow being set up. Maybe by his brother. Ruin Jack's business by making him look like a criminal, withholding evidence. Or maybe the Wheeling town council. They'd been wanting to take his store for over ten years — turn it into a visitors' center. Prime property, Jack's store. And if it was a setup, Jack had already taken the bait money — all two hundred fifty dollars. Christ, how much of an idiot was he turning out to be?

"All I want is the name of the man who sold you the brush," Adam repeated.

Jack hung up the phone.

"I want what I paid for," Adam said.

"You didn't pay for *nothing,*" Jack answered. He was sweating. The gun shifted uneasily in his grip, while Jack wondered whether to pull the trigger. The man was a thief, damn it. He broke into the store.

"My daughter's in trouble."

"I don't sell stolen goods," Jack said. "And I didn't have anything to do with kidnapping anyone's kid."

"I didn't say — "

"Who the fuck are you to tell me anything?" Jack shouted. "You think I'm dumb? You think I don't see what's going on?"

"Nothing's going on — "

109

"Bullshit," said Jack.

"Ten days ago, a man kidnapped my daughter."

"I don't want to hear," he said.

"The brush and the sweatshirt —"

"Shut up," Jack said.

"They were taken from my daughter by a man with black hair and —"

"Shut *up*."

Jack pulled back on the gun's hammer. He aimed the weapon, almost ready to fire.

"Get out of my store," Jack said.

Adam finally understood. He stepped back toward the door.

"No," Jack said. "You came in through the window, you go out the window."

Adam obeyed and Jack moved forward, keeping his gun ready.

"Don't you ever come back here, okay?" Jack said.

Jack shoved him in the face and Adam tumbled over the windowsill. A minute passed before Adam moved, and Jack worried that he had again been suckered — that maybe Adam wanted to be hit, so someone could take pictures.

Adam crawled to his feet, looked a last time at Jack, and walked away. Faded away, Jack thought.

And then Jack fell heavily on his stool. He turned to his coffee maker and poured himself a fresh cup. Was it over? Jack fought the shivers. With his gun tucked in his belt, he went back to the window and slid a filing cabinet in front of it. Should call the police, he thought. Maybe phone in a few things as missing; collect on the insurance.

"Fuck it," he said, sipping his coffee and heading back to his office. He'd spend the night here. In the morning, he'd look into security systems — something he should have done years ago. Do a little business, and then get away for a few days. And if anyone bothered him, he'd always have the gun.

So Jack spent the night in his office, with the television as company and all the lights on. Because he was up all night, he opened especially early, managing to make a few sales before working hours. In fact, he did a healthy load of business, which impressed him— mostly from teenagers who needed to hock electronics to return the cash they'd stolen from their parents. He bought maybe four hundred dollars in good merchandise and gave out only eighty. In three weeks, he could sell it all for a hefty profit. It was enough to consider hiring a part-time worker for a morning shift.

But who could you trust with the safe and the cash, Jack thought. Besides, there was no room for amateurs in a business where every deal was negotiated and so much depended on a person's skill in handling merchandise.

Jack stopped his daydreaming at ten o'clock and the first rush of tourists. There were three scheduled tours through his store—the last, thank God, at two o'clock. Jack would close his store at two fifteen.

"How much are the bicentennial flags?" someone asked.

Jack gave the price, took the money, and settled by his coffee machine. He remembered wanting to buy a security system, but in the daylight, burglars didn't seem important. Wheeling, after all, wasn't a high-crime town. Besides, no one could break into his safe, and security systems didn't come cheap.

"You got any books?" someone else asked.

Jack pointed to a carton behind the clothes rack, then made it back to his cash register before the next wave of tourists. He was in the rhythm of the day. He had almost forgotten the stranger—Adam Druit? Was that really his name? Jack didn't believe it. He didn't even consider phoning the police. Besides, he was still richer from the experience. To make sure no one took that away, Jack would throw the girl's hairbrush in the dump.

"Hey, watch what you're doing," Jack warned. He had been dozing — his head on the glass counter, his cup of coffee cold. The long night had finally caught up with him. Fortunately, a sixth sense woke him in time to catch a kid playing with a ceramic dish. Jack looked for the tour guide. It was closing time.

But someone caught Jack's eye. The tourists were leaving the store — about fifteen people, he'd guess. And damned if one of them wasn't Adam Druit.

"Hey!" Jack shouted.

A few of the people turned, but not the person Jack wanted.

"Hey, Druit!"

Jack went to the door, but didn't dare leave his store — not with people still inside. What's the point of catching one thief, just to set loose a dozen more?

"Adam Druit, you fucking crook!"

The customers watched him like he was part of the tour show. Jack was sick to death of them, and he began pushing people out the door. Once alone, he fastened the bolt and went back to his perch near the coffee machine. Damned if he knew what Druit had been doing in his store. Be returning too, Jack was certain. Jack held his gun and felt safe. He should have killed the man last night, when it would have been legal. Well, so much for doing favors. It had been a hard lesson, but this time, Jack wouldn't screw up. If Adam Druit ever showed his face again, it would be the last time.

Jack poured a fresh cup of coffee. He wanted as much caffeine as his blood could take. He drank, wondering if he should just jump in the car and leave town, like he'd planned. Give Druit time to blow away. Even more important, give Jack a chance to collect his thoughts and figure out how to protect himself.

"Should call the police," Jack said, taking another sip.

No, he thought. Because if Druit was telling the truth, then Jack did have the girl's hairbrush, which would make Jack an accessory. At the very least, he'd get in trouble for selling stolen goods. And the brush had been goldplated. Quality merchandise, which Jack stored in the safe.

He had to get rid of it and the ticket. The solution was to sell the brush secretly to another broker; then he could let the police know someone had broken into the store and threatened him. That way if Jack did shoot Druit, everyone would know it was self-defense.

That's it, Jack decided. Get rid of the brush and the ticket, then call the police. Finally, a plan of action. He finished his coffee, put down the cup, pushed off his seat . . .

And dropped to the floor.

Jack was shocked. It was as if there were no muscles in his legs. Everything from the waist down had turned numb. He could feel the deadening sensation crawling through the rest of his body.

A heart attack, he thought, having no real idea how one would feel. Part of him panicked, and part of him said relax. Take deep breaths and inch toward the telephone. Or at least the gun. Fire a few shots, and someone would break down the door and save him.

But the tickling pain now ran through all of him. Complete paralysis. Christ, he needed a doctor. What would happen to him? He didn't want to be a quadriplegic. To never walk or touch or move. What about his life? His *store*.

"Help me," he said, the words barely spoken. He took another shallow breath, but this time couldn't speak.

He heard someone at the door. He could hear the

doorknob turning, and he thanked God for the lucky break. Another tourist, Jack thought. Jack would give him anything he wanted. Anything and everything for a doctor.

The doorknob twisted to the left and right, and again, and again, and . . .

Locked, Jack remembered. He had locked the fucking door.

Jack heard the visitor tell someone else the store was closed and walk away. Now, no one would rescue him.

I'm gonna die, Jack thought. I'm really gonna die.

The numbness was entering his lungs. Another five minutes, and he'd stop breathing. How long did it take a person to choke to death? Would it be painful? Shit, of course it would be painful. This wasn't dying in bed — he was face down on the floor, barely in control of his own mind.

Then Jack heard something. Glass breaking. It was the same sound he had heard when the stranger broke into the store, except not as gentle. Before, a corner of glass had been cracked; now, Jack heard half the frame shattering.

The last of the glass fell and he heard a person falling inside. Jack was in silent tears. Suddenly there was another way to die. If he didn't get it from a heart attack or suffocating, he'd have his head cracked open by a thief. He thought of rolling behind the counter — somehow hiding himself. But the intruder was already in the store, and the sound was so close. The shuffling steps, hesitating . . . Jack could feel the intruder looking down at him.

Make me invisible, Jack thought. Make him look through me.

Adam rolled Jack onto his back.

"Where do you keep the tickets?" Adam Druit asked.

Jack stared up at him. Adam's face was inches away,

114

the details frightening. Psycho, Jack thought. Druit's face was flushed, his eyes bloodshot.

"The tickets," Adam said again, his breath unbearably stale.

"Top cabinet," Jack mouthed.

Adam stood and walked away. Jack prayed Adam found what he wanted. For the first time, it occurred to Jack it wasn't his heart; he had been *poisoned*. And if Druit had poisoned him, maybe he could also save him.

"It's not there," Adam said.

No, Jack thought. It's there. I misplaced it; that's all.

Adam checked a second time, shuffling all the tickets on the counter, looking for the one marked for a gold brush.

"You've hidden it," Adam said.

"No," Jack groaned. He managed to shake his head. The stranger reached down and held Jack's chin.

"Relax," Adam said. "Take short, regular breaths."

Jack obeyed. He was trusting Adam with his life.

"In the safe," Jack managed. "Ticket's in it. On the brush."

"What's the combination?"

One by one, each with its own breath, Jack gave him the numbers, and Adam again left. Jack waited. The ticket was tied to the hairbrush. That's why it wasn't in his files. Adam would find what he wanted, then phone the ambulance. Jack didn't have to die; if only the stranger found what he wanted. But suppose he didn't? Why the hell was this taking so long?

"Help me," Jack squeaked.

No answer. Fuck, Jack didn't hear a sound.

"Help," he tried again.

Nothing.

"Christ," his lips motioned. "Gonna die. Gonna die."

Adam pinched Jack's face. Jack could see the ticket in his fingers. "What was his name?" Adam asked.

115

Jack struggled to remember. "Vince . . . Vincent . . ."

"Vincent Braitman," Adam said. "Is that what the ticket says?"

Jack nodded.

"Did he show you any identification?"

"No," Jack said. He coughed and Adam slapped his back.

"What did he look like?"

"Dark hair," Jack said. "Mustache."

"Did he have a girl with him?"

"No girl." Adam pressed his cheeks more tightly. "No girl," Jack insisted.

"Where was he going?"

Jack shook his head. He was losing it. "Call a doctor," Jack said.

"Where was he going?"

"Don't know."

"Where—"

"God," Jack groaned.

He made a last effort to lift himself, then dropped back, unconscious.

Adam studied Jack, probing his neck and feeling the temple. Finally, he rolled up Jack's sleeve. By Adam's side was a black attaché case. Adam turned the clasps and reached for a clear vial with a rubber cap. He opened the wrapping to a disposable syringe, punctured the cap, and filled the syringe to 50cc. Then he squeezed Jack's arm until he found the thickest vein.

When he was done, Adam dropped the syringe in a plastic bag and put it in his pocket. He took Jack's pulse a last time and, satisfied, went to the coffee machine. He removed the pot and poured the last of it down the sink. Then he scrubbed the pot.

Finally, he went to Jack's office, taking a seat by the telephone. In his pocket was a map of New England and an AAA travel guide. In the guide was a list of Wheeling motels.

He began with the Travelodge.

"Hello," Adam said. "I'm looking for a Vincent Braitman. Mustache? Drives a blue station wagon. . . ."

Chapter 9

It was remarkable how the right drug brought new insight to even the most obvious thoughts.

Adam was in the Wheeling Police Station — had been there over four hours — waiting for word on his daughter or at least about her kidnapper. A lieutenant had contacted the West Bay station, verifying Sherry's disappearance; now, everyone believed Adam was not only sane, but seriously close to finding her.

He had explained several times what had brought him to Wheeling. First, he assumed his daughter had been kidnapped — a presumption that saved a number of days the police otherwise wasted. Second, he decided that his daughter had been kidnapped by a complete stranger. Sherry had, after all, disappeared in a strange town, at a gas station, after spending the night away from home with Casey. If Sherry's abductor had known her prior to the disappearance, there would have been ample opportunities when she was closer to home.

The kidnapper was also a stranger to West Bay. Adam had driven through the area looking for a blue station wagon, and after a last search of the streets, he felt reasonably sure the kidnapper had just been passing through. The logic worked. You didn't risk a kidnapping at a local gas station, near witnesses, in a relatively small town, if you were a familiar face. Possible, but it was more likely that whoever kidnapped Sherry was a stranger to everyone. Someone who had pulled in for gas, found a prize, and left. An impulsive act, Adam imagined; something the kidnapper couldn't control. His daughter was the victim of chance. One more missing child, taken away by an anonymous person in an anonymous car.

Anonymous. The word was the end to a burial, after the dirt was patted down and all you could see was a long grass field dotted with markers. At least if someone in the area had kidnapped her, there was hope Sherry could be freed and the kidnapper captured. If she had been taken out of West Bay, and if her kidnapper was unknown . . .

So they were checking his story. Indeed, they had spent hours checking the story. But Adam didn't let them waste his time. While the police made their phone calls, he went to the rest room, chose his pill, and swallowed. Then he returned to the hallway bench, sitting comfortably and letting his imagination take off.

It was like flying up on a cloud, taking a seat next to God and looking down on the planet. Suddenly, he knew who everyone was and why everything happened. Hell, it was *being* God, except he didn't want to create a universe, just a kidnapper.

With his new power, he made a man as only He would do it: molding with clay. Adam started with the feet. A poor man, he had decided. The clue wasn't the hairbrush, it had been the sweatshirt. The shirt couldn't have been worth two dollars; still the kidnapper had bothered selling it. The man needed money, and Adam fit his kidnapper in a pair of tattered black shoes.

Because the man was poor, Adam tailored the pants short, revealing a pair of white cotton socks that were soiled from too many weeks without cleaning, but no dirtier than the pants themselves. Khaki pants—comfortable for driving, or running short distances to steal children.

Those were the easy parts. Now, was the kidnapper a heavy man or thin? At first, Adam thought heavy, and his clay figure expanded. But then the kidnapper had also been fast on his feet. He had stolen a child in less than a minute; run to the side of a car, reached in, and kidnapped Sherry without anyone's seeing. A strong man, too. Trim, but from choice. Decisive. Deadly quick.

The figure became firmer, with muscles that filled a flannel shirt.

Adam had the body. He could see his creation standing upon the earth, the chest lifting with its first breath. But the body wasn't finished.

He still hadn't decided on the face.

The hair was simple. Jet black, and so wet it dripped down the sides of the head. Adam combed it from the left side, satisfied with what he had done.

But the face. The damned face.

The figure knew it was incomplete. It stood there, waiting, its heart beating, its breaths patient. Yet Adam couldn't finish the job. He still didn't know the mind of Sherry's kidnapper, and he couldn't create a human's face when it all seemed so inhuman. He lifted its head so he could press his thumb and forefinger into the clay, making dents where the eyes belonged. Then he carved a mouth—a ragged line, neither human nor animal. Simply a cut, without a hint of an identity.

The mouth moved. Adam's kidnapper could speak. An incomplete masterpiece—a creature with two sockets for eyes and a wound for its mouth—reached toward him, taking a last deep breath and speaking, the sound deepening as if it were Adam's own voice . . .

"Mr. Druit?" said an officer.

Adam opened his eyes and saw two plainclothes policemen looking at him. An empty chair was by their desk. One of the officers adjusted the chair.

"This is Detective Brooks," the man said. "I want you to tell him what you told me."

Adam stepped cautiously forward, his feet unsure of the floorboards, his legs almost forgetting the motion necessary to walk. Finally, he sat on the chair and took a moment to study both of them. It was like looking at a single amoeba that had split. Indeed, the whole precinct could be a massive organ, with people carrying papers and charts like blood cells transporting bacteria.

"I understand you've been on the trail of a kidnapper," said Brooks. "Doesn't look like you've had much sleep."

Adam waited for his mind to settle comfortably back in his body. He had absolutely no memory of Detective Brooks. What was it, he wondered—too many drugs, or too much time in police precincts?

"My daughter was kidnapped last Sunday," Adam said. He talked slowly and clearly, as if remembering how to speak. "The West Bay police searched the area for any sign of the vehicle. When the police finished looking, I did my own check."

"His daughter and the kidnapper were seen in a blue station wagon," said the other officer.

"I realized," said Adam, "that either my daughter was somewhere close to West Bay or had been taken out of town."

"Both good possibilities," said Brooks.

"The West Bay police could only handle West Bay," said Adam. "If it came to doing a search outside the district or outside the state, my daughter was gone for good." Adam again closed his eyes, wishing he could take a Benzedrine. Now that he was again on the ground, his body was tiring him. The only way he could talk was to pretend he was addressing himself, assessing his progress to turn up a new clue. "The kidnapper was a drifter," Adam continued. "A drifter doesn't just drift; he goes forward from place to place, maybe bending with the roads, but that's it. I thought that a drifter who drinks goes from one town to the next looking for bars. A drifter who kidnaps, he goes looking for kids."

"Sounds right," said Brooks.

"So I checked the newspapers."

The other officer moved closer to Brooks and acted as interpreter. "He means he checked about a *hundred* newspapers."

The officer smiled as if Adam had broken some Guinness world record. Adam thought only of his daughter. "I looked for a trail. Any other missing children during the previous months. I found some, they fell into the right time sequence, I saw a movement that led up the Interstate and—"

"Excuse me," said Brooks. The scope of the task had sunk in. "You actually went through a hundred newspapers in—"

"Only eight-three," said Adam. "Covering a two-month period."

"You read them in a week?"

"The librarian let me stay after closing hours. Whatever newspapers they didn't have I found in Providence."

Brooks struggled a moment, now certain Adam Druit was crazy, wishing to God he wasn't the one who had to explain how hopeless this would be. "Mr. Druit," he said, "kids disappear every day. The chances of finding yours—"

"I looked for a pattern," Adam said.

"The chances of those disappearances being related to each other are *phenomenal.*"

"That's why I concentrated just on kids about Sherry's age. Girls in particular. I figured out a rating system for disappearances. Once I saw the pattern, I

122

stopped looking."

"You mean the kidnapper heading north on Route 95."

"I'm sure of it," Adam said.

"Because of this hairbrush?" said Brooks, lifting the brush Adam had stolen from the pawnshop.

"I gave that to Sherry's mother. She gave it to Sherry. Casey said Sherry kept the hairbrush in her purse. I also found the sweatshirt she wore the day she disappeared."

"I've seen the sweatshirt, too," said Brooks. "I've also seen the pawn ticket."

"The ticket's only two days old," said Adam. "If we can just get a little help further upstate, then—"

"And I've also seen the owner of the pawnshop," Brooks said. "He's at home, sick. Said something about a burglar breaking in his store."

Adam waited, saying nothing.

"Said he doesn't know who broke in," Brooks said, "but he's missing some jewelry and a stereo. He's filed a report for the insurance claim."

Brooks stretched his back and walked to the water cooler for a brief break. When he returned, he ordered the other officer to phone the state police and have a patrol car dispatched. When he sat down again, he said, "I saw Jack Kiley and he wasn't just upset about the burglary, he was terrified and looked like hell. He's also not stupid enough to file a claim unless someone did break into his shop. I told him you had shown up with one of his shop tickets and some of his merchandise."

"I paid Mr. Kiley two hundred fifty dollars for—"

"It's all right," said Brooks. "He said he gave you the receipt. I don't believe it, because Jack doesn't give things away. Maybe you paid for it. He's too scared to say anything else. I don't know what the hell happened over there, but all he wants now is to collect his insurance and take a vacation."

"I want to find my daughter," said Adam.

"I'm sure you do," said Brooks. "And *we'll* do our best finding her and the kidnapper. You understand?"

"A blue station wagon," said Adam. "He was here just two days ago. If you phone the state police—"

"We did," said Brooks. "Just understand, all right? Maybe you got something, maybe not. *Probably* not. No matter what, you're not doing your daughter any good by causing trouble."

"If I hadn't come up here—" said Adam.

"You don't know that," Brooks answered. "And you don't know for certain that's your daughter's brush. I've seen brushes like that everywhere. My wife has one."

"A *gold* hairbrush?"

"Hey, that surprises you? I look poor?" said Brooks.

"Then what about the shirt?" Adam said.

"What about it?" Brooks said. "What makes you so certain it's hers? Maybe it is, but can you really tell? I bet there are thousands of them out there." Brooks grinned and stood up. "Come on. I'm taking you to a motel so you can sleep. You need it bad."

"I'll stay here," Adam said.

"Do yourself a small favor and go to the motel. We won't be hearing from anyone for a few hours. The moment we get a call—"

Adam left the chair, balanced himself against the desk, then walked across the hall to the bathroom. Once by the sink, he found his tabs of amphetamines and swallowed two, cupping his hands together to drink water from the tap. He also splashed his face to bring color to his cheeks.

When he returned to the bench, his body ached from lack of sleep, but his mind was again alert.

Brooks and Adam exchanged annoyed looks, then Brooks went about his business. Adam kept at his post, putting on sunglasses to guard his sore eyes from the glare of an overhead lamp. It also let him look into people's faces without fear. He saw them talking, laughing, working . . . all behaving so normally, while Adam felt so helpless.

If only he had seen Sherry when she was alive. If only he had let her know she wasn't alone.

" 'Was alive,' " he said softly. " 'Was.' " A yesterday word. But Adam knew there was a chance of his daughter's being dead. It was the conclusion to his logic that neither he nor the detective discussed. After all, if Sherry had been kidnapped by a drifter, then the odds were very good the man had kidnapped before. But there was no one else reported in the station wagon. The kidnapper had been alone.

"Mr. Druit?"

Adam lifted his head. Brooks was touching his shoulder, gently shaking him. Perhaps Brooks thought Adam had been sleeping. When Adam removed his sunglasses, it was clear Adam hadn't slept a moment.

The clock said ten o'clock. Adam looked at Brooks, expecting the detective to tell him again to check into a motel, saying that the night's work was finished.

"Mr. Druit, we've found a car that may match your description."

Adam listened. Despite working so hard to find the kidnapper and being so sure of the trail, he couldn't react.

"A blue station wagon with out-of-state plates," said Brooks. "We have a patrol car keeping it under surveillance. I'm heading there now. I thought, if your daughter really is there, you might want to come along."

"Where is it?" Adam finally managed.

"Two counties away. Forty-minute drive if —"

Adam stopped the detective. "For God's sake, let's get out there," he said.

125

Chapter 10

The station wagon was parked behind a roadside bar called the Blue Ridge Tavern. Whoever had left the car clearly wanted to keep it out of sight, because almost all the other cars were out front by the highway. The station wagon was by itself, behind a dumpster, more than a hundred yards from the nearest light.

"Where's the patrol car?" Adam whispered.

They were sitting in Brooks's car, lights out. They had been at the lot for only a few minutes, giving Brooks a chance to assess the situation.

"Down the road," Brooks said. "We're getting a check on the car. Connecticut license plate."

Adam glanced at Brooks, remembering Pecco's hallucination. He had been blinded by the memory of a light blue glow emanating from the back of the station wagon. Light blue was also the color of a Connecticut plate.

As for Brooks, he didn't mind having Adam along. The detective was also a father, and while, if he was working in Boston, he would have been obliged to leave Adam at the station house, one of the advantages to working in Wheeling was the flexibility of the job. Besides, if the roles were reversed, Brooks would have insisted on going.

Brooks left his car, and with the door open, Adam could hear the noise from the tavern. It was a busy night. Through its windows, he could see the shadows of a crowd.

Was the kidnapper inside? Adam wondered. If so, how the hell could Adam identify him? Adam had only the faintest notion of what the kidnapper looked like. There was only one hope of making the catch, and that was if Brooks sealed off the tavern and took everyone into custody. Yet Brooks had no intention of taking such action. No need, Brooks said; they were only looking at a car, that's all.

Brooks approached the patrol car and leaned into the window. After a brief conversation with the driver, he headed for the back lot, waving for Adam to follow. Adam left the car and ran across the gravel. "Let's take a closer look at the station wagon," Brooks said.

They walked along the outer edge of the parking lot, near a line of trees, to avoid a block of light that shined from a rear kitchen window. Once behind the dumpster, Brooks turned on a penlight. He used the narrow beam to do a second check of the license plate. After writing it down, he went to the side of the car and tested the front door. It opened.

"Keep alert," Brooks told Adam, then crawled into the front seat. A ceiling light illuminated the inside of the car. Brooks slid across to the glove compartment, hoping to find the registration. Instead, he found a sheathed bowie knife.

Adam pulled the knife out of Brooks's hand.

"Give it back," Brooks said.

Adam stepped away. He scratched the steel of the knife with a thumbnail, then ran his tongue gently on the edge.

"Give it or this is all over," Brooks warned.

Adam held the knife tightly. For a moment, Brooks thought Adam had lost his mind; that Adam was looking at the detective, but seeing the kidnapper.

"I tasted blood on the blade," Adam said. He slipped the knife back into the sheath and returned it, handle up, to Brooks.

Brooks put the knife in his pocket. "Seats look clean, but you can't see much in this light."

Brooks searched under the seat. He found a road map, some used napkins, and a fast food receipt for two hamburgers and a soft drink. On the floor of the backseat was an empty paper cup and comic book.

He looked for Adam and found him lifting the hood of the car.

"What are you doing?" Brooks asked.

Adam reached inside, pulled out the ignition wires, then slammed down the hood. "I'm making sure he doesn't drive anywhere."

"And suppose this is the wrong car?"

"It's the car," Adam said. He kneeled to the ground and rubbed a handful of gravel between his fingers. They both saw a light turn on from a second-story window. The light spread across the dumpster and car, and Brooks could see a man rummaging through a closet.

"You're crazy," Brooks said to Adam.

Adam ignored him. His body was asleep, while his mind retreated deeper into a depression. He was part of the ground, part of the car . . . part of everything he touched, but no longer Adam Druit.

"My daughter was killed in this car," Adam said. It was a note being jotted in his memory. He touched the car's chrome with a tenderness others might show a tombstone.

It was all so clear. The car, the knife . . . And in the rear of the station wagon, Adam had found a pillow, blanket, and nylon cord. Kept her alive for a night, maybe two, Adam thought. Trundled her up and kept her hidden. Tortured her? Perhaps not. That was one thing he never allowed himself to imagine. But the kidnapper had kept his girl alive. Maybe he had intended to keep Sherry—to love her and bring her up as his own child. Instead . . .

Spare the rod, spoil the child, Adam thought.

Perhaps she had cried one too many times, or asked for the wrong dinner, or refused to eat her dinner, or whispered when she should have talked, or talked when she should have said nothing.

Spare the rod, spoil the child.

It would have happened on a side road, not far from Route 95—the kidnapper never drove far from this route—but far enough to dispose of the body once he was done. Sherry, bound by the cord and covered by the blanket, wouldn't have realized where they were or what was to happen. She may have been asleep, even as the kidnapper stopped the car and opened the glove compartment for the knife.

Adam wondered how the knife felt in the killer's hand. Comfortable, he imagined. After all, Adam had also held the knife. He knew the softness of the leather grip and the slight wear in the pommel. The man who owned this knife cared for it. The grip was formed to the fingers, and the edge of the blade was uneven from too many strokes against a sharpening stone. The knife fit the hand, as tight to the fingers as the cord that must have wrapped Sherry's wrists. And grabbing Sherry—feeling underneath the blanket for her head, fondling her hair, finding her throat and sliding the blade across it as if it was just a slight stroke . . . The touch of a doctor, marking the skin for surgery . . .

"There's someone out there," Adam said.

He surprised himself, just as he surprised Brooks. The words were a whisper, but enough for both of them to hear. Adam had seen movement in the short expanse of woods near the front of the tavern. A person was balanced on a fallen log. It was the movements of a bobbing ghost without dimensions. When the man moved, it was hard to tell if he walked toward the dumpster or away. He turned out of the woods and stood absolutely still, reminding Adam of a deer caught in the headlights of a car.

Adam pointed at him. "He's watching us."

Brooks held Adam still, then stepped into the kitchen light. "Hey!" he shouted.

Brooks reached in one pocket for his badge, the other for his gun. There wasn't any need for the gun, but it was like spending hours listening to ghost stories; you didn't believe it, but you still moved differently, your mind keen on danger. Now he behaved as if the "ghost" in the distance was actually a kidnapper and a killer — a crazy possibility. The world spent millions trying to track down the sort of people who kidnapped Sherry Druits. There was no way an angry father could spend an afternoon in the library, then play Sherlock Holmes and find the man who stole his daughter.

But when the "ghost" on top of the log ran into the woods, Brooks believed. He fired once in the air and started running across the parking lot. The headlights of the patrol car flicked on and the other officers joined the chase. Adam followed Brooks, his legs not fully awake, moving like a runner with cramps.

It was a ridiculous scene, in part because no one seemed certain what to do — not the suspect, not Brooks, not Adam. Brooks imitated the motions of a movie hero — pausing at the log, cocking his head for the sight and sound of the villain, then glimpsing the shadow just at the edge of the road. It was a cop's fantasy; from the illusive menace, to the smell of a recently fired revolver. Then, as the Blue Ridge regulars came out to watch the action, more car lights flicked on so everyone could see what was happening. One of the circles captured their prey, and the touch of the light froze him. He turned and faced the headlights, wavering in place, until he leaned forward and covered his mouth. By the time Brooks reached him, he had vomited.

Brooks needed a moment to catch his breath and reason. Adam seemed ready to attack the man, but another patrolman kept him still so Brooks could handle the suspect. For his part, Brooks bent down to take a closer look at his kidnapper and realized almost immediately that it was a fuckup. For one, the man was wearing a suit and tie, and somehow Brooks didn't imagine a drifter as being especially well dressed for the occasion. Then Brooks recognized him. He had seen the man working at a bank; in fact, had seen him on the job last Friday, and there wasn't any way in hell a bank teller would have the time to weave a cross-country trail of terror between deposits and withdrawals.

Nonetheless, Brooks did his duty. He pulled the man straight and asked for a name and identification. His name, it turned out, was Haining, and his driver's license identified him as a local.

"You the owner of that blue station wagon?" Brooks said, nodding back toward the lot.

"No, sir," Haining said, and Brooks took Haining's car keys. He gave them to one of the officers, who went back to try them on the station wagon.

"Where's my daughter?" Adam shouted at the suspect.

Haining glanced into the headlights as if they had been the source of the question. The longer Brooks studied his kidnapper, the more embarrassed he felt. Haining was maybe five-foot-three, heavyset, and in his late thirties, early forties. He had a face that had grown soft and featureless from years of desk work. A set of glasses fit tightly on the nose, and the stems pressed into his skin, like long varicose veins that stretched back to the ears. And while Brooks couldn't really know, he imagined that Haining's face was only a hint of the overall pillow softness of the whole man.

"What were you doing at the tavern?" Brooks asked him.

"I'm always here Tuesday nights," Haining said.

"And why were you in the woods?"

Haining looked about for help, then again faced the detective. "Urinating, sir."

Brooks heard the crowd laugh. He glanced at his kidnapper's crotch. The fly was open, and the front tail of a shirt jutted free. A trail of piss marked one leg of his pants.

"Don't they have toilets for that?"

"Toilets were busy."

"But you ran when I identified myself," Brooks said.

"I didn't, sir," said Haining.

"You were in the woods watching that car, and you saw us and took off."

"I thought you were car thieves," Haining said.

"I said I was a police officer," said Brooks.

"If I'd heard that, sir, I wouldn't have run."

"Haining," someone shouted, "they're gonna confiscate your prick for evidence."

Brooks turned as if ready to arrest everyone. When the other officer returned with the car keys and said they didn't fit the station wagon, Brooks acted as if this were the final piece of evidence for conviction.

"Let's go to the car," Brooks ordered his prisoner.

"I don't want to be arrested," Haining said. "I didn't do anything."

"No one said anything about arresting anyone," Brooks said. Everyone overheard, including Adam, who again shouted at Haining. Haining wanted to turn and run, but Brooks tugged him toward the patrol car, and while the patrolmen restrained Adam, Brooks spent five minutes convincing Haining that he was damned lucky not to get arrested, and if Brooks ever caught him again pissing in the woods, he'd run him down the streets with his pants down.

Adam, meanwhile, began to understand. His mind was moving slower than Brooks's, but once it had caught

132

up, his fury at Haining left with one deep breath, and his suspicions turned on the customers drifting back to the bar.

Brooks finished with his suspect and found Adam stationed by the front door of the Blue Ridge.

"He's in there," Adam said.

Brooks didn't answer. He walked away, then returned with the patrolmen.

"Mr. Druit?" said one of the officers, taking his arm.

Adam, surprised, looked to Brooks for help.

"You're going to the station house," Brooks explained.

"I'm staying here," Adam answered.

"You're interfering with an investigation," Brooks said.

The patrolman tugged at Adam. Adam resisted, absolutely certain that within a few feet was the kidnapper. If only he knew what the man looked like. If only he had a drug that brought back memories with the clarity of perfect vision.

They all walked back to the patrol car, and Adam overheard Brooks radio for assistance. It made the trip to the station easier knowing that despite the chase, the investigation would continue. This was the one thought that consoled Adam as he took his seat on the hard wood bench in the station house.

Adam leaned over the armrest, barely holding his weight. At the first sign of relaxation, his body had declared itself closed. There was little else he could do now but sleep. At least an hour's worth. He closed his eyes, and let his mind join the rest of his body. No more pills — not now. He couldn't let himself die without first seeing the man who'd killed his daughter. And Christ, what if she had survived? Maybe the kidnapper tried killing her, but Sherry managed to escape?

"Sherry," he whispered, hoping her name would send

133

him into a dream. But the station house stayed. The colorless walls, the tired, late-night boredom, the sound of a television, the coughs and pains of a shelter for the homeless and drunk. . . . Adam was held in place. He had forgotten how to sleep.

Someone mistook Adam's slumped posture for rest. When Brooks returned to the station house, he found Adam covered by a blanket. Brooks stopped briefly by the sergeant's desk to ask for a set of forms, then touched Adam's shoulder.

"Mr. Druit," he said gently.

Brooks was exhausted, but there would be no sleep for him tonight, either; not after the hours of interrogation he'd finished.

"Mr. Druit."

Brooks pulled back the blanket. Adam had buried his face in an arm. Brooks slipped his hand under Adam's head and tried lifting him, thinking Adam had only to sit to wake up. He cupped Adam's chin between his hands and met a stare that had been uninterrupted since Adam arrived in the station house.

Brooks slapped Adam's face. "Druit?"

Nothing. Brooks recognized it as shock. He slapped Adam again, and Adam slumped to the side. "Holy shit," Brooks murmured, listening to the heart. He lifted Adam off the bench and dropped him on the floor. "We need an ambulance!" Brooks shouted to the sergeant.

Brooks straddled Adam, then punched down on his chest. He heard a plastic bottle break and reached into Adam's breast pocket. Pills spilled onto the floor.

"We may have an OD," Brooks added, again punching down.

Adam showed no response, except in his eyes. They began to tear.

Chapter 11

For the kidnapper, it was like staring into a department store window.

A room full of babies, lined up in rows like so many groceries in a store. Clean, soft skin; eyes squeezed tightly shut, with only wisps of hair on their heads and blood vessels lining their skulls. Hands no larger than a silver dollar and fingers as fragile as wood matches. Some of the babies slept, some cried. Birth had been a painful, exhausting process.

"Time to change wraps," said a nurse, covering her mouth with a paper mask and entering the ward. The babies were oblivious to her presence, even when she lifted them, one by one, to pull free a sheet or change a cotton dress. Occasionally, she'd lift a baby and hold the child toward a glass partition, so a father could have a better look at his hours-old son or daughter. The father would tap on the window and point, as if he were picking his child on the spot, rather than by birth.

The kidnapper did the same, tapping the window and pointing at a baby in the far corner of the room. A baby girl, with faintly reddish hair. In her hands was a knot of blanket, twisted between her fingers and pressed in her mouth. The nurse freed the sleeping child, lifted her gently, and let him see her. "Lovely,"

135

the nurse said silently, exaggerating the word so that he could understand.

He smiled. She was so much younger than the rest and wouldn't dare cause the trouble he had with all the other little girls.

This time, he would raise the perfect girl—no noise, no crying. She would be trained as his alone, and when she grew older, she'd first be his daughter and then his mistress. One child, one family. It was an idea that could have worked the other times, if only he had been more careful. But the other girls had been spoiled by their parents. Undisciplined.

This time, there would be no problems.

He waved good-bye to the child and the nurse, and turned down the corridor. There was no fear in the kidnapper—no concern that he might be identified for a past crime or remembered later for a new one. He was anonymous in every respect—part of the secret to his success. He dressed in gray clothes, wore a gray rain cap, and hid his eyes behind tinted sunglasses. Even if someone looked his way, he would be forgotten. The kidnapper never met anyone's stare—not directly. He saw through people, and they saw through him. The few who did notice him were perhaps attracted to his sheer size, which was greater than most men. Yet they looked only briefly, before stepping out of his path.

Not that he ever would attack a passerby. He wasn't interested in most people—just children. They were his prizes. And his last prize had been a good one, hadn't she?

He stopped at a water fountain, took a short drink, and looked to either side of the corridor. The hallways seemed to twist into infinity, the way two mirrors reflect forever until the images warp into nothing. There was no one in either direction. The hospital, and the girl, were his for the taking.

"Clarissa," he said to himself, choosing his child's name. There was really no reason for saying it aloud; he used the same name for all his children. That had been the problem with the last little girl. No matter how many times he called her "Clarissa," she refused to answer. She used that other name, "Sherry." Sometimes she said "Sherry Druit." Stupid, stupid girl.

The kidnapper opened the stairwell door and walked to the fourth floor. Before he claimed his prize, there were other things to do.

He waited for an intern to pass, then, again alone, entered the hallway and looked for Room 4012. When he found it, he opened the door quietly, careful not to wake the patient. Then he unsheathed his knife.

He walked between the rows of hospital beds, each isolated by drawn curtains. The long, mesh sheets curled against the wind of an air vent, and the kidnapper ran the tip of his knife across the fluttering cloth. When he bent to read the chart, his fingers never touched the paper. "Druit, Adam S.," it read. There was more information, but that was all the kidnapper needed. For the past two weeks, Adam Druit had made his life miserable. His way of life, and the life of his future child, were being threatened. Perhaps Adam Druit was even considering murder. He wondered if Druit struggled with the idea of death. Did Druit have the courage to drive a knife into a person's stomach and drag it slowly through the belly, or would he be like the others—set on vengeance, until someone handed them the gun or knife. So gutless, they couldn't kill a killer.

He slipped between the beds and to the side of the curtain, ready to strike. The movements would be automatic. First, a pillow across the face; then the knife across the throat. Routine. Just as he had killed the children.

The kidnapper silently pulled back the curtain and slipped his hand about Adam Druit's neck.

Adam opened his eyes.

The pillow hit his face and the knife just cut the edge of his throat. Yet Adam managed to fall off the bed, the IV tube pulling out of his arm and the bottle shattering against the bed rail. The knife came down again, tearing through the curtain. Adam could see the steel cutting downward and toward his chest, the fist of the kidnapper tangling in his shirt, ripping it open.

Adam screamed, pushing away the hand and rolling under the bed, watching the blade hit the floor. He heard the kidnapper curse him and then watched the blade pull free of the floorboards. The knife disappeared from view, and all Adam could see was the bend of the bedsprings. The kidnapper had climbed atop Adam's bed and was moving about, devising his attack. Adam could see the left springs relax, and the ones on the right sink. It was a slow, fluid shifting, like slow waves running across an ocean. As the springs bent more toward the right, Adam moved to the left.

When the knife again came slashing, Adam was far enough away to miss the blade.

He finally began screaming for help. Then he noticed the bed's emergency alarm dangling free and within his reach. Without considering the risks, he reached out from under the bed and grabbed the buzzer, pressing the button and holding on tightly, as if it was a lifeline. A nurse's bell rang in the hallway. He hoped to God that she came with an armed guard.

The bedsprings again shifted and Adam rolled to his safe position in the center of the frame. When Adam shifted to the right, the springs rippled back in his direction. Adam responded by again moving to the center. He watched the mattress, thinking they had reached a stalemate, knowing it would just be a matter of seconds before his rescuers arrived. But no one arrived. And while Adam stared at the mattress, the bedsprings suddenly shifted one last time with the kidnapper's weight, and then completely relaxed, as if there was no weight at all left on the mattress.

Adam waited.

Still nothing moved. Nor was there a sound. Adam prepared for the worst until the anticipation finally forced him to action. Cautiously, he slid from under the bed, then rolled completely free, getting quickly to his feet in preparation for a fight.

The room was empty. Adam moved carefully through it, then fled the final few steps to the door, throwing it open and rushing into the hallway.

Before him, lying on the floor, was one of the nurses — her neck crushed and head twisted back.

Adam almost fainted. Blood was smeared on the linoleum, leading him, in a line, through the corridors. He followed, giving the corners a broad berth, stopping before two more bodies: interns surrounded by broken bottles and unraveled gauze.

Adam approached the bodies as if they were dangerous. The murders were fresh — only minutes old. The kidnapper had caught the young men completely by surprise and killed without hesitation. A murdering machine. For all Adam knew, he was the one person to escape. Was this a gift from the kidnapper or a mistake?

Or was the killer saving Adam for last?

Near one of the bodies was a scalpel. Adam took the knife just as a door clicked closed. He followed the sound to a stairwell, but he couldn't tell if the noise came from above or below him. By luck he saw the second floor door swing shut. It never occurred to Adam that he was meant to see the door shut — that the kidnapper killed not because people were in his way, but to leave a trail.

Adam opened the second floor door and entered the hallway. There were no footsteps, but he knew where the killer had gone the moment he spotted the sign in the north corridor. MATERNITY WARD, it read.

Adam ran, turning down the corridor and finding more blood smeared on the floor. Adam held the scalpel pointed away from his chest, ready to attack. He found two benches heavy with dead fathers. And behind the glass partition, a room so recently alive with newborn babies was a slaughterhouse.

Adam screamed and turned.

"Come on," the nurse said, wiping his forehead. "Calm down. No more crying."

She pushed him back against the bed, soothing him, trying to calm him.

Adam finally opened his eyes and looked about the room. Everything was fine; everything safe.

Safe.

He locked on to the thought while the nurse took his pulse and called for the doctor.

Chapter 12

It was a semiprivate room. Air came from a vent in the ceiling, which circulated the odors of the hospital. Antiseptics, medications, anesthetics, petroleum jellies, detergents, food . . . Adam knew the hospital just by smelling. Odors were like drugs that stimulated the senses.

So why wouldn't they give him any drugs?

Adam lay in his bed, eyes open, looking at his window. The curtain was closed, but an outline of light painted the edges so he knew it was day. He also knew that thirty-two hours had passed since his admittance—time that should have been spent tracking his daughter's kidnapper.

Who cared if he fainted? It was no great medical mystery; he hadn't slept in days. That wasn't the fault of drugs, it was his own fault. Why did Casey tell the doctors he needed rehabilitation—as if she was the one with the degree in pharmacology, and he was a junkie who had fallen at her doorstep. And who had invited Casey to the hospital? He didn't want Casey here; didn't need her. He certainly didn't want her signing papers as if he was still her responsibility.

Rehabilitation. A murderer running after children, and they wanted to rehabilitate Adam. The whole idea disgusted him—made him sweaty and dizzy, want to wretch from anger. What he'd give for something to calm his stomach and get rid of the shakes.

Damn it, he *needed* medication.

The door opened and two nurses entered—one with a lunch tray, the other with medication. The first nurse propped Adam in his bed and delivered his meal—baked chicken, green beans, and cherry gelatin. "Enjoy, sweetheart," she said, tucking a napkin under his chin and leaving the room. As for the second nurse, she walked past Adam and over to his roommate. "Time to wake up," she said. Adam could only hear the man, because a curtain kept them separated, but it was just as well—the nurse had been carrying a paper cup with two light-blue capsules. Likely Cyclospasmol, a cyclandelate used to increase blood circulation. Since his roommate had circulatory trouble and was in the hospital, Adam suspected he had either a severe trophic ulcer or cardiovascular difficulties. Either way, he wasn't the sort of person who wanted conversation.

"Come on; take your pills," the nurse ordered.

Adam heard the man struggling to wake against a narcotic. Ridiculous, Adam thought. The man should be getting intravenous, not oral, medication. A patient in his shape could choke on a pill.

There was an awful gargle of water, followed by a gasp for air. The nurse patted her patient's back, then insisted he swallow a second pill. The patient must have complied, because Adam heard all the sounds of a drowning man. When the patient again regained his breath, Adam heard him fall back against his pillow, then saw the nurse emerge from behind the screen, prepared to leave for the rest of her duties.

"What medication did you give him?" Adam asked her.

The nurse didn't answer. She was offended by Adam. She had no respect for someone in the medical profession who had abused his privileges. She had only once acknowledged his background by offering him a copy of the *Journal of Pharmacology* — a gift Adam initially interpreted favorably. Later, he realized the magazine was meant to be a reminder of the professionalism he had abandoned.

"What is he?" Adam insisted. "Diabetic? Is it arteriosclerosis?"

"It's none of your business," she finally said

"You should stop giving him pills," Adam said. "Put him on an IV preparation of isoxsuprine hydrochloride. It'll be easier for the both of you."

"I'll pass your advice to his physician," the nurse said.

"Then you can also tell him I'm tired," Adam said. "I need more sugar and protein. I could also use ten milligrams of methamphetamine."

"Oh, absolutely."

"I'm not joking."

She smirked, and without another word, left the room. Adam leaned back against his pillow, staring at the food, thinking of his daughter's kidnapper. He was certain the only way to find the man was to be absolutely fit. "Superman" fit, he thought. His mistake had been in letting everything go at once and making a dash for the kidnapper, instead of giving a steady chase.

Of course, before, Adam thought his daughter was alive; now . . .

Adam wiped his face, wanting to cry but stopping. The doubts he could handle. No, there were other problems worse than the doubts. Problems like the police.

They had tried discussing the case with him. A local sergeant, Phillip, and Casey had surrounded Adam's bed like executives in a board meeting. They spread their manila folders on the bed sheets and carefully told Adam the "facts." Fact one: five people in the Blue Ridge Tavern had matched the description of Adam's kidnapper, and none could have been in West Bay at the time of Sherry's disappearance. Fact two: Adam's station wagon was indeed a stolen vehicle, but the knife Adam had found in the glove compartment showed signs only of animal blood, not human. Furthermore, there was no evidence whatsoever that any child had recently been inside the car. No stray hairs, no fingerprints . . . True, there had been a comic book, but adults also read them. The car was basically clean, unlike Adam's attaché case, which the police had confiscated.

He listened to these "facts" as best he could. They were meant to put him off the trail, not help his pursuit. "Adam's kidnapper," they said. "Adam's station wagon." "Adam's hunting knife." Everyone talked as if the world was his property. Stupidity, Adam would later think. But when he first listened, he cared foremost about how Casey was giving up hope.

When the sergeant finished the lecture, the man settled back in his seat, confident in the completeness of the facts.

Adam turned to Casey. No one else mattered. "I

can catch him."

The sergeant looked uncomfortable. "Mr. Druit, please stop this."

"The kidnapper's close," Adam told her. "I'm certain of it."

Phillip wrapped his arm around Casey. "You don't know that, so don't say it."

"There was no human blood on the knife," said the sergeant. "There's no reason to suspect your daughter was in the car."

"I wish you would stop this," Casey told Adam.

Adam reached for her. "Casey . . ."

Casey began crying, and Phillip took her out of the room. Adam was alone with the sergeant—a circumstance that made both men uncomfortable. The sergeant gathered his papers. "Mr. Druit, we're doing all we can."

Adam focused on him. "Did you check the pawn ticket? Did you locate Vincent Braitman?"

"It was looked into," said the sergeant.

"And?"

"And we don't think there is a Vincent Braitman. We think it's a false name."

Adam again looked thoughtful, and the sergeant tried to cut him off.

"That doesn't mean anything, Mr. Druit," he said. "Most of the names on those tickets are false. People don't like to be caught selling their mother's china."

"It means something this time," Adam said. "Did you try calling other shops? Maybe he used the same name twice? Or maybe something a little different, like 'Bratting' or 'Brayman' or—"

"We did some checking."

"How much is some?"

"As much as we could," the sergeant said, irritated. "There's a limit to our jurisdiction, Mr. Druit. But I notified the state police and the neighboring jurisdictions, and nothing's turned up yet."

"Maybe that's because he's not nearby," Adam said. "By now, he could be out of the state. He's probably—"

"I told you; we're looking into it," said the sergeant. "Now you've got to stop what you're doing here before you get hurt. And you've got to cut out the amphetamines and barbiturates and whatever else we found in that bag."

"I'm a pharmacologist—"

"You're a vigilante."

"—and I'm a concerned father," said Adam. He glared at the sergeant.

The sergeant softened. "Look, I'm willing to bet your daughter's alive. But I also know that if you keep playing your games, you're gonna end up dead and buried. And she's gonna need a father after what she's been through. Think about that."

Adam thought of one thing—that the sergeant was a fucking idiot. What did people expect; for him to relax and sit still? Why didn't Casey help, instead of trusting people who couldn't care less about what happened to Sherry?

Shit—people told him to stop taking pills as if drugs were something bad. But the drugs made it possible for Adam to understand the common link between the kidnapper and the world, then use this knowledge as a testing ground for ideas. It let Adam realize details no one else seemed capable of imagining.

The drugs also made Adam stronger, and that was

another feeling no person had ever given him, not even Casey. It was a feeling he needed now, for his daughter, dead or alive. Things were happening in the world, and they were all happening outside the hospital, not in it. Adam needed strength.

If he couldn't get it from his friends, he had to find other ways.

When he was alone, Adam covered himself in a bathrobe and checked his bed chart. Then he left the room, in search of the pharmacology station.

It was an odd trip for Adam—lurking through the hospital, dressed as a patient instead of the professional. As a medical professional, he had always been conscious of his white smock uniform, especially when physicians came for advice, or when he saw the patients dressed in gray bathrobes, giving way as he walked toward them. The white smocks and the gray bathrobes created two distinct classes of people in the hospital. Adam often saw himself and the physicians as wardens in a jail, and the patients as felons—imprisoned until the doctors saw fit to declare them rehabilitated.

Now Adam was the prisoner dressed in gray, and as he drifted toward the pharmacy counter, he entered an area of the hospital where gray was forbidden.

It was an alcove, just off the main hallway and almost in view of the nurse's station. A medicine tray rested near a wall—an aluminum and steel traveling cart, waist high, with a set of drawers for storing drugs, stock medications, and syringes. There was a plastic box for disposing of used needles, cups for measuring dosages, and an open file of patient profiles, specifying the prescriptions for the floor.

147

Adam left the alcove and went to the visitors' room, where he found a newspaper. When he returned to the alcove, he opened the newspaper and made himself comfortable against the cart, pretending to read sports while thumbing through the prescriptions. "Bixley, R. E. 053-44-6756. b.i.d. magnesium sulfate, 30 mg. Dr. S—" Something to help constipation; a problem that hadn't yet bothered Adam, although he imagined everything was a matter of time. He searched farther in the cards. "Petrunski, J. 443-33-5536. q.6h. Luminal, 400 mg. Dr. S—" Luminal was phenobarbital, a sedative primarily used for calming convulsions. It could help him relax—get the sleep he couldn't get before his trip to the hospital. But even better was a prescription for flurazepam.

He memorized the prescription numbers and bent down to look in the cabinet. Inside were several trays, each marked for the appropriate patient. He looked for Petrunksi's number and reached for a plastic bottle of spherical white pills.

"What are you doing?"

Adam turned, the pills in his hand.

"I was just looking for aspirin," Adam said. He knew the answer sounded stupid, but he also knew the cart should have been attended, and it was in everyone's interest for the nurse to believe him.

The nurse frowned at him as if he were an eight-year-old and warned that if he had swallowed the drug, he might have suffered a seizure—an extremely unlikely action, even with an overdose. Adam thanked her, returned the pills, and feigned continued interest in an article. Slowly, he drifted back to the alcove.

What he wanted more than anything was painkillers and amphetamines, and it was the prescription pad that would get them for him. The blank pad rested near the pharmacy window. Like at his own clinic in New York, the pharmacist's assistant and the drugs were behind a Plexiglas window. There was no chance of Adam's simply wandering inside the pharmacy and stealing what he needed; however, a prescription pad, left on the counter for the physicians . . . Adam approached the window, his smile on. "Hello?" he called to a young woman behind the Plexiglas. "I ran a hospital pharmacy in New York."

She smiled back, giving him more than the usual attention.

"Are you the director?" he asked, knowing she wasn't. She laughed at the compliment, and the ice was broken. Adam began asking her questions about the pharmacy—size of staff, shipments, laboratory work—all the time flipping the pad of prescription paper and figuring out their system for leaving orders. It was either more complicated than Adam realized, or merely a matter of the physician writing his order, the assistant stamping acceptance, and the order being dropped in a shoe box. As if to assure Adam of the system's simplicity, a doctor borrowed the prescription pad, scribbled a request, and pushed it through a slit in the window. The woman stopped the conversation long enough to read the prescription, stamp it, and drop the paper in a box. There was never a conversation with the doctor or a question asked by the woman processing the requests. An old-fashioned assembly for processing prescriptions, Adam thought.

Satisfied, he finally asked for the name of the director. She told him, and he reacted with planned delight—insisting he knew the man, and could she please see if he was in the pharmacy. Without hesitation, she left her post and walked through the aisle toward the back offices. The moment she was out of sight, Adam took the pad. "Druit, A. 551-12-0323. b.i.d. Biphetamine, 20mg. Flurazepam, 30mg., before bed. Dr. S—," he scrawled, not attempting to write a name, only to imitate a few circular lines.

When the woman returned, Adam was still by the window, and the prescription was on her side of the partition. "The director's not in," she said, looking at the paper, stamping it, and dropping the prescription in the shoe box.

"Maybe later," Adam said, easing himself out of the conversation. He was soon back in his bed, pleased with himself.

Leave in the morning, he thought. Stash the pills until needed, then figure out what the hell was going on. Patience—that was the key. Patience, and keeping to a pace. Forget the day that was lost. Forget the damn station wagon and the knife; even stop wondering whether Sherry was alive. Just go back to where he lost the trail and pick it up. After all, it's only been a few days. The kidnapper couldn't have traveled far.

"Mr. Druit?"

The man was staring down at Adam—a tall, balding doctor, with a stethoscope cradled about his neck.

"I'm Dr. Schorr," the man said.

Adam tried recalling the face.

"I talked to you earlier, briefly, while you were recovering from sedation. You woke from a nightmare," said Schorr. "Something about a maniac in the hospital."

"I remember," Adam said.

"Have you had that dream again?"

"No."

"From the look on your face, I thought you were having it now."

"I'm all right."

Schorr shook his head. "I know that's a lie." Schorr dropped a piece of paper on the bed. "You could go to jail over something like this."

Adam glanced at the prescription he had written.

"What are you?" Schorr asked. "An addict?"

"I just wanted them for later, if I needed them," Adam said.

The doctor nodded, having anticipated another lie, no matter what Adam answered. "I'm not reporting this because I know what happened to your daughter," said Schorr. "But I also don't want you winding up in intensive care."

"You don't have to worry," said Adam. "I'm leaving town tomorrow morning."

"That's not what I meant," said Schorr. "You came in here a mess. Blood pressure down, heart palpitating . . . You probably think you're okay, because you feel better than you did before, but your body's not clean. Whether or not you're an addict, you've been on a junkie's diet."

"I know how to take care of myself."

"Yeah," said Schorr. "You've really impressed everyone." He walked to the door, bumping into the floor nurse. She apologized and pulled back the curtain that hid Adam's roommate.

"Your judgment's off," Schorr told him. "You

151

drift in and out of sleep, you're paranoid, you're compulsive, and you're reckless," he said. "Has that always been your personality profile?" Schorr stopped his lecture to watch the nurse coax Adam's roommate into taking more pills. As before, the man choked on the medicine.

"Nurse," Schorr said, "I told you to change that."

"Dr. Schorr, I don't remember—"

"IV preparation of isoxsuprine hydrochloride," said Schorr. He looked at Adam. "Some of us know when to take advice."

Schorr left the room. Adam lay back in bed and closed his eyes.

A junkie's diet, Schorr had said. But there was a big difference in being addicted to a drug or merely dependent on its benefits. It was enough of a difference to free Adam of guilt now, or when he had been a director at his own hospital—experimenting with the drugs, seeing how they affected him or seeing how new combinations benefited the patients, losing interest in everything that had once mattered. His career, his wife, his child.

His child.

"What are you doing?" Phillip asked.

He stood at the doorway, not so much waiting for an invitation as leaning against the wall, arms folded, threatening Adam. Adam didn't know what to make of Phillip's expression. Was it jealousy? Appreciation? Anger?

"I asked a question," Phillip said. "Why are you killing yourself? Do you think it's helping anyone?"

"I'm trying to save Sherry," Adam said, "and for the life of me, I don't know why everyone finds that such a problem."

"Maybe if it was someone else, they wouldn't."

"Very funny," Adam said.

"You think so?" Phillip said. "I want to know what you're trying to prove, Adam. I mean, what makes you better than the police?"

"I care."

Phillip looked incredulous, but he also felt Adam's intensity. In fact, it warned Phillip to keep his distance. "You care," he repeated, not coming close to believing Adam. "Well, I've got news for you; that isn't enough."

"It's still important," Adam said. "I've talked with the police, Phillip. I've talked with them in West Bay and Calverton and here and the harder it gets, the less they try."

"That's *not* true."

"They're treating Sherry's kidnapping like a car theft," Adam said. "But it's going to take more than that now. Everything I had to work with—the car, the license plate, Sherry's clothes . . . They're no good. There's only me."

Phillip considered saying something, hesitated, then said, "You may be surprised, but I didn't come here to talk you out of this nonsense. I know better than to try that."

Adam listened.

"I just want to say one thing," Phillip said. "On the incredible long shot you do find Sherry . . . If you get anywhere close, before you do anything, I want you to phone the police."

"What does that mean?"

"I mean don't do anything yourself," Phillip said. "Don't touch her."

Adam still didn't understand, but Phillip was insistent. "Just don't touch her, okay? You're too much of a mess to be trusted. The way you're popping pills . . . Look; just phone for help, phone the police, or I swear to God . . ."

This time, Phillip stopped himself. He still wanted to say something, but instead waved away Adam and turned back toward the door. "Christ," he said. "What's the point of talking. You won't know what the fuck you're doing anyway."

With that, Phillip left, closing the door, leaving Adam.

As for Adam, he stared at the door. Once again, he was alone.

Well, that was fine too. In fact, that was exactly what he wanted.

And the day he left the hospital, he wasted no time getting back into action. Of course, the local sheriff wanted him out of town quickly, but Adam wasn't going anywhere yet; not until he had an idea of which way to go.

For that information, he went back to the Blue Ridge Tavern.

This time he went inside, walking up to the counter and waiting for the bartender. "Excuse me," Adam said. "A few days ago, the police arrested a man outside—someone they thought was a kidnapper."

"I remember," said the bartender.

"Who was working the bar when that happened?" Adam asked.

"You're talking to him."

Adam stared at the man. He was young, muscular, sturdy . . . A cigarette habit, but that would be all. "I'm the father of the kidnap victim. I was wondering if you'd answer some questions about that night?"

The bartender shrugged. "I already talked with the cops."

"I know, but I think they asked you about identifying a particular man." Adam rested his hands on the counter. "I was hoping . . ." Adam eyed the man, waiting for his name.

"Mike," the bartender said.

"I was hoping, Mike, that they missed something. What did the police ask?"

"They wanted to know about anyone with black hair, kind of slicked back. One or two other things, like the car, and the—"

"Did they show you a picture of my daughter?"

Mike shook his head.

"Did they mention the name Vincent Braitman?"

"No, but it doesn't mean anything to me anyway," the bartender said.

"Did they ask you about anyone who looked a little different?" Adam said.

"Different how?"

"Like someone who didn't have slicked-back hair?" Adam said. "I mean, maybe by the time he got here, he had changed his appearance?"

Mike shook his head. "I don't see how they could," he said. "The place was pretty crowded. I mean, if you don't know what he looked like . . ."

Adam opened his wallet. "This is her," he said, showing the picture of Sherry.

Mike stared at it.

"Did you hear anyone talking about children? Did anyone drop the name Sherry, or mention a young girl, or—"

155

"Not a thing," said Mike. "I'm still thinking about the hair, though."

"What are you thinking?"

Mike concentrated, squinting, trying to remember. "There's a guy named Frank Beatty who does a midnight haul up to some outlets in Maine."

"You think the man who took my daughter could be—"

"No, not Beatty," said the bartender. "But I just remember him sitting at a table, spreading family pictures, talking with some guy." Mike thought harder, then shook his head. "You might want to ask Beatty; he's usually in by eight, so you might want to come back then."

Yes, Adam would. But that was only the first step. He also needed to go back to the library; to read the newspapers, to study the maps and, most important, to search through the shelves. He wanted books. Criminal profiles, case studies, psychological analyses . . . Something to help mold the clay—to press and shape Sherry's kidnapper, to make him more real, to help Adam understand and predict the man's moves.

He leafed through more than a dozen manuscripts, ranging from a clinical look at the criminal mind to a fictionalized account of a cross-country murder spree. He tried to draw something from each of them—a clearer motive for Sherry's kidnapper, a sense of direction, an understanding of how he made his choices . . . a confirmation of Adam's own thoughts and ideas about why the kidnapper picked a particular road, or chose a particular child. . . .

Finally, he went back to the maps. He studied where he was, then played a game, trying to predict where Sherry's kidnapper might go. He stared at the map, reading the names of towns, taking note of the landmarks and other markings, looking for his destination. A place of innocence, he thought. A place where the children were young and available and, foremost, unprotected.

He stared at the map until he found his point, then drew his circle. Only for a moment did he hesitate. There seemed something wrong about the mark—as if Adam was veering off the trail, even though he was only guessing the trail's direction. Then he understood; for the first time, he was turning off Interstate 95. Indeed, even before Sherry's disappearance the kidnapper had kept to his highway; but now Adam was guessing another route. Adam was actually gambling the kidnapper was changing directions—that, perhaps, Adam had gotten too close and the kidnapper had felt it was time for a deviation. Or, more simply, that the promises of another road would demand that the kidnapper detour.

Adam was gambling that he knew the kidnapper so well that he knew when it was time for the pattern to change.

He tore the map from the book and stuck the sheet in his pocket. Then, an hour later, he was back in the Blue Ridge Tavern, sitting at one of the tables, listening as a trucker told him all he needed to know.

"He kind of followed me in," Frank Beatty said. "We both showed up maybe two hours before the police came by."

"What did he look like?"

"Kind of middle-aged, with dark hair," said Beatty, "but nothing wet or greasy, like you was say-

157

ing. Blown back is more accurate. We walked in, sat down, and he started buying me beers, just like you're doing."

"That's it?"

"Then we started talking families, and I showed him pictures of my kids, and he showed me pictures of his."

"Were any of his children a girl?"

"One was."

Adam showed his picture of Sherry and Beatty stared at it.

"If you're asking me if it's the same kid, I couldn't say," Beatty said. "It could be."

"What happened next?"

"Next I got up to leave, and he asked for a ride. Said he was hitchhiking. Said his car busted and he had to get home. So I gave him a ride." Beatty again looked at the picture of Sherry. "Didn't have any little girl with him."

No, but that didn't matter, Adam thought. He could have locked Sherry away someplace, or maybe he was going back to see her now. "Where did you drop him off?"

"Up 93, first exit past Windham," Beatty said. "I'm not sure where it goes."

Adam jotted down the number and later that night, pulled off the exit, stopping before a sign.

WELCOME TO BIRCHMERE POP. 2200

He stared at the sign, then unfolded the map he had taken from the library, finding the town he had circled.

"Birchmere."

He closed the map and reached for a bottle of pills.

He needed to calm his nerves. He needed to stop wondering how he could be so good at second-guessing a monster. He had to stop asking why it was proving so easy to understand someone who had performed such awful things on his daughter.

Above all, he had to remind himself of how unlikely it was that he was on the right trail.

Still, if the kidnapper was here . . . If Frank Beatty really had carried him to Birchmere . . . And if Adam had managed to follow him all this distance, with so few clues, with so little help . . .

It was enough to keep Adam awake until morning.

Birchmere was thirty-five miles north of the hospital. It was a New Hampshire town, near Manchester, with one church, one main street, and two schools. One of the schools was an all-boys boarding school—children ages nine through eighteen, tuition $10,000 per student, and all activities regimented between a schoolhouse, gymnasium, cafeteria, and the dormitory. There was barely a moment when the boys were unguarded, and children were as carefully tended as the manicured land upon which the school rested.

Visually, it was an odd sight against the New England mountainside. The lawn itself was the school's border, and the grass fields—trim as a golf course—stretched in all directions from the main houses. The grass served several purposes: it separated the school from the otherwise rural township; it made truancy from the school impossible; and it protected the school from outsiders. People who were lost knew immediately they had missed the proper turn off, and parents searching for the school understood, without any words passing between them and the schoolmaster, that fathers and mothers were needed only for the two-month summer vacation.

In comparison, the public school—four miles away—was merely an afterthought to Birchmere's local playground. It was an elementary school, and while the town itself wasn't especially poor, neither was it rich. Some of the school's windows were broken, and the fence around the playground had been irreversibly bent from the weight of too many children scaling its side. A driveway circled near a building extension, where many of the children were dropped off in the morning and picked up in the afternoon. Just as many children walked to school, in pairs or alone, by crossing a grass football field that stretched behind the school. It was a field that would never have the trim of the boarding school lawn.

A tar parking lot bordered the east side of the school. This was used more as a play area for the youngest children, who would take turns kicking a large red ball, or would run around bases that had once been painted on the concrete, but were now drawn in chalk. A teacher was always with these children when they played outdoors, but this wasn't true for the older boys and girls. During lunchtime and after school ended, the older children—ten and up—were free to play on the field, or, if they lived nearby, go home. There was no boarding school regimen because it was hard enough teaching the children math and English. Nor did anyone feel a need to watch them. These boys and girls hadn't been taken from their homes. The school was part of a community, and the community was at ease in a part of the world where the most common crime was drunk driving or an occasional breaking and entering.

It was, in short, a town where the only things that came from the outside were money and children, and usually they came together. For someone like Adam Druit, or for that matter any visitor, there was no reason for a prolonged stay in Birchmere.

Unless, of course, one had a special interest in young, unprotected children.

That was why he had circled the town. One of the map's landmarks had been the preparatory school. Now, sitting at a luncheon counter, just inside the doorway of the Birchmere Fountain and Lunch Shop, he tried to think less of how he found Birchmere, and more about what to do next. Adam would just have to be alert, that was all. He would have to learn Birchmere, then be awake for any sign of trouble. Every minute would count.

Which made him think of the time: two fifteen in the afternoon.

"Excuse me," Adam asked a counter boy. "You said there's a public phone?"

The boy pointed toward the rear. Adam paid his bill and went to the phone, deciding to chance a call to Casey.

It took some courage calling her. Once again, she had seen him at his worst, and Adam couldn't think of a time when she needed more strength and support. Christ, she was the one supporting *him*. She had come to the hospital, she had talked with the doctors. . . . Adam also knew she was the one footing the bill. Yes; he had definitely failed her, and the longer Sherry's kidnapper ran loose, the longer he failed.

"Hello?" Casey answered, her voice too faint, even for a long distance call.

"It's me," Adam said.

Casey needed a moment to recognize Adam's voice. Adam didn't know if his voice had changed, or if Casey's memory was weakening from fatigue. Maybe it was only natural for her to forget him. Without Sherry, perhaps all of the past would fade.

"I'm sorry about the hospital," he said.

"I know." Casey sounded understanding. "It's all right."

"I just wanted you to know I appreciate it, and that I really am okay. I didn't overdose."

"Adam . . ."

"I mean it, Casey. I know what I'm doing. I'm not saying I'll be able to find Sherry, but I'm giving it my best shot."

"Adam, where are you?"

"Don't worry about that," Adam said.

"You're sick," Casey said. "You've been sick for years, and now this thing with Sherry's making you worse."

Adam glanced at the clock. Two twenty-five. "Look," he said, "I don't want to argue; I called to say thanks and to let you know that if anything turns up, I'll phone."

"What do you mean if . . ."

"I guarantee I'm okay. But this could take a while. I know that now."

"Adam, what are you doing?"

"*Nothing*," Adam reassured. "Just keeping my eyes open."

Adam knew she was unconvinced; she had to be,

162

because Adam had to strain for the right sound of sanity. At the same time, Casey knew she had little control over him. They were miles apart, and they were divorced; she could only pick up the pieces after he fell apart, until she no longer cared.

"If it's any help," Casey told him, "I know she's still alive."

"I think so too," Adam said.

"But I *know* it," Casey said. Her voice grew fainter. Adam could hear her crying.

Adam looked again at the clock. Two thirty.

"I'll call you later, Casey," he said. He hung up and headed back to his car. On the front seat was a thermos, a clipboard, and a pad of paper. The paper had several phone numbers, the address for a motel, and directions for Birchmere's two schools. In the backseat was Adam's overnight bag. He hadn't asked the police for his attaché case.

Adam picked up the clipboard and read the directions to the public school.

He reached the school by two forty and parked by the wire fence. He arrived in time to watch as the children left school—some meeting their mothers, most walking home alone, unprotected.

It was perfect timing. He opened his thermos and took a sip of herbal tea. He studied the children carefully, adopting them, remembering moments with Sherry that he had almost forgotten.

And he watched the road, waiting.

163

Chapter 13

Jerry Talbot drove fifty miles out of Boston to try and save his company $450,000.

This was the likely cost of the malpractice claim against Adam Druit, a claim that would be paid by the insurance company for whom Jerry worked as an investigator. The trick, Jerry knew, was to prove beyond a reasonable doubt that the patient knew and accepted the inherent risks in the chosen therapy. If they could relieve Druit of his part in administering the drug, then it would just be a matter of reiterating the patient's near-death state and comparing Druit's unorthodox therapy to similar experimental tests on dying patients.

Put simply, if all other treatment had failed, and the patient was already days short of death, who the hell cared if the patient played guinea pig and died a little early?

The beauty of the argument was that it avoided Druit's competency as a pharmacologist. Instead, it concentrated on the patient's willingness to take risks and Druit's ability to explain the drug's dangers—something that required minimum oratory skills. Jerry turned off the pike and slowly pumped the brakes to his Pontiac Seville—a large, black car, heavy with every available option. He drove, wondering if Adam Druit would be reasonable. Hell; *could* Druit be reasonable? A tricky question, considering it had taken two investigators just to find him. Jerry had been one of them, and while he appreciated the overtime pay, he hadn't appreciated all the telephone calls to the hospital, Druit's lawyer, the police. . . . Most of all, he had hated the phone call to Adam's wife.

It was something he had avoided until all the other calls failed. Phoning her should have been his first course of action, but Jerry had heard about the child's disappearance and who wanted to walk into something like that? Fortunately, Jerry dealt with her calmly—never mentioning the kid or apologizing for the phone call. Mrs. Druit—or the former Mrs. Druit—responded in kind. "He didn't leave me a phone number or an address," she told him, "but I know he's not too far from the hospital."

Precisely fifty miles from the hospital, Jerry learned after phoning the motels and hotels. Jerry talked with Adam Druit and arranged to meet him at a place called the Toll House Inn. Adam agreed with only one precondition: Jerry was to be there by one thirty, and Adam was to leave precisely at two o'clock. Jerry, pleased to make contact, offered no argument and managed to reach the Toll House on time. Despite the punctuality, however, identifying Adam still proved difficult. Of course

Jerry had a picture of him, but Adam Druit was a man known to take drugs. When you added an emotional profile just shy of suicidal, the combination tended to change a man's appearance. Jerry searched the restaurant looking for someone who looked like he had crawled out of a garbage bin. Then he tried a new tack—sitting alone at a booth and waiting for Adam to find him. He sat there for five minutes before noticing another gentleman, two booths away, staring intently out the window.

Jerry opened his attaché case and double-checked the photograph. The man in the booth was not only cleanshaven, but tailored in the kind of gentle weekend clothes one would expect of someone who had spent every summer in the wholesome seclusion of New England. It was an effective disguise, if you didn't notice how tired he looked, and the bloodless pale of the skin.

Jerry left his booth and approached him.

"Mr. Druit?" said Jerry.

Adam glanced at Jerry, nodded curtly, then continued staring out the window. Jerry followed the direction of Adam's gaze. He was watching a gas station. Several cars were parked in a line, and four children were racing for the toilets. Adam didn't stop watching until the children were safely back in their family's car.

"He could have spent days here," Adam said.

"Excuse me?" said Jerry, not close to understanding.

"This is where he'd sit. In this booth, looking out at the highway. He could count the children

166

going by and think about stealing one from any of the cars at the station." Adam looked toward the counter, where a chalkboard advertised the day's specials. "You'd think he would drink coffee, from all his traveling, but he doesn't need it. The children keep him awake. That's probably his problem; thoughts of children keep him awake days and nights." He turned to Jerry, who still didn't follow Adam's thoughts. "They're his ghosts," Adam told him. "He may have even tried escaping them, but you can't run from children. They're everywhere and always within his reach. Maybe he hears them calling his name. Or maybe he calls them, and they answer." Adam looked again at the gas station. "This place needs guarding," he said.

A waitress approached the booth and asked if they were ready to order. Jerry asked for coffee and a donut.

"I'd like two hard-boiled eggs and a cup of hot water, please," Adam said.

The waitress and Jerry stared at him. Adam, however, was again turned to the window. Finally, they exchanged looks, and Jerry shrugged. When the waitress left, Jerry cleared his throat and feigned a smile. "Mr. Druit," Jerry asked, "are you on drugs right now? It doesn't help our discussion if you are. I've done a lot of driving today, and I don't want to waste my time talking if you're—"

"You're already wasting time," Adam said. "You've got about twenty minutes."

Jerry took the cue and opened his attaché case. "All right," he said. "But you don't want to rush this, Mr. Druit. I'm not just here for the company.

167

Your career is at stake. There are also criminal charges to consider, and—"

"Coffee and donut," said the waitress, pushing the cup in front of Jerry. She leaned toward Adam and lowered her tray. "Two eggs, hard-boiled. One steaming cup of water."

"Thank you," Adam said.

Jerry watched Adam open a paper bag. Inside it were sandwich bags, individually filled with powders, leaves, seeds, and what looked like twigs or pieces of bark. Adam placed the plastic bags in a neat row and opened them.

"What I'm saying is that it's in your best interest to cooperate."

"Is that what you came to tell me?" said Adam.

"I came to get a few details about the death of the patient," said Jerry.

Adam paused, letting his mind recall the details of the death. "He died because I brought into this country a drug that hadn't been classified by the FDA. His heart couldn't take the metabolic changes."

"No one knows if he died because of the drug," said Jerry. "He was ready to die."

Jerry edged uncomfortably in place, stealing a look about the restaurant to make certain there wasn't someone listening. Adam measured his powders and leaves, and added them to the cup of hot water.

"Look," Jerry whispered. "It doesn't matter if the drug killed him or not. Personally, I don't think it did. The real issue is whether or not the patient knew the risks."

Adam shook his head.

"He was warned, wasn't he?" said Jerry.

"I wouldn't give any drug without explaining the risks."

"Then I need to know precisely what you told him," said Jerry. "Did you tell him the nature of the risks? That the drug could produce palpitations or a strain on the heart or a weakness in the circulation?"

"Of course."

"Don't say that," said Jerry. "Nothing's 'of course.' Do you remember if he discussed the therapy with anyone else in the hospital?"

"He talked with his son."

"His son's the one who's suing us," said Jerry. "Did you talk it over with a nurse?"

"Maybe he did."

"I need more than 'maybe's.' "

"I talked it over with the patient," Adam said. "I gave him some articles to read. . . ."

"Which articles?" said Jerry.

"One in the *New England Journal of Medicine,* another in the *Times,* one in—"

"I want copies of the articles," said Jerry.

"I don't carry them around."

"Did he sign a letter of consent?" Jerry asked. "Do you have anything on paper that indicates his level of understanding?"

"He wrote letters to his family," said Adam. "That's the best I can do."

Jerry wiped his face, ready to give up. "I don't think you realize, Mr. Druit, that I might be the only person on earth who can save your ass."

169

"I don't think you realize, Mr. Talbot, that I don't want my ass saved."

"We're not just talking career; we're talking criminal charges."

Adam finished his drink, reached in his pocket, and dropped two dollars on the table. "You've got three more minutes."

"Okay, okay," said Jerry. "Two last questions. The first is that we're going before a mediator in about two weeks. I already told you the issue isn't if you administered the drug or even if the drug killed him. All that matters is if we can establish that the drug had the potential of doing good and that the patient was aware of the risks when he accepted therapy."

"What's your question?" said Adam.

"My question is can you be in New York City when we go before the mediator?"

"I don't think—"

"Don't answer me now," said Jerry. "You want to think about it. You got a whole life ahead of you and you don't want to trash it in the Toll House Inn."

"Then what's your second question?" Adam asked.

Jerry pointed at Adam's emptied cup. "What the hell was in that?"

"Nasturtium, watercress, and meadowsweet, stirred together with a stick of cinnamon," Adam said. "An antibacterial tea, for cleaning the system."

"Sounds healthy," Jerry said, not believing it.

Adam left the table. Jerry followed after him.

"Where are you going?" Jerry asked. "Can I reach you at that motel?"

"You can try," Adam said. "I'll call you if I'm interested."

"Mr. Druit, I still don't think you understand how important it is for you to—"

Adam put a hand against Jerry to stop him. "I understand that you've got a half million dollars to protect. I couldn't give a shit about your money. But I'll think about it."

"It's more than money, Mr. Druit. That's the point."

"That's for me to decide," Adam said. "Right now, I've got about eighty kids to watch."

Adam turned and walked out the door.

He glanced at his watch. He knew he had to get back to the school yard by two, but for the first time in a long time, he was thinking about his former profession.

Adam called it his "former profession" not only because of Jerry Talbot, but because he thought of almost everything these days in the past tense.

Now Talbot had Adam thinking about the wrong things. Lawsuits. Professions. Money. He had Adam thinking of himself, when every thought should be about Sherry. The kidnapper was here, in Birchmere. And if he wasn't, then he was nearby. Adam knew it.

But his thoughts again slipped as he walked across the parking lot to the gasoline station.

On the side of the building was a pay telephone.

He dialed the operator, gave the telephone number, and deposited his change. The call was answered almost immediately.

"Main Pharmacy," answered Murray.

Adam said hello. Murray asked who was calling, and Adam identified himself. Murray laughed.

"I didn't recognize your voice," said Murray. "You sound different."

"How are things?"

"Things are all right," Murray said. "Prescription's closed, but as long as can keep selling the shelf stuff, I still call us the Main Pharmacy. Figure you'll be coming back soon, anyway."

"Sure," Adam said.

"Got your daughter's picture by the window. You missed the search. About a hundred people got together and checked the woods for clues."

"I've been doing my own search," Adam said.

"Put a reward out, too," said Murray. "Five hundred dollars."

"You can't afford that."

"If it works, we'll split it."

"Look, Murray, I didn't call about my daughter," Adam said. "You ever see a Chinese kid come by?"

"I see Chinese kids like I see other kids," said Murray.

"His name is Michael. The grocer's boy, about two blocks from your shop."

"I know the shop, and I know the kid, but I haven't seen him. What's the matter?"

Adam didn't even want to try and explain. "He was going to do something for me, that's all. I thought he might have stopped by."

"You want me to check on him?"

"Don't bother," Adam said. "I shouldn't have called in the first place. I need to get somewhere."

"Then get going," Murray said. "But call me back. I'm keeping tabs down here on your daughter. You never know when something might turn up."

"I appreciate it."

"Of course you do," Murray said. "And remember—you can come back here any time you're ready. You got a job waiting."

"Right," Adam answered. He was ready to hang up, but he didn't. Instead, he thought a moment, while Murray waited. "Murray?" he finally said.

"Still here."

"Murray, I'm going to catch him and I'm going to kill him."

"Of course you are," said Murray.

"I've got an edge, Murray," he said. "Sometimes, when look inside myself, I can picture what he looks like; what he wants to do; what makes him move. Sometimes I even know what he feels. I mean, it's nothing hard, but I can still use that. I can use it all to get him. That's my secret, Murray. That's my edge."

Murray paused, considering what Adam had said, then chose his words carefully. "Your kid disappeared," he said slowly, deliberately. "You're a father chasing after his daughter. Things may not be as clear as you think. Understand me? Can you follow that?"

Adam didn't answer.

"Adam?" Murray shouted. "Hey, will you please

relax?"

But Adam glanced at his watch, hung up the phone, and walked quickly to the door. He was already ten minutes late.

Chapter 14

The routine was simple at Birchmere Elementary. At two o'clock, the preschool children were brought outside to the playground, where they stayed until their parents arrived to drive them home. Two thirty, and the kindergarten class was dismissed. Two forty-five, and the rest of the school was freed.

The older children were more difficult to supervise. Some of them were driven home, but most were trusted to themselves. For a half hour, an adult watched the playground; then the children were left alone.

That, thought Adam, was when the school became dangerous.

Adam knew the routine because he had been in the area five days. At least he guessed five. He knew the days by their events, and most had been uneventful.

He was also becoming familiar with the children. He had even overheard some of their names. Most, however, he knew only by face, and for these, he had given his own names. One dark-haired, quiet boy—pencil thin and a fast runner—he called Tony, after a classmate from his own childhood. A large, overweight girl he named Elyse, a name Adam found beautiful, and which he believed could help promise the girl an easier, thinner future.

There were scores of children, and Adam guarded them all. But only one of the children he named Sherry.

She had brown hair, her favorite color was blue, and she wore dresses that were as light and colorful as a clear sky. She had more energy than Adam's daughter—at least more than Adam remembered—and was older; perhaps ten. But this was part of his attraction to the girl. No one could be Sherry at the time of the kidnapping. That memory was too sacred. But a girl could be Sherry a few years older.

When Adam first saw this particular girl, he saw the resemblance instantly—the girl who should have been his daughter; the impossible possibility. Now he watched her with special fondness, knowing what she looked like a few years ago, imagining what she would be in a few years. He became her godfather. On the days when she left school late— when her friends were gone and there was no one to guard her—Adam followed her home, always keeping out of view. Then he would return to the playground and continue his vigil until the last of the children had also gone home.

Inevitably, one of the children noticed the car that seemed to be parked forever at the far side of the grass field and the child mentioned this to a supervising teacher. Adam, however, had anticipated the discovery and stopped by the principal's office, where he identified himself as a writer and said he wanted to observe the children for a few weeks.

Adam had been concerned his story would need more substance, but there was no suspicion from the faculty. The wrong people simply didn't come to this part of the world. Besides, Birchmere was familiar with the odd interests of writers; every presidential election, the town teemed with reporters interviewing everything short of the cows. The teacher told the children not to worry, looked to Adam, and waved. Adam waved back.

When word spread that Adam was writing a book, some of the parents even stopped by his car, especially during lunchtime, to see how the project was going, to ask if he had noticed their own children, and to offer something to eat. Adam handled the questions without losing his cover. When he bought a camera and began taking pictures, it fit perfectly with his assumed occupation, and no one minded. The few children who were nervous at his presence soon ignored him, and he became a part of the landscape that edged the field.

Adam used this freedom to take pictures of everyone and everything. He wanted a comprehensive chronicle of the town to help him know when something changed. On his first day of picture taking, the children were especially easy to photograph, because school let out early for a severe storm warning, and the children waited outside, in a line, for their parents to pick them up. Adam proved to be a patient photographer, waiting until each child turned fully toward the camera before pressing the shutter. He took several of his daughter's new namesake, and also of the parents as they arrived and left with the children, so that he could identify the true mothers and fathers of Birchmere.

Then there were also the nearby woods and roads. When he finished taking pictures, he used his zoom to survey the fields and study the bushes and alleys of every nearby house. Even in a simple, small town such as Birchmere, the number of places to hide were remarkable.

This particular afternoon, the playground emptied earlier than usual. The parents came and collected the preschoolers, the older children played only a short while and then left. As in previous days, "Sherry" walked alone, and Adam left his post briefly to follow her home. By the time he returned to the school, however, the playground was empty, and rain clouds had brought an early dusk. He was considering a second watch point when someone came up to the passenger side of his car and knocked on the window. Adam recognized him as Franklin Sayles, the principal of Birchmere School.

"Drive me home?" Sayles asked.

Adam could only agree. Sayles climbed into the car, then directed Adam from the passenger's seat, all the time examining Adam's camera.

"You must have a lot of material by now," Sayles said. "You've been out every day this week."

"I haven't counted the days," answered Adam.

"The teachers have," Sayles said. "They don't really mind. At least they didn't until you started with the pictures."

"I'm not taking pictures of the teachers," Adam said.

"Free country anyway, right?" Sayles said. "I was

thinking, though; maybe it would be good if you spent some time inside the school. That way you could balance whatever disorderly activities these kids are doing on their own time."

"My book really is about children at play," said Adam.

Sayles smiled to show sympathetic understanding. "The teachers would appreciate it, that's all," he said. He rested an arm on the front seat and looked about the car. "So where's your notebook?"

"Pardon?" Adam said.

"Your notebook," Sayles said. He turned to search the backseat. "Don't you take notes about the kids?"

Adam thought a moment, just to be certain his lies wouldn't cross. "I do that when I go back to my motel room," Adam finally answered. "You can't watch children if you're spending half the time with your head over a notepad."

"You got one hell of a memory," said Sayles, in clear admiration.

Adam stopped in front of Sayles's driveway.

"Thanks for the ride," Sayles said. "Let's talk Monday about having you visit the school. Maybe an assembly would do the trick."

Adam, as an afterthought, reached in his pocket and pulled out a photograph. "Mr. Sayles, I don't suppose you've seen this girl, have you?"

Sayles studied the picture. It was a school portrait of Sherry, and Adam waited, hoping for a look of recognition. "No sir," Sayles said. "She's not one of ours, is she?"

"She'd be with a man. Dark hair, maybe

179

greased down."

"Someone who lives around here?"

"I don't think so," Adam said.

"Because there're plenty of guys who fit your description—maybe a quarter of the state—but I've never seen the child before." Sayles handed back the picture. "Why? Are they—"

"I'm asking for a friend, that's all," Adam said. "I do it wherever travel. Missing child."

Sayles appeared sympathetic. "If it'll help, we can put a notice up at the school."

"Let me think on it," Adam said. "I'll tell you tomorrow."

Sayles grinned. "Not tomorrow," he said. "It's Saturday. School's closed."

Sayles patted Adam on the shoulder and left the car. Adam sat a moment while the car idled.

The weekend. Adam had completely forgotten about it. Two days with the children on their own, unguarded, free to roam the woods or the streets or where ever they wanted. If the kidnapper appeared now, what could Adam do? Where was the best place to guard his adopted town? And come Monday, would all his children be back at school, or would one of them have disappeared?

The rain fell harder, and Adam knew there would be no watch during the evening. Still, he wasn't ready for going back to the motel, just as he wasn't ready for a weekend.

Adam turned the car and drove toward Manchester, pulling into a shopping mall and taking his film to a developer that promised morning delivery. Then he went to a pay phone and dialed long distance to Providence. "Eddie Hearns, please," Adam told a secretary.

Adam was put on hold a moment, and he turned his attention to a nearby video arcade. The entrance to the arcade had all the attraction of a peep show, with flashing neon lights and loud, vibrating rock music. Another prime area for a kidnapping, Adam thought. The only person watching the teenagers was a fat, tired old man who turned dollars into quarters. The quarters disappeared into the machines, and the kids stared steadily into the monitors, oblivious to danger.

"Adam?"

"Eddie," Adam said.

"I tried reaching you at the pharmacy, but the owner said you're out of town."

"Just testing other locations, that's all," Adam said.

"Heard about your daughter. If there's anything I can do—"

"I appreciate it," Adam said. "But I'm near Manchester, and what I really need is a local distributor who can give me some samples, cheap."

"What kind do you have in mind?"

"Warfarin sodium, phenobarbital, levarterenol . . ."

"Wait a minute," Eddie stopped him. "You're talking hospital supplies, not pharmacy."

"I'm selling to hospitals," Adam said.

"Levarterenol?"

"I know what I'm doing, Eddie," Adam said.

"It doesn't sound like it."

"Either take the business or don't," Adam said.

"I've been buying from you for five years. I don't see your problem."

"I might not even have these drugs. The barbiturates we have, but some of the others . . ."

"I haven't told you about the others."

"All right, so tell me," Eddie said.

Adam read off his list, and Eddie wrote down the names while running up a bill on a calculator. When Adam finished, Eddie told him the total price.

"No problem," Adam said. "Credit me and I'll pay you when I'm done with business."

"Adam . . ."

"I'm working as a pharmacist, Eddie," Adam said. "For a living, I count pills behind a counter. What the hell am I going to do—run off with a handful of samples and lose the best wholesaler I know?"

Eddie hesitated. "Okay," he said. "Give me a call tomorrow morning and I'll see what I can work out. You understand that anything I can deliver has to be skimmed?"

"Sure."

"That means can only give you extras. You may not be too lucky. People don't usually overstock on warfarin sodium."

"Anything you can do would be appreciated."

"I'll do what I can," Eddie said. "And I meant what I said about your daughter. Anything at all . . ."

"I'll remember," Adam said, hanging up.

He turned and stared a moment at the arcade, then walked through the mall with the slow gait of a police officer. He made one stop—at a natural foods store. He went through the canisters of spices and bought himself cinnamon, fennel, mint. . . . He also bought two bottles of nutmeg and mace.

In the evening, back in his motel room, he used a hot plate to boil water and dissolved two teaspoons of nutmeg and mace. He drank the tea and turned on the television, patiently waiting for the chemicals myristicin and elemicin to begin their hallucinatory effects. It would be a punishing high, Adam knew. When the pleasure disappeared, and the mirage faded, the nutmeg and mace would leave him hunched over the toilet, retching his dinner and making him feel close to death. But there would still be the pleasure beforehand, and at the moment, that meant more to Adam. The two spices would at least keep him happy until his supplies came in.

"Back into the fire," Adam murmured, knowing too well this was the sort of behavior that could lead him again to a hospital. More than that— hadn't this also led to his quitting work and leaving his family?

But there were so many children and so much danger, and the drugs . . . they not only kept him going; they gave him the edge. They intoxicated him with hope, with conviction . . . with the same feelings Adam suspected the kidnapper felt—an utter confidence over the world; a certainty that he could only win and would get what he wanted.

And that was good. Adam wanted to feel like the kidnapper. He wanted to know his thoughts, his feelings, his actions. . . .

"Back in the fire."

No; high and above the fire. Free floating, farther than Sherry and Casey and all his colleagues would ever permit.

And maybe there would come a time when he'd stop. If another month passed, and Sherry was still gone, and he no longer had his strength, he might have no choice.

For now, though, he trusted his pills. Off he floated, for the moment free of all pain. And below, a hundred thousand miles away, somewhere in the tiny speck called Birchmere, was the kidnapper.

Below him was the man Adam Druit felt certain he would kill.

The following day, he retrieved his photographs from the mall. He sorted the pictures of the children and matched them, whenever possible, with their parents. A number of the photographs had been taken as the children gathered to climb into the cars. Adam had on his bed the whole progression of the routine, from the boys and girls leaving the building, to the rides in the playground, to the parents whisking the children away in their Fords and Chryslers.

He noticed it the second time through the pictures. One dark blue car, parked behind the others, never moving until most of the children had gone; then, Adam had a picture of it pulling from the school's driveway, with the driver still alone.

The car was in seven of Adam's photographs. The driver was a white male, but in none of the pictures did Adam have a clear shot of his face. The oddest thing about the photographs was how the man's position in the car also never changed. His head remained still, his hands kept their precise position on the steering wheel. It was as if the man were a part of the car; as if by sitting still, he would remain unseen. And if that had been the intention, it had worked quite well. Adam hadn't noticed him, and it appeared none of the parents or children had, either. Adam suspected that even if the man had been waiting for a son or daughter, the child would have the same difficulty seeing the man; his manner was so discreet, his presence so forgettable, that he could be invisible. A statue in the park.

Adam studied one of the photographs more carefully, trying to guess the direction of the driver's eyes. The other men and women clearly knew their families, but this man seemed to claim the entire yard of children. Finally, Adam noticed the car's license plate. It was a New Hampshire plate, but the plate number was R-66789. The "R" meant the car was a rental.

The "R" meant Birchmere had another visitor.

Chapter 15

"Eighty-five ninety," said the saleswoman.

Adam handed her a credit card, and she handed him the attaché case.

It was almost identical to the one confiscated by the police. Black, professional, with brass edge protectors on the corners. For ten extra dollars, he could have had his initials added to the lock near the handle, but there was no point to the extra touch. This attaché case was needed only while Adam pursued Sherry's kidnapper. Once the man was caught, the attaché case, like Adam, could retire.

When he got back to his motel room, Adam pulled the curtains and chained the door. He removed the bottom drawer to his bureau and rested it on the bed. Underneath a layer of shirts were his supplies.

For stimulants, Adam had purchased amphetamine, phenmetrazine, and pemoline. The pemoline he bought as an amphetamine substitute—a less potent alternative to the other drugs.

Adam had also purchased a bottle each of picrotoxin and pentylenetetrazol—convulsants that, in

186

low dosages, counteracted his depressants, but in high dosages could punish and kill his enemies by choking away their breath.

Alongside his convulsants was a small vial of oxymorphone, a synthetic opiate six times as powerful as morphine. Adam preferred the drug to meperidine, which he had also bought. Meperidine brought back too many memories of colleagues hiding in the storage room between floor assignments, injecting each other, somehow convinced the drug was nonaddictive. They continued believing this, even after the fun had cost their jobs and they were on the street looking for other opiates.

Adam also had four different tranquilizers and three types of sedatives. With the sedatives were four small bottles of chlorpromazine hydrochloride—25, 50, 100, and 200 mg tablets. The drug was normally used for combating schizophrenia and tended to settle a patient into a laconic stupor. In place of energy, one was overwhelmed by a sense of disinterest and detachment; a total lack of fear, but also no motivation to act. Simple existence, as uncomplicated as a patient sitting on the edge of his bed, staring tirelessly at a wall.

For most of the drugs, Adam had imagined a purpose. The tranquilizers and sedatives had the most obvious uses, especially for Adam. Yet Adam also bought drugs on instinct, without a clear idea of why he needed them. For instance, the warfarin sodium was an anticoagulant that inhibited a person's ability to stop bleeding. With the warfarin sodium, he bought its antidote: a bottle of vitamin K. There were also three bottles of heart medicine: one for speeding the heart, one for slowing it, and a third for easing trauma due to a heart attack.

It wasn't just a sampling out of a supply catalog; it was an arsenal of drugs designed to bring radical change to every part of the human body. Adam had even purchased a supply of ketamine, a surgical anesthetic with the side effect of causing vivid hallucinations.

Any legitimate wholesaler would have panicked at the order Adam had submitted and recognized the supply for what it was: weaponry. But the wholesaler wasn't legitimate, and the supplies had been skimmed from the purchase requests of various hospitals. Those that weren't skimmed from order forms were bought from hospitals that had overstocked. Or they were purchased from the diversion market — drugs purportedly sold abroad at substantial discounts, then rerouted back to the United States and sold without any attached paperwork.

Adam unscrewed the bottle of amphetamines and swallowed one of the small white tablets. It helped him concentrate on his job while blocking the distractions caused by memories. In one of the desk drawers was a scissors. He shook his pillow out of its case, tore off the ticking, and began cutting the foam into squares. He spaced the squares inside the attaché case, making a kind of checkerboard. Then he placed the drugs between the foam pieces.

By the time he finished the job, the amphetamine was at its peak. It gave Adam the clearness of mind to do a more careful written inventory, and to code the bottles before he forgot how to identify them on sight. He taped this list to the inside of the attaché case, put a last sheet of foam on top of all the bottles, and closed the lid.

The lock clicked shut.

Adam lifted the case and carried it to the bathroom, where he could stare at himself in a body-length mirror. He imagined wearing a suit, with white shirt and tie, and the briefcase gripped firmly in his right hand. It was heavier than a normal businessman's attaché—heavy the way Adam imagined a bomb: not so much by the explosives as by the weight of its potency.

"You've got my daughter," Adam whispered. "Where is she?"

He looked at himself as if he saw a stranger, and the stranger was hiding his daughter.

"Where's Sherry?" he demanded.

But it was only a mirror. He could just as easily have talked to the sink or the toilet.

Adam studied his face. A useless, foolish man who had failed his wife and his daughter . . . And now all he could do was hide out in a motel and pretend he was doing something for her, when it was all really for himself. A way to relieve his guilt; as if there weren't a hundred and ten things for him to feel guilty about.

But the guilt for Sherry . . .

Christ, he hated his reflection. It made him realize his true mission. He didn't just want Sherry's kidnapper; he wanted the man in the mirror to die saving her. It was the only fair retribution. It was what he deserved.

He lifted his attaché case and smashed it into the glass. The mirror shattered, the pieces showering

189

the sink and floor.

Adam held the wall. Shit, what had he done now? He stepped out of the bathroom, cradling the attaché case, certain he had broken every bottle in it.

But when he checked the bottles, they were fine. His packing had been superb. The arsenal was intact, and now it was just a question of when he should strike. The kidnapper was as good as dead. So was Adam.

He picked up a piece of broken glass and again stared at his reflection.

Nothing broken.

It was enough to make him think his luck was changing.

By Sunday, the sky was clear, with only a hint of the previous day's rain. Adam used the nice weather as an excuse to visit the brown-haired girl he called Sherry, pretending the trip was necessary to learn more about the area, not bothering to wonder what information he lacked. He prepared himself by taking a low, .2 milligram dosage of ethchlorvynol—a nonbarbiturate depressant—as a temporary relief from two days of amphetamines, hoping a depressant would counter the strain he saw whenever he dared look at his own reflection. In the midst of this precarious balance, he parked by the driveway and stared at the girl's home.

The house was typical for this area of Birchmere: a ranch house protected by a pine fence that wrapped about the front yard. It was a suburban street that fitted as uncomfortably in the New England woods as the private academy. There were eight houses, all of similar design, that followed each other up an incline before succumbing to a dense forest. For this distance, the road itself was briefly transformed from gravel to a paved road; but when the forest brought an end to the neighborhood, the paved road transformed back to dirt and gravel.

Adam left his car and tested the door. Unlocked. He supposed all the houses were this vulnerable. These weren't just eight houses; it was a completed world, which began at Birchmere and ended at the forest. A safe world. Who needed locks? Who needed alarms or guns or guards?

It was nothing less than a kidnapper's delight. How easy to break the calm; how easy to snatch a child. . . .

He took his hand off the knob just before the door opened.

"Can help you?" the woman asked.

Adam stared at the woman. He had seen Sherry in the child, and now looked for a hint of Casey's face in the mother. The resemblance had to be there; but there was such a haze in his memory. The woman before him had reddish hair—was short, heavyset, and had a skin rash from too much sweat, sun, and motherhood. She regarded Adam without fear. There was, perhaps, a shade of suspicion, but only because she mistook Adam for a salesman.

"My name's Adam Druit," he finally said. "I've been down at the school working on a book."

Whatever reservations the woman had disappeared. "I've seen you by the playground, haven't I?"

"Probably."

"Amanda told us about you," she said. She extended her hand. "Molly Ballinger."

Adam shook Molly's hand. Behind the woman, sitting on a kitchen stool, was the girl. Amanda watched Adam for a moment, then ran away. Adam could hear the sounds of other children, and one of them—a boy, no more than five—came stumbling out of the kitchen to wrap himself about his mother's legs. He stood there whispering to himself, peeking at Adam and smiling, finally tugging at Molly's pants.

During this, Molly talked to Adam, her concentration tuned to a sound other than the noise of her children. The Ballinger house was normally in a state of semichaos. There was nothing wrong with yelling or fighting, so long as no one went deaf and bones weren't broken.

Molly led the conversation. First, they talked about Adam's book and his week of watching children. Adam handled the questions easily. His book was already a well-practiced lie, and by this late date, he had also invented a publisher and coauthor. As for his observations of the school, Molly was impressed with the amount of detail he had memorized about the children. While Adam didn't know their correct names, from the manner in which he described them, she had no difficulty at all knowing whom he discussed. If there was any question at all about the legitimacy of Adam's work as a writer, his precise descriptions ended them.

"Now that I've had a chance to see the children, I thought it would be good to meet a few of the parents," Adam explained.

"Of course," Molly said, inviting him inside the house. "But my husband isn't home. Won't be back until Tuesday. He's a trucker."

Adam followed her into the kitchen and took a seat by a small Formica table. She went to the refrigerator, opened a bag of cookies, and poured them into a cereal bowl. The coffee was already heating on a hot plate, but Adam preferred milk. He was concerned the caffeine mixing with the ethchlorvynol could completely confuse his body and start a fit of vomiting.

"People have been very nice to me," Adam said. "No one seems especially worried about strangers."

"Well, Birchmere's not like Boston or New York," she answered. "You don't have the crazies around here. Maybe there's a little of that in Manchester, but Birchmere's quiet."

"You never know what's going to come up the highway," Adam said.

"That's how a city person thinks."

"So you don't worry about your children?"

"Kids gotta grow up," Molly said. "Do you have any kids?"

"A daughter."

"How old?"

"Seven."

"Well, then you ought to know," Molly said, sitting down in a chair and folding her arms. If there was one thing she knew, it was how to raise children.

"Amanda reminds me of my daughter," Adam said. He opened his wallet and found an old picture of Sherry and Casey. Molly studied the picture and nodded her approval.

"Beautiful little girl," Molly said. "And this is your wife?"

"We're divorced," Adam said.

Molly pretended she hadn't asked the question. "Beautiful daughter."

"Her name's Sherry."

"I can see the resemblance between her and Amanda," Molly said.

"Do your other children go to school?"

"They're too young," Molly said. She leaned toward the doorway and shouted the children's names. In a moment, Amanda and her two younger brothers had crowded behind Adam, the youngest boy holding tightly on Amanda's arm. "Bobby, stand up straight." Both boys shuffled in place, neither standing any straighter. "Bobby's the older," Molly told Adam. "Amanda, this is the man you told me about. The one who sits in the car."

Amanda didn't answer. She looked to the floor, avoiding any kind of contact with Adam. Adam stared at her, stunned by memories of Sherry. Sitting at the kitchen table, with the children nearby and Molly making conversation . . . it was so easy to imagine Amanda as his own child. He reached out to her. Amanda stood still, letting him run a finger along her cheek. Her skin was so soft. It was like touching the skin of Sherry's ghost.

"You can go now," Molly said. "Take the cookies with you." Amanda slipped past Adam and stole the bowl of cookies. Molly brushed her hands and smiled again to Adam before noticing the strain in his face. "You feeling all right?" Molly asked.

The illusion had disappeared with the children. Instead of looking at Amanda, he stared at the floor. Suddenly, the family and the house became quite foreign to him. Not his children, he thought. Not his wife, not his house . . .

Molly's smile also became strained. Having a stranger in her house was unusual by itself; also having him near tears . . . It made her think again of what Adam had said about dangers traveling along the roads. "Well," she said, sitting straight and attentive.

Adam looked at her.

"Now that we've had a chance to meet . . ." Molly said.

Adam waited, knowing Molly wanted him to finish her sentence.

"Didn't you come here for a reason?" Molly asked.

Adam tried to think of why he had come. To meet Amanda, he thought. To see how much of his daughter was inside her and to see if this family was like the one he used to have. But the real reason was he wanted a few minutes to live someone else's life.

"I'd like to take a picture," Adam said. "One of Amanda with her family."

This brought back Molly's true smile. "What a delightful idea," she said. "This is going to be in your book?"

"And hopefully an article," Adam said. "The

Boston *Globe.*"

Molly looked proud. She immediately left the kitchen and called after her children. Adam returned to his car for the camera. He stood for a moment and imagined all the ways someone could break into the house. In addition to the open door, there was a sliding glass porch door, no security lights, and no dog. Adam wanted to steal something, just to teach the family a lesson. How he would love to steal Amanda.

Almost ten minutes passed before Molly returned. It occurred to him that perhaps she hadn't gone back for the children; instead, she could have tried calling the *Globe.* However, she had only taken extra time to clean the children and dress Amanda in one of the girl's favorite blouses.

All the children were beautiful. Adam needed his strength to hold the camera steady. He went through the motions of being a portrait photographer. "Everyone together," he said, pressing them in. Molly stood behind the three children, her own hair neatly brushed and one hand pressing in her stomach. Adam took three portraits of the family, then asked Molly's permission to take separate pictures of the children.

"By all means," Molly said, stepping to the side.

Adam took three pictures each of the boys, then positioned Amanda by the window for better light.

"Hold your head up, dear," Molly encouraged, lifting her daughter's chin. Amanda fully faced the camera, staring through the lens and into Adam's eye.

"Put your hand on your waist," Adam instructed,

his voice barely audible. "Curl your hair, just a bit behind the ear."

If Molly had remembered Adam's picture of Sherry Druit, she might have seen how Adam posed Amanda in a way that mimicked the photograph.

"Can I get copies of these?" Molly asked.

Adam kept taking his pictures.

"I'll pay for them," she said. "I don't have any professional pictures of my children."

"I'll send you copies for free," Adam said, moving to the side for Amanda's profile.

"I never heard of such a thing," Molly said, obviously pleased.

"It's no problem," Adam answered automatically. All the time, he kept taking his pictures. He was fascinated by Amanda. She *was* Sherry. His pictures were of a life that existed and a life that lived in Adam's imagination.

He didn't stop taking pictures until he ran out of film.

The stranger was again at the school—farther away from the parents this time, parked by a home Adam knew to be empty. Clearly, the man did not want to be seen. He even faced away from the school yard, to feign interest in some other part of the town. But Adam saw him there, at the noon recess. Adam watched the man adjust his rearview mirror so that he could watch the children without turning his head; so he could see every face, without anyone else seeing his.

"Jesus," Adam murmured. He let his head drop

197

against the steering wheel, resting for a moment before continuing the vigil. He was pushing himself toward the same exhaustion that had landed him in the hospital. His remaining good sense warned him of this. There were ways to beat good sense, though. An amphetamine diet was proving the most effective.

He didn't feel hungry—hadn't had an appetite for at least two days—but he wasn't a fool, either. Adam knew that an amphetamine could kill an elephant's hunger. He opened up a paper bag and unwrapped a sandwich.

In separate cars, on different streets, Adam and the stranger ate lunch together.

For Adam, it was as if they were sitting at neighboring tables in a dinner theater, with the stranger one seat closer to the stage. With his telephoto lens, he could see the man's head bob down for his food, then draw back, his jaw chewing at the bread. Adam guessed the stranger was a pudgy man, with soft skin that could hide any expression of joy or deceit.

Adam himself chewed for minutes on a single bite, finally swallowing and putting his sandwich aside. Plenty of time to eat later, he decided, promising to have a large dinner, if other matters didn't come up. He reached into his open attaché case and found his small plastic bottle marked methylphenidate. Just one tab, he thought; to calm his nerves and to make that bite of sandwich last him the afternoon.

The tab sat on his tongue for a moment, and Adam lulled it to the back of his throat and swallowed. He ate the pill with more enjoyment than he could get from any lunch.

"Relax," he told himself. He acted as his own best friend, his own therapist, his own doctor. "Long breaths; calm the nerves." The children's lunch hour was still busy, and the boys and girls ran tirelessly about, enjoying games without rules or end. The stranger kept eating—now chewing on a pickle, the juice wetting his lips.

As for Adam, he kept fidgeting. He refused to let his head touch the steering wheel again, but the price of the methylphenidate was another hour's worth of painfully keen alertness. It was more energy than he needed at the moment, and it would have been nice to store it deep inside his body for a more useful time. But the pill didn't work that way, and Adam would be on edge until it wore off. Maybe this time the peak would die earlier—his body, after all, was building up one hell of a resistance. Then the crash would be even worse, unless he took another tab, or perhaps two tabs.

"Amanda," he whispered, pleased just to hear the name. The name sounded rough when he spoke it; his throat was dry, and there was a sickly harshness to his voice. Still, somehow, the name made the pain honorable. He could see the girl against the wall of the school, walking slowly about a free jump rope, undecided whether or not to play. She took no notice of Adam; they had met once, and Adam was again becoming a forgettable fixture in the school's backyard. The other girls, however, seemed to take special notice of her. They avoided Amanda, forcing her to play alone. Adam suspected the reason—word had gotten out that the out-of-town writer had given her special attention.

I'm ruining the child's life, Adam thought.

But then he remembered the stranger.

The stranger had finished with his lunch, all except for a cup of coffee, which he sipped from a Styrofoam cup. He moved with the impatience of someone who had suddenly become bored; who had tired of watching and was ready to *do* something. Adam watched, expecting the stranger to jump out of the car, grab a child, and head for the small roads in the forest.

All he did was drink his coffee and readjust his mirror—turning it so he could watch one child in particular.

He's watching Amanda, Adam thought.

Adam shouldn't wait another minute. He should run to the stranger's car and pull open the door. He should kill him now, before the stranger had time to turn the engine; before he'd even have time to wipe his mouth.

Sherry's kidnapper, Adam thought. Maybe her killer. And now he was stalking Sherry again, in the guise of a girl named Amanda.

But Adam didn't.

What happened to your guts, Adam thought.

Adam didn't know. Maybe he needed a show of proof, just to be certain it was the kidnapper? Or maybe, deep in his heart, Adam didn't really want to catch him? With the kidnapper caught, he wouldn't have a reason to stay near the playground. It would be time to leave Amanda, go home and go to work.

Or time to go in the woods, take an overdose of pentylenetetrazol, and die.

He watched as the stranger crushed the Styrofoam cup and steered onto the street, driving away from the school and disappearing behind a corner house. Adam felt for the key to his own car, his fingers numb and swollen. He had to concentrate hard to make them close on the key ring and start the car. He leaned back in his seat a moment and tried to shake clean his blood; then he shifted into drive and began to follow the stranger.

They turned south on the highway and soon were driving the speed limit, taking a fifteen-minute trip to downtown Manchester. Once in the city, the game became more difficult. City streets brought city traffic, hiding the stranger's car behind buses and vans. Adam also found it difficult driving in the city. Driving had once been second nature to him; now, he had to remind himself to accelerate, decelerate, turn on the blinker, stop at the lights. It was easy enough to do on country roads, when he could take his time progressing through the steps; on downtown streets, however, every street corner and stoplight was an agonizing challenge, especially with his attention already focused not on driving, but on tailing another driver.

The stranger curved around a left-hand corner, and Adam followed, starting his turn from an inside lane. He cut in front of a van, and the other driver slammed on his brakes. Adam flinched from the distraction, but nothing more. He didn't believe in accidents. If he was going to die on the road, there had been plenty of opportunities before this.

They traveled north, then west, then north again, heading to the far side of the city. Twice, the stranger barely made it through a changing light, and twice Adam followed after the signal had changed red. Both episodes should have caught the stranger's attention, but they didn't appear to, and when they neared a train station, the stranger finished his trip by turning down a side road and parking at the curb.

When the stranger stopped, Adam rounded a corner and parked illegally in a bus zone. He sat for a moment, waiting for the stranger to make his next move. The stranger finally did, opening the door, collecting garbage from his car, and climbing out of the front seat. He locked the doors and walked away from Adam. His last gesture before turning a distant corner was to throw his garbage in a trash can.

Adam left his car quickly, not even bothering to close the door. First he ran to the trash can, sifting though the top of garbage for some unknown clue and finding nothing. Then he continued his pursuit, just in time to see the stranger enter the eight-story hotel. RAMADA INN — MANCHESTER, said the block letters. Beneath the sign was a marquee: WELCOME TRU-PRODUCTS CONVENTIONEERS. Adam followed the stranger through the revolving doors and found himself in a wide lobby, with a coffee shop to one side and a set of elevators on the other. Before him, at a long, marble counter, was the front desk.

The stranger was by the message booth. Adam could see the man asking a brief question and the clerk responding by going to a wall of mail slots.

Adam walked across the lobby as if he was a guest, avoiding the stranger's attention, but keeping sight of the clerk. The clerk thumbed a mail slot, pulled out a message and returned to the stranger. The stranger took the note and turned toward the elevator.

Adam left the motel.

He found a bench near the train station and sat down. Things were starting to happen, and it was frightening. Adam knew what he *had* to do, yet nothing was coming easy; as he got closer to the end, he felt more unsteady.

He wished he could forget everything. The stranger, the school, Amanda, Sherry.

He shook his head. How could he get scared, now that he finally had what he wanted?

A room number; that was all. Number 808.

But it meant that the stranger no longer had a place to hide. No matter where he went during the day, in the evening, Adam knew where to find him.

Now it was all up to Adam.

Chapter 16

Casey answered the phone on the fifth ring. "Who is it?"

Adam didn't talk right away. Casey had changed. Her voice was too calm; too free of pain. It frightened him, because the moment they started pretending everything was all right, that was the moment Sherry would disappear forever and the kidnapper would escape. Didn't Casey understand that?

"It's me," Adam said.

"Adam?"

"Yes, Adam."

"Oh," she said.

Her tone infuriated him. She could just as easily be talking about a summer vacation as the disappearance of their child.

"You've been getting phone calls," Casey said. "You got a call from an insurance lawyer."

"If it doesn't have to do with Sherry, I don't want to hear about it."

"The lawyer said he needs you to testify," Casey continued. "He said you could get everything cleared up in New York."

"I don't care about New York."

"You could practice again, Adam."

Adam struggled with his temper. He was getting dangerously close to shouting. He wanted to remind Casey that her daughter was gone; that Sherry might have been stabbed and molested and who knew what else.

"Put the letters in the garbage and tell the lawyer to fuck himself," Adam said. It was the sort of half-assed remark that should have brought the phone call to an end, which was exactly what Adam wanted.

"Maybe you ought to tell him yourself," Casey said. "He's been calling a lot, Adam. How have you been?"

Her voice was so clean and easy; a woman without worries. Adam began to realize what had happened.

"Casey, who else is over there?"

"Phillip's here," she said.

"Put Phillip on the telephone, all right?"

She did what she was told—no arguments, no questions.

"Adam?" Phillip said.

Adam heard the caution in Phillip's voice.

"What did you put her on?" Adam asked.

Phillip had anticipated the question; he just hadn't decided whether to answer it. "There's nothing to worry about," he said.

"What the fuck have you done to her?"

"Nothing," Phillip insisted. "She's on sedatives."

"What kind and how much?"

"Lorazepam, six milligrams."

"Six?"

"She needs it," Phillip said.

"And how would you know?"

205

"She's lost a daughter," Phillip said. He talked low, so Casey couldn't hear them. Adam thought it was absurd; with six mils of lorazepam, Casey couldn't make sense of a train roaring past her bed. "It's a rough time for her. She needs something to calm her down."

"You're not calming her down; you're knocking her out."

"I'm doing what I think is best," Phillip said. Now Phillip was angry.

"Put Casey back on the phone," he said.

"Forget it," Phillip said.

"Don't push this," Adam said.

"Push what?" he answered. "If you cared so much about her, Adam, where've you been for the past year? Where were you when Casey and Sherry visited?"

The questions were meant to hurt Adam, but they had lost their bite since Adam had already asked them for weeks. Still, he could hear Casey screaming and knew the questions were tearing her apart. Casey was begging Phillip to stop; but Phillip, like Adam, was too busy enjoying the pain he caused.

"Don't bitch to me about lorazepam," Phillip said. "It's not half the shit you're living on."

"I'll call Casey later," Adam said.

"The hell you will."

"I'll call when you're out and she's awake."

"*Forget* it," Phillip said. "Over my goddamn—"

Adam hung up.

It took a long time to calm his nerves. He stood absolutely still in the phone booth, listening to the street traffic, his eyes shut painfully tight and his hands in fists, as if all the agony could be squeezed out of his body. If Phillip could have seen him, he would have taken pleasure in the show.

Adam wasn't hurting from rage; an awful weakness doubled him over. For a moment, there was no more strength in his body. He survived on willpower, and unless he took care of matters quickly . . .

Adam opened his eyes. The weakness passed and with the passing came back his self-control.

"Room 808," Adam said aloud, looking across the street at the hotel. Several hours had passed since learning the stranger's room number. In that time, Adam had wallowed in indecision. If he hadn't been properly dressed, he likely would have been questioned for vagrancy. A bellboy had taken a great deal of interest in him earlier in the evening; at first, wondering if Adam needed help with bags, then wondering if he was waiting for another guest.

But now there was a desk clerk, and come evening, Adam—still stationed across the street—was only a silhouette, as harmless as any evening shadow. And the hotel didn't care about shadows; it was an omnipotent structure of steel and glass, with lights that glowed from most of its windows and people who milled about the lobby, secure in their safety.

How easily people are fooled, Adam thought—the only one who knew better.

"Room 808."

So Adam understood what he would do, but not with something risky, like an overdose of a cardiovascular drug. People could have amazing resilience to drugs. Adam couldn't chance it.

He would need a gun.

That normally wasn't a tall order; not in the "Live Free or Die" state. But it was late, and Adam also didn't want just any gun; he wanted an untraceable one. After all, he was going to commit murder, and a part of him—a less brave part—wondered what would happen after he had killed the killer. And as much as he hated it, he had started wondering if his testimony really could make a difference in New York.

An untraceable weapon. There was something so right about it. Murdering a mystery killer with a mystery gun, probably smudged with the fingerprints of another criminal.

He needed that gun, and he had only one idea about how to get it.

He returned to his car and drove crosstown, knowing what he was looking for but not certain where to find it. Finally, he was there. He recognized it more by what he didn't see than what he did—the dark streets, the teenagers huddled together. No matter where you went anywhere in the United States, you were never far from one of these: a junkies' corner, where the shadows were dangerous, and the buildings were storehouses for little plastic envelopes worth thousands of dollars.

Adam parked near the one street lamp, opened his attaché case, and removed four dark, plastic bottles and a handful of disposable syringes. After a long breath to calm himself, he left the car.

It was odd walking the street. For the first time in a long time, Adam felt as if he was slipping into his element. He was in a neighborhood thick with junked-out desperadoes and it felt as if he had walked into a family reunion. Adam knew these people well. He knew them like a personal family physician—all too aware of the types of drugs that diluted their blood, the dependencies they felt, the thrill of the high, the fear of the drop. He also knew them as a member of the brotherhood, and while Adam didn't have to break into cars and still didn't consider himself truly dependent on drugs, he could understand why other people succumbed.

Yes; from physiology to psychology, Adam knew these people. They had no surprises for him. In fact, if anyone had surprises, it was Adam. The drugs he possessed made him powerful. He was like a millionaire walking through a slum, ready to throw a thousand-dollar bill to anyone who took care of him. And Adam would be a very soft touch tonight for anyone willing to make the right exchange.

The shadows were clearer now that he had joined them. He passed a corner crowd in favor of a fellow resting on the stoop of a closed pet store. The man was a far cry from the sort of addicts Adam remembered from New York; part of a New Hampshire breed that reminded him of young, wayward lumberjacks, minus the outdoor crispness. In the pet store, two puppies slouched against the shop window, their snouts curled into their bodies. The man had taken a similar position, except his nose was smothered in the crook of an uncovered arm. Adam guessed he was chewing needle sores.

"I'm looking to make a deal," Adam told the man.

The man kept running his lips up and down his arm, not interested in what he heard, presuming he heard anything.

"I want to make a purchase," Adam said again. "Who do I talk to?"

The man murmured something, and Adam waited a moment, hoping the man would speak again.

"Do you understand me?" Adam tried.

This time, the man nodded.

"I want to buy something," Adam said.

"You want to buy something," the man repeated.

"Who do I talk to?"

The man threw back his head and cracked it against the storefront glass. The puppies woke briefly, then rearranged themselves into fresh curls of fur.

"Who?"

Adam was ready to give up, but now the junkie wavered side to side, the question slipping in and out of focus. "Who?" he said loudly. "Who?"

" 'Who' what?" someone else picked up.

The corner crowd began shifting its attention. The junkie started hooting like an owl.

"Why you bothering him?" the same person asked. "You looking to buy?"

Adam didn't answer immediately. He was either about to make a deal or be robbed.

"He's a cop," a voice whispered.

"He ain't no fucking cop," another voice answered.

"I'm talking to you," the first person said. He stood dead in front of Adam, his hand hidden and probably tight on a knife. "What you want? Pills? Crack? Dust?"

"I'm not looking for drugs," Adam said.

"Not looking?" the person repeated. It was a thought that didn't go down easily.

"Not for drugs," Adam said.

The person hesitated. Adam, in turn, considered his words carefully. The junkies were now his audience, and he could keep them going so long as they enjoyed themselves. "I need to buy a gun," he said.

"You want a gun, go to a store," the leader said.

"I wouldn't be here if I could go to a store."

"You would if you didn't know where the fuck you are," someone else said. Adam only looked to their leader, and everyone else shut up. Then Adam smiled. He was standing in the same business suit he had worn for the hotel, surrounded by junkies, in possibly the worst neighborhood in the state, and he'd never felt more confident. It was the sort of situation he had been seeking since Sherry's disappearance. Win or die; no in-between, no near wins or losses.

Adam turned as if to leave, and the leader grabbed his arm.

"I don't talk well with crowds," Adam said.

"You talk when I say," the leader said.

"Shake him down, Abbie," someone said.

Abbie pushed Adam toward an alley. Adam offered no resistance. It was as dangerous in the alley as anywhere else; what difference did it make where he was? At least Abbie left his friends on the street, so they could be alone. The crowd was happier away from the action, shrieking as they told Abbie to kill him and imagining the results.

When they were behind a dumpster, Abbie finally revealed his knife.

"If you're a cop," Abbie said, "you better speak up, because that's about the only thing keeping you on your feet."

"I'm just looking to make a deal."

"Okay," Abbie said. "Then let's start by emptying your pockets." He held up the knife and reached into Adam's breast pocket, pricking his finger on one of the disposable syringes. Abbie did a comedian's double take. If Adam had wanted, he could have used the moment to wrestle Abbie for the knife.

Abbie began laughing. "Shit, what else you got?" he said, checking Adam's pockets. The knife was still held like a weapon, but the tip pointed away from Adam. After all the bullshit, Abbie thought the whole thing had become a joke; that despite the airs, Adam was here for dope like everyone else. That made it easy for Abbie. It wasn't like he was shaking down someone; now he was just forcing another junkie to pay his dues.

"Take what you want," Adam said. "That's just part of my payoff."

Abbie examined one of the vials, shook it, took off the cap, dabbed it on his thumb, and tasted it. Adam watched. The knife was completely forgotten.

"What is it?" Abbie asked.

"A mix I made, with a meperidine base."

Abbie looked confused. Adam guessed the question.

"It's a morphine substitute."

"So you came here to sell it?" Abbie asked.

"Trade it," said Adam. "I got more elsewhere."

A change of attitude came over Abbie. He switched from street punk to businessman. He straightened his back and held the vial above his head, so that the glass could catch the light from a distant street lamp. It was a meaningless gesture— there was nothing special to see, and Adam doubted Abbie had any idea what he was doing.

"People got smack if they want it," Abbie said. "No one's going to buy this substitute shit."

"I'm not trying to make a sale."

"People trade for cash, not for garbage."

"That's good," Adam said.

"And how do I know it?"

Adam watched Abbie swirl the drug against the light. It was the act of an idiot. He walked forward, pushing past Abbie, not thinking twice about the knife.

"What're you doing?" Abbie shouted.

"Going," Adam said.

Abbie reached out, grabbing Adam with the same hand that held the knife. They both knew Adam's life wasn't in danger; only Abbie's chance at a deal.

"How do I know it's any good?" Abbie said.

"Try it," Adam answered.

Abbie grinned, as if he was too bright to be suckered.

"You try it," Abbie replied.

Adam again pulled free to leave.

"Wait a minute," Abbie said quickly. "I got a way to test."

Together, they left the alley. The crowd approached Abbie for the details, but stopped talking the moment Adam emerged from the alley. Abbie saw their disappointment and chased them away. Then he took Adam to the closed pet store.

To make the test easier, the junkie's sleeve was already rolled up.

"Okay," Abbie said, giving Adam the vial, "put it in Frankie."

Adam froze. The man—Frankie—was still talking to himself, his face pressed against the storefront window. One of the puppies licked the window as if it could lick Frankie's cheek.

"Come on," Abbie said. "You'll be doing him a favor." Abbie squatted next to his junkie. "Frankie," Abbie said loudly. "Want a free hit, man?"

Frankie came vaguely to life. His eyes actually opened, and even in the poor light, Adam could tell they lacked any vision. When Abbie repeated the question, Frankie finally understood. He put his hands on the stoop and tried lifting himself. In his own mind, Frankie probably felt like a superman and was ready to follow Abbie anywhere on the earth for his freebie.

Although he didn't have to, Abbie rested a hand on Frankie to keep him in place. "We deliver," Abbie told him. Abbie turned to Adam as if they had shared a joke. "Come on," Abbie ordered.

Adam had, in fact, already torn away the paper that protected the syringe. He unscrewed the vial's cap and dipped the needle into the drug. He pulled back on the plunger, not at all certain how much of the drug to administer. The man was already helpless; he needed treatment, not another high. At the same time, if the meperidine mix didn't do its trick, then Adam would still be without his gun. And the odds were the dosage had to be potent, judging from Frankie's stupor.

It was a choice between playing it safe and risking failure, or playing it dangerous and risking a junkie's life and maybe helping his daughter.

A moment later, he approached Frankie with a full syringe.

Abbie stepped back, and Adam examined the junkie's arms. "He's filthy," Adam said.

"What a surprise," Abbie answered.

Frankie's eyes managed to put the syringe into focus, and he watched it waver above him—his mouth wide open, his face an expression of complete awe. It was as if Frankie was being visited by God.

Adam continued his examination. "Half his veins are collapsed," Adam said. "He's lucky he can still move his fingers."

Abbie, annoyed with the delays, examined both arms, dropped them, then lifted one of Frankie's legs. Frankie fell backwards, but his eyes never lost sight of the syringe. Soon one of his pants legs was drawn up, and Abbie had tightened a cord around Frankie's knee. Veins appeared like ridges.

"Let's get on with it," Abbie said.

This time Adam obeyed. The skin was relatively clean, and there would be no chance of missing a vein or hitting an artery. He moved down to the leg and pressed the needle in place. Frankie started to panic; not from the feel of the needle, but because he had lost sight of it. He started moaning, certain that it had all been a trick and that he had lost his free hit. He wailed as if his best friend had been killed.

Then he stopped. First his voice grew faint; then it completely disappeared. His mouth held the shape of his last spoken word, until all his muscles relaxed, and Frankie leaned comfortably on his side. Whatever pain Frankie had felt was gone.

Abbie untied the cord, and Adam dropped the empty syringe on the sidewalk, stepping on it.

"Hey, I could have sold that," Abbie said.

That was precisely why Adam had destroyed it, but he didn't bother taunting Abbie with this fact. Instead, he concentrated on Frankie, watching the man as a doctor watches a patient fighting for life. Adam took the junkie's pulse and then checked his eyes. Abbie, meanwhile, slapped Frankie's cheeks. "How do you feel, man?"

A minute passed before Frankie could answer. "Fucking fantastic," he finally said, then drifted totally off.

Abbie and Adam stood up, both satisfied.

"I want a gun," Adam said again. "One that can't be traced and in good shape."

"Any kind in particular?" Abbie asked.

Adam hadn't thought about that. It hadn't occurred to him there would be a selection. Besides, when he murdered Sherry's kidnapper, he didn't plan on doing it from a distance. When it came time to pull the trigger, he wanted to be up close. "One that shoots," Adam answered.

Abbie laughed. "That's funny," Abbie said, patting Adam's shoulder. "Let me ask you this, okay? Are you supplied? Do you got the stuff now? The man I'm taking you to likes to taste what he buys."

"I've got more samples," Adam answered.

This pleased Abbie, and he started walking down the street. When Adam didn't follow, Abbie stopped and waved him along. "You want your gun, right?" Abbie asked.

Adam followed. He walked a pace behind Abbie, which Abbie also found amusing. For ten minutes, they walked down side streets, with Abbie acting as the silent guide for his misplaced tourist. They passed streets even Adam wouldn't have considered walking — rows of abandoned warehouses and boarded buildings, distinguished only by the graffiti on their walls. Then midway down the block, Abbie turned into one of these buildings. He stopped, expecting Adam to freeze outside the door, too terri-

216

fied to enter. But Adam was right behind him. So close that Abbie felt suspicious.

"You hold it one second, all right?" Abbie said.

Adam, in no position to argue, did what he was told. Abbie proceeded to pat Adam's pockets, chest, arms and legs, looking for weapons. What he found was the other vials and syringes—four of each.

"This everything you got?"

"That's all I'm carrying," said Adam.

"If you're hiding any, they're just gonna find it."

"I'm telling the truth," Adam said.

Abbie nodded, accepting this; not so much because he trusted Adam, but given the situation, it was the expected answer. He also knew it didn't make much difference if Adam had a little something extra hidden on him; in a few minutes, it would be off his body.

They continued inside and were almost immediately met by a muscle man. King of the lumberjacks, Adam thought. Abbie greeted the man, waved Adam in, and continued upstairs. Adam started to follow, but the guard blocked his way. Although Adam had just been frisked, the guard insisted on repeating it. When the guard was done, Abbie again called for him and the guard reluctantly stepped aside. They went upstairs, walking toward a dim, purple light.

The hallway reminded Adam of some forgotten drug enclave lost from the sixties. Swirls of bright orange and green colors had been painted on the otherwise crumbling walls. The floors and steps, while sagging with every step, had been partially covered with the remains of a shag carpet. At the top of the steps was a velvet poster of a naked woman, her breasts thrust ridiculously high and a leopard curled about her waist. From what he could tell, a number of customers had done their shooting while staring at those velvet breasts. At the woman's feet were forgotten needles. To her side were the outlines of four doors—formerly apartments, now shells that echoed their own peculiar noises.

Abbie led him past the poster and toward the farthest door. The building was a junkies' hotel. The first room was the guest room—a shooting gallery with eight people sitting inside, enjoying various stages of high. In the center of the room was a Bunsen burner. They could have all been collected about a campfire. Near the door was their camp counselor, another of New Hampshire's lumberjacks. He sat with his eyes half shut and stared vacantly over the sleepy scene. The real work would come if one of the customers became sick or died. Then the eyes would open wide and the arms would unravel, either beating the junkie back to life or dragging him outside and away for disposal.

The second room was the hotel's office for lower management. The concierge, the bell boy, the front desk . . . all the jobs were handled in this small apartment, protected solely by a 100-watt light bulb—the only decent source of light in the place. One small, patient man, relaxed in a chair, guarded the supply of towels, sodas, beer, aspirin, and other sundries. Along a wall were bundles of clothes, shopping bags, and other items left by the customers in the first room. The man used pieces of playing cards for his tickets, and a spread of royalty, representing all the suits, decorated the mass of possessions.

"Good evening," the man said politely to Adam.

218

The courtesy was so misplaced that Adam instinctively returned it. Abbie and Adam continued past the next room. Although the door was closed, Adam guessed it was the supply closet because of two dead bolts. It was the only door with this much security. The door itself was reenforced with aluminum sheets that gave the room an illusion of being a large safe.

Abbie turned Adam toward the last room, and they entered a small office. It was decorated by furniture that had been abandoned on the street, yet all the pieces were there—a wood swivel chair, a metal desk, a file cabinet, and a desk lamp. The lampshade was tilted toward a couch covered with newspapers and small packets of marijuana. There was also a strongbox on the couch. The box was the only new item in the room—a shiny steel container, with the warranty still glued on the side.

When Adam entered the room, the owner of the box was locking it. There were three other people in the room besides Abbie and Adam. Adam had time to examine each of them carefully, as no one seemed rushed to speak.

The hierarchy of the establishment apparently depended on body weight. One man in the room, about five feet ten, kept a calm but careful eye on Adam and Abbie, and seemed in charge of making sure that the business afforded no surprises. Abbie called him Billy. Billy looked the most uncomfortable with Adam's presence, because Adam was the epitome of surprise—an incongruous, fully suited businessman in the middle of drug alley.

Opposite Billy, resting against the desk, was a thin, lanky fellow, dressed in white slacks and a print shirt. Adam took particular notice of the man's dress because he was the only person who didn't look ready to sleep in the street. The man had about an inch on Billy. Adam didn't have the slightest idea what he did, aside from make the room look pretty. The only thing he did now was stare at the strongbox, which was being mothered by a man Abbie called Freedo.

For height and weight, Freedo had everyone beat. He looked like an aging bike king, someone who had been forced out of the club because there wasn't a motorcycle built that could support him. Instead, he had moved off the highway for a quiet place in the country. The drug ring would be Freedo's idea of semiretirement.

"Gimme some hash, Tom," Freedo told the man opposite Billy.

Tom reached in the desk drawer and found a sandwich bag stuffed with hash. With anyone else, he would have tossed the bag across the room. When it came to Freedo, Tom did everything gently. He walked to the sofa, opened the sack, and left it on the strongbox.

Freedo rolled himself a joint and gave his guests the slightest attention. "Abbie," he said, the word breathing out easily with his first puff of smoke.

"Got you some business," Abbie said.

Freedo was expressionless; or if there was an expression, it was hidden beneath his beard. Freedo only leaned back, enjoying the hash, letting Abbie search the room for a friendly face. "Customers stay up front," Freedo finally said. "You know that."

"He's not here to buy drugs; he wants to sell them."

"That's not quite right," Adam said.

220

Abbie showed Freedo the drugs he had collected from Adam. Freedo examined the vials with the same useless gestures Abbie had employed. It only convinced Adam that, despite the show, he was less in a den of connected suppliers than misplaced punks. Nonetheless, when Freedo waved Adam forward, Adam showed all the reverence he might give a Mafia chieftain.

"What's your story?" Freedo asked.

Adam explained he was looking for a gun. He said it made no difference what kind of gun, so long as it had bullets, could fire, and was untraceable.

Freedo listened, stubbing the end of his hash stick in the couch arm. "And in return, we get what?"

"I can get you ten more dosages of my stock," Adam said. "Its base is meperidine, a morphine substitute. You can use them yourself or pass them off as heroin."

Freedo looked at Abbie. "His stuff any good?"

Abbie, his reputation on the line, gave his most professional nod, as if he had taken each vial and run it through an exhaustive series of laboratory tests. Freedo digested this bit of information as slowly as he had digested the hash. Finally, he seemed to bestow on Adam a supreme honor—Freedo stood from the couch. But it wasn't for Adam's benefit; Freedo left his seat to talk with Tom. Tom, in turn, talked with Billy, and then Billy went behind Adam to shut the door.

Tom pulled a gun from his pocket.

Adam still hadn't caught on. He thought this was to be his payoff. He walked toward Tom, extending a hand as if to take the weapon.

Billy caught him by the collar.

Adam looked to Abbie. "What the fuck is this all about?" he demanded.

Abbie had no idea. He turned to Freedo for help. Abbie looked like a real estate agent who had just lost a commission.

"Get out," Freedo told Abbie.

Abbie knew better than to argue. He didn't even give Adam a last look of sympathy. The moment Freedo told Abbie to leave, Adam was on his own.

When Abbie left, Freedo relaxed. A smile crept through his beard and he chuckled slightly. Adam waited, figuring it was best not to talk until spoken to. It proved smart, because Freedo mistook Adam's silence for respect. Freedo allowed Adam to sit, then made himself another hash stick. After enjoying the first few inhales, he leaned forward, so that all Adam could see was wall-to-wall Freedo.

"Okay," Freedo said. "So what's your real story?"

Adam stared at Freedo, not sure how to answer.

"Don't piss with me," Freedo said. "Did you come here alone, or is there someone else?"

"I'm not here to sell drugs," Adam said. "All want is to buy a gun."

Freedo squeezed Adam's cheeks, twisting the skin, forcing Adam to pucker like a fish.

"Don't give me this pistol bullshit," Freedo said. "Abbie caught you selling on my corner, right?"

Adam tried to answer, but couldn't move his lips.

"You think I worked all these years just to lose my business to some dumb fuck dressed for Wall Street?"

Freedo shoved Adam away, and Adam tumbled back, falling against Billy.

"You're getting this all wrong," Adam said.

222

But Freedo wasn't listening. "Keep him out of sight," Freedo told Billy. "As long as he gets us supplies, he lives. Maybe his fucking partner will come looking for him." Freedo looked at Adam. "You're a prisoner, asshole. Understand me?"

Adam nodded.

"You live as long as the cash comes in. Can you get me some more of your stash on the phone?"

Adam again nodded. Freedo, however, was losing interest in Adam. Either Adam delivered or died. No matter what happened, things worked out for the better. Freedo decided to enjoy himself. While Billy emptied Adam's pockets, Freedo again examined the vials.

"Fuck," Billy said. He had stabbed a finger on one of Adam's syringes. Freedo, alerted to more treasure, pushed Billy to the side and dug into Adam's pockets. He found the needles, examined them with the same caution he had used with the vials, then spread them on the couch.

"He's a walking grocery store," Freedo said.

Freedo rolled up a sleeve, then examined the vials, trying to decide which one held the biggest Christmas present.

"These don't all look the same," Freedo observed. He weighed the vials individually, then opened one, smelling the liquid. Adam watched, waiting for Freedo to quit playing chemist and ask for help. In fact, Freedo was waiting for Adam to volunteer the information; by the time Freedo did bother asking, he was embarrassed and out of temper.

"All right," Freedo asked, "which is the good stuff?"

Adam hesitated, not certain Tom and Billy would

allow him to cross the room. But Freedo was getting more impatient, and Adam figured it would be in everyone's interest to keep him happy.

"Give them to me," Adam said.

Freedo looked as if Adam was out to steal all the toys.

"Come on," Adam insisted. "Tighten the belt and give me one of the syringes."

"I can do this myself," Freedo said.

"I can do it better. I'm a doctor."

This small lie made a difference to the conversation. When a man in a business suit is merchandising drugs, finding out the man's a "doctor" made sense. It also made the man more trustworthy. Even Freedo knew doctors took oaths.

"Which one is the good stuff?" Freedo said.

"The thin one." Adam uncorked the smallest vial, dipped a needle in it, and drew back the stopper. He moved without the hesitation he had displayed with the street junkie.

Freedo offered Adam an arm and said, "Pick your target." Adam leaned closer and waited for a vein to appear. It never did. Freedo was a man who had enjoyed years of self-abuse and most of the veins were invisible. Adam should have abandoned the arms and tried Freedo's legs, but Freedo wouldn't let him. It was a matter of pride for Freedo to take it in the arm. One more way to tell him from the other junkies. Let the shits on the street poke their pricks. Freedo's arms would last forever.

Adam pierced Freedo's skin, probed, then brought back the needle without releasing the liquid.

Freedo frowned. "What are you doing?"

"I'm looking for a vein," Adam said.

"What the hell am I, a dart board?" Freedo slapped Adam's forehead. "Tom, put the gun to his head. He pulls this shit again, you kill him."

"If the belt was tighter . . ."

"Screw the belt," said Freedo, taking it off.

Tom and Billy watched more closely. Adam examined Freedo's arm again, almost seeing a small vein roping about Freedo's elbow. He again lowered the needle.

"Hold still," Adam ordered.

The needle plunged into Freedo's skin, and Adam massaged the area to make it painless. When he was satisfied with the target, he pressed down on the plunger and withdrew the syringe. Then he leaned back on the sofa waiting for the reaction.

The drug took effect almost immediately.

"Oh, *shit,*" said Freedo, the words singing out with the first rush. There was a look of surprise, and then a smile. "Shit." He laughed, closing his eyes. "Man, this is good, good stuff."

Adam didn't answer. Billy and Tom hovered behind Adam, the gun still cocked. Even with their boss in heaven, the sentry duty didn't end.

"What'd you call this? Meperidine?" Freedo said. "Man, I didn't know anything could be like *this.*" He leaned back on the couch, throwing his legs up on a pillow. Although it was still early, Freedo's hands were on his stomach, his breath starting to quicken.

"Actually, it's not meperidine," said Adam.

Freedo might have heard, but it was hard to tell. The smile had disappeared. It took Billy and Tom a moment to notice the change. Freedo's quick breaths became gasps, and his arms clamped tightly about his chest.

"Hey, Freedo," Billy said. "Freedo, you okay?"

Freedo heaved forward, his face twisted as if someone had taken a screwdriver and stabbed him in the spine: Tom dropped next to him and slapped his face. Freedo didn't respond. His body had become too tight. He simply stared back at Tom, his mouth wide open as he gasped for breath. His face had turned red.

"He needs water," Tom told Billy.

"No; he needs air," Adam said. Billy and Tom looked at him. "He's on a narcotic analgesic called sufentanil. It's about a thousand times more potent than morphine." Adam studied Freedo calmly, letting Freedo's terror sink into Tom and Billy. "At this dosage level," Adam finished, "it also stops a person from breathing."

"Oh, Jesus," Tom said.

It took Billy a moment longer to understand.

"You fucking poisoned him?" Billy asked.

Adam didn't bother answering. Tom was in hysterics, on his knees and ordering Freedo to breathe. Billy was more matter-of-fact. He knew his orders. Without hesitation, he pressed the barrel of the gun against Adam's head.

"That wouldn't be smart," Adam told him. "Not if you want him to live."

The trigger didn't pull, and Adam could almost hear Billy thinking.

"You can save him?" Billy asked.

"If I work quickly," Adam said. "Once he stops breathing completely, and the oxygen can't reach his brain, then he'll be dead."

Billy considered this, and Adam did his best to be patient. He didn't want to appear desperate; at the same time, Freedo was dying.

"So Freedo's choking," Billy said. "But you can stop all that."

"One of the drugs I brought along is a muscle relaxant," Adam explained. "If I give him the drug, and one of you provides artificial respiration, you should be able to get him to a hospital."

"Hell, we can do the whole fucking thing ourselves," said Billy. "Give me the goddamn drug."

"Not until you give me the gun," Adam answered.

Billy suddenly understood the game. He became furious and knocked Adam on the floor, pointing the gun dead center at Adam's chest and ready to pull the trigger.

"Don't do it," Tom screamed.

"Don't worry," Billy answered. "I'll kill him and then we'll put the drug in ourselves."

"Maybe," Adam said. "But I have three vials left. Only one of them is right. The other two are meperidine. Give him meperidine now and he doesn't stand a chance."

"Goddamn it, Billy; do what he says," Tom said.

Billy was still undecided. He was being asked to disobey Freedo, and he wasn't certain Freedo would approve.

"He's *dying,*" Tom said.

"If I give him the gun, then he could shoot us," Billy said.

"He's not going to shoot anyone," Tom said. "Christ, he's a *doctor.*"

"I wouldn't wait much longer," Adam warned.

Billy still pointed the gun, but his anger had given way to confusion. "But if I give him the gun—"

Tom left Freedo and pushed Billy against the wall.

Billy now turned the gun on Tom, but Tom was furious.

"If you shoot the fucking doctor," Tom said, "you better hope Freedo dies, because if he doesn't, I'm going to tell him exactly what happened. And even if you fucking kill me too, he's going to figure it out on his own, because there's only one Grade A asshole here, and everyone knows who it is."

But Billy *still* didn't let go of the gun. At the same time, Tom and Adam knew Billy had lost the courage to fire it.

Tom pulled it out of Billy's hand and gave it to Adam. Adam kept the hammer cocked.

"Put your faces on the ground," Adam ordered.

All Billy's anger returned, and he gave Adam and Tom a hateful stare. If he had been a fool with a gun, he was even more of one without it.

"On the floor," Tom ordered, already lying down.

Billy joined him. The moment he did, Adam went into action. He opened a vial, filled a syringe, and pulled up one of Freedo's pants legs. This time, there would be no guesswork. Adam found a vein right away and made the injection.

Adam left Freedo to stand by the door. "All right," he said. "I'll phone the hospital and tell them what's going on. In the meantime, one of you start breathing air into him. Pull his head back, hold his nose, and cover his mouth with your own. Just blow into him long and hard until an ambulance shows up. You understand?"

Billy sat up on his knees, wishing he had another gun to take care of Adam. Tom, meanwhile, rushed back to Freedo's side, taking deep breaths and blowing into the massive mouth.

"Thank Freedo for the gun," Adam finished.

It wasn't smart throwing a final insult in Billy's direction. Another word from Adam, and Billy would charge him, gun or no gun.

"Fuck," Billy murmured, settling despondently on the floor.

Adam was gone.

Chapter 17

"I left an important bag in Room 808," Adam told the desk clerk.

The clerk was a short man, wearing glasses that sat on his nose with magnetic strength. He stopped checking messages long enough to face Adam and give his most soothing smile—an automatic response that went into action with numbing faithfulness.

"A brown doctor's bag," Adam said, "with the initials 'AD' at the clasp."

The clerk wrote diligently on a card. "Contents?"

"I'm a cardiologist," Adam said. "was carrying some medicines for heart seizures. Metharbital, mephenytoin, paramethadione . . . That's why I need I the bag. If someone gets into it . . ."

"I can check, but I don't think we have it," the clerk said.

"You can see why it's important," Adam answered.

The clerk excused himself and went to a back office. Adam waited, playing with a hotel pen, bending it to the breaking point. He wanted *in* to that room. He had to see it all. He had to be *sure*.

The clerk returned with the manager—a man almost identical to the clerk, but with another ten years. The manager extended a hand. "You are Dr.—"

"Druit," Adam said.

"Dr. Druit, no one has reported finding a medical bag in the hotel," the manager said. "Even if they forgot to write a receipt, we would have noticed such a claim immediately."

"I'd still feel better checking the room myself," Adam said.

The manager considered this, consulted briefly with the clerk, then walked back to his office. A minute later, he returned to the lobby. "The room is occupied," the manager said, "but the tenant says it's all right if you go upstairs."

The manager gave the key to the clerk, and the clerk walked around the counter, leading Adam into the elevator. Adam followed, trying to keep calm, but thinking too hard about Sherry's kidnapper. What if Sherry was actually upstairs? Was there any chance of such a thing? Christ, what would Adam do? Would he just kill the bastard on the spot or—

"Why are you in town, Dr. Druit?" the clerk asked.

Adam glanced at the clerk—a blank look. One of confusion.

"A convention," Adam said.

"A convention here?" the clerk said, knowing his own hotel hadn't booked a medical conference.

"No, I only stayed here," said Adam. "The convention was at another hotel."

The clerk nodded, wondering where the conference had taken place. There were no neighboring hotels. It bothered the clerk, just as it bothered him when the elevator doors opened and Adam showed no lingering knowledge of the hallways. The clerk, however, continued playing the role of good host and led him to the room. He knocked on the door until a voice announced it was unlocked. With the clerk leading, they entered.

"I'm sorry, Mr. Waters, but the gentleman has misplaced a—"

"The manager told me. Please go ahead and look," Waters said, beckoning them. He was shaving, and his cheeks were smothered in cream. Adam passed him, glancing quickly in the bathroom, then immediately scanning the room for any sign of Sherry. Finally, he stood dead center in the room and turned all his attention on Waters, studying his prey, trying to imagine every moment of his coming revenge. But the images weren't clear. Perhaps he had thought too often of the moment—considered too many possibilities—and now he couldn't keep his ideas in focus. Or perhaps it was the shaving cream masking the kidnapper's face, keeping Adam from truly identifying the man.

Adam concentrated, needing to make the best use of his time. Except now that he was in the room, he wasn't sure what to look for. In an instant, he knew Sherry wasn't here. But did that mean anything? If Waters was smart, he would keep her elsewhere rather than risk having her seen.

Proof she had been here—any kind of proof—was all he needed. And if not concrete evidence, then something that showed Waters had been in the vicinity of Providence at the time of Sherry's disappearance. Or something that showed his fixation with little girls. Just a small clue, that was all. A forgotten skirt in the closet . . . . a pile of news clips, similar to Adam's own collection of kidnapping stories . . . Adam looked hard—wanting little, hoping for anything.

But there wasn't a hint of trouble. Waters' clothes were neatly folded, with a pile of clean shirts sitting in an open drawer, bordered by a line of wrapped socks.

Near the bed, by the night lamp, was a picture of his own wife and two daughters, neither child older than three and both absolutely adorable. And there was Waters himself — nothing less than the prototype salesman, even without his shirt and pants. Adam could guess his history. A tattoo on Waters' right arm, probably dating back to some ancient stint in the navy. There was a scar across his abdomen from having an appendix removed, and another scar across his chest; perhaps a bypass operation. A bottle of bicarbonate served as testimony to an ulcer. When Adam put it all together, he saw a middle-aged middle-class family man who lived almost all his life on the road and who probably wished he could be back home.

This was Sherry's kidnapper?

"Where did you say you left your bag?" the clerk asked Adam.

Adam turned in a slow circle, then decided to search the closet. With his body blocking the clerk's view, he went through Waters' clothes and suitcase, finding nothing.

The clerk waited . . . impatient, less certain of Adam with each passing moment. Finally, he said, "Can't find it?" The remark was meant to hurry Adam, but it made no difference. Adam kept going through the hanging suits, purportedly to check the floor of the closet, but really searching the clothes for stains or tears.

"The closet was empty when I moved in," Waters shouted from the bathroom.

"You can't be too careful," Adam answered, moving from the closet and looking under the bureaus. "Been here long?"

Waters washed his face and rubbed the spots of cream away with a towel.

233

"About a week," Waters said. "From Wisconsin. I'm here covering sales."

"Wisconsin?"

"Ohio originally," Waters corrected. "Got transferred to the east a few months ago." Waters turned and saw Adam digging through the bureau drawers. "I thought you were looking for a bag?"

"A small bag," Adam said.

Adam took another look at Waters. This time, Waters was unmasked. The most distinct feature about Waters was his cheeks—soft and round, flushed from the warm water and shave. It gave him a Santa Claus face, one you immediately trusted.

Adam tried to imagine this man with slick black hair, barely living each day, so desperate he sold clothes at hock shops. The man wasn't there. In fact, Waters was the opposite of everything Adam had imagined. Even his eyes were gentle, although steady and concentrated. Adam was discovering that now, as Waters took a closer look at him.

"You said you're a doctor?" Waters asked.

Adam searched under the bed. He wasn't the least concerned about medical questions. He could play a doctor in his sleep.

Waters, however, didn't doubt Adam. Instead, he surprised him with another question. "Have a daughter?"

Adam froze. All of his hatred surfaced, and for a quick moment, the clerk saw Adam's fear and rage. Adam had his back to Waters, but Waters also sensed a change. "I saw you looking at my family picture," Waters explained. "Have two myself."

Adam continued his search. "One daughter," he said. He reached under the bed frame and pulled out a large gray box. Waters thought Adam was looking behind the box; instead, Adam opened it.

"That's mine," Waters said.

Adam didn't listen, lifting the lid and tearing through the sheets of packaging paper.

"That's a present for one of my girls," Waters said, sounding annoyed.

Adam pulled out a child's white dress and spread it carefully on the bed, brushing the cloth flat with his fingertips. He stared at it, overwhelmed. Lace-embroidered sleeves and small plastic pearls buttoned all the way up to the collar. Around the waist of the dress was a silk sash, already tied in a knot. It was the sort of dress Adam had once dreamed of buying Sherry, but at the time was too busy dreaming instead of doing.

Waters pulled the dress off the bed. Adam, still on his knees, looked up at the kidnapper.

"Ever been to West Bay?" Adam asked softly.

Waters took away the dress. "Your bag's not here," he answered.

"How about Calverton?" Adam said, his anger clear.

Waters returned the stare, invincible to the hatred. He turned to the clerk. "If you're done, I'd like to have my room back."

The clerk gave a nervous smile and nodded, taking the cue. Adam followed the clerk to the door, but he walked backwards, like someone backing out from a bar fight.

"Her name is Sherry," Adam said. "I don't know if she ever had a chance to tell you, but that's her name."

"I don't know what the hell you're talking about," Waters said.

"She would be in school now," Adam said. "I loved her. And I'm still going to find her."

Waters again looked to the clerk. "This guy's a

lunatic," he said. "Get him out or I'm phoning the manager."

The threat gave the clerk enough confidence to pull Adam the remaining distance through the door. Adam didn't fight back; he was too lost in his fury.

"Her name is Sherry," Adam shouted.

Waters slammed the door.

It was the dress that had given him away. "That's a present for one of my kids," Waters had said, but Adam had seen the picture of Waters' two girls. They were babies, still ready for rides in the stroller.

The lace dress Adam had held was for a girl at least seven years old.

Nor did Adam care if Waters had mistakenly said daughter when he meant someone else. In Adam's court, a mistake was a deception, and a deception was an admission of guilt.

Well, Adam had heard the deception, and now he needed the guts to administer justice.

A lace dress, Adam thought. Who was it for? Sherry, or some other little girl? Was it possible Sherry was being held captive—perhaps in a neighboring hotel room—and the dress was meant to win his daughter's good behavior? Oh, don't fall for that trick, Sherry. Stay strong. I'm coming after you. I'm going to—

Adam shook his head violently, standing outside in the cold, trying to break his wandering thoughts. Pay attention to the lobby, he told himself. And when the time came to kill Waters, act without hesitation. Let Waters drop on his knees and plead for mercy . . . beg for a second chance, maybe for a cop to cart him off to jail. But don't give him that chance. This was not a time for sympathy. A quick shot, in the back of the head. Maybe in an alley, where it was dark. Or if Waters went to his car, Adam could fire through the window. Or—

Adam again snapped awake. He had dropped forward, almost collapsing in sleep. Damn the clorazepate. Except he couldn't blame the drug; it was his own fault for not sleeping. It was night, and whatever life was left in him wanted to be tucked into bed.

He began pacing. They were the wavering, uncertain steps of a drunk. Adam knew there was only one solution—to counter the sedative with an amphetamine. He hated playing that game and knew where it would end; still, it didn't matter, because his attaché case was in the car, and the car was parked out of the hotel's view. He double-checked his pockets and managed to find one loose tab of pemoline, an amphetamine substitute, but it was only a child's chewable. He popped it in his mouth anyway, chewing the drug like gum, convinced his only option was to abandon his post long enough to get the attaché case out of the car and administer an intravenous dose of energy.

"Waters," he kept repeating. "Waters, Waters . . ."

He leaned behind a lamppost and watched a man leave the hotel lobby, turning toward a garage. The chant had worked. Adam waited for Waters to reappear behind the steering wheel of his rental car; then he ran back to his own car, and before Waters could slip from view, Adam drove onto the avenue.

Waters pumped the brakes for a corner and turned down a side street, but he was out of view for only a half minute. When Adam reached the corner, he turned in time to see the rental bob over a set of railway tracks and make another turn. Adam followed, having no idea where they were going, only knowing that it would end with a bullet in Waters' head.

At first, Adam thought they had driven to another

corner of Manchester's drug alley. But the teenagers were scarcer, and the only real action came from wandering hookers — women who bore only the faintest resemblance to the whores Adam had seen on New York streets. These were country girls who either couldn't make it in Boston or had mistaken Manchester for the big city. Adam imagined that during the day many were either housewives or factory workers. Either way, they were strong, heavy, and weather-worn.

Adam watched as Waters began a conversation with one of them.

Adam parked far enough away to avoid being seen or solicited. He watched as Waters — the family man with two daughters — paid an advance, left the car, and followed his date into a bar. Adam hadn't seen the bar until Waters entered it. There were no lights advertising the name, and the only hint of its existence was the flash of neon that colored the street as the front door opened and closed. Adam left his car and followed Waters inside. He found his target at the counter, a finger raised to the bartender while the hooker squeezed his thigh.

There was no chance of Adam's being seen. Just as it had been dark on the street, the only real light in this bar was from a single bulb hanging just shy of Waters' head. Adam could sit on a stool, tucked alongside a blaring jukebox, and watch without fear. Nor was he the only one using the darkness. Between the partitions, the shadows were full of movement. And if the hooker had her way, Waters would be joining those shadows.

She tugged at Waters' arm, and they carried their drinks to the most distant corner of the room. Adam could see the hooker loosening her dress. She wasn't wasting any time, Adam thought. It was a lesson he could use himself. She pushed Waters deeper into the stall, then followed him behind the table. Her head dropped, and Waters rested against the wall.

Adam left the bar and waited outside.

"Five minutes," Adam promised himself, glancing at his watch so he could count the time. If he didn't see Waters by then, he really would go back inside and finish him.

Meanwhile, the other prostitutes passed him slowly, sensing he wasn't a customer, but not sure why else Adam would be in this part of town. Adam avoided any eye contact — even the passing exchange of a smile. His sole interest was in the time. But when the five minutes passed, he gave Waters more time, the way an executioner might give a death row prisoner a last request. It was more generosity than Waters deserved, Adam knew; but Adam also needed the time. He was growing more doubtful about what to do. He wanted a chance to think about the choices.

"Three more minutes," Adam said to no one. One of the girls glanced at him, thinking he had talked to her and was ready for action. He gave a look that turned her away for good.

And then Waters emerged from the bar, tucking his shirt in his pants, the whore following close behind. Adam thought of hiding, but there wasn't any need; Waters' mind and imagination were far, far away. There wasn't a hint of fear that someone could recognize him. No concern that his marriage would be ruined, or that his life was in any danger.

"You take care, sweetheart," Waters told the hooker. She walked away as Waters took his seat behind the driver's wheel.

Adam moved. He went to the passenger side of the car, opened the door, and dropped into the front seat alongside Waters.

Waters needed a moment to register the scene. He was still snug in his memories; so snug that he regarded Adam with the same silly smile that had been on his face in the bar. The smile didn't disappear until he saw the gun. In a clearer presence of mind, Waters could have easily knocked the weapon away.

Instead, Waters screamed, leaning against his side door and falling onto the sidewalk. Adam watched as Waters scrambled onto his feet and, with surprising speed, started running down an alley.

Adam jumped out and chased after him.

It was a short alley that emptied onto a major avenue. Adam could see Waters' silhouette as the man leaned against a wall to catch his breath. Adam felt like he was a football field away from Waters, still he stopped and pointed the gun. "Stop!" But Waters was back on his feet and around another corner.

Adam followed, surprised at how well Waters ran, just managing to keep him in view. All the time, Adam was disappointed in himself. He should have killed him in the car. Did Waters show the same mercy with Sherry?

When he reached the avenue and found it empty, Adam stood absolutely still and showed the cool caution of someone who killed for a living. Before he had been a pedestrian with a gun; now he was a tracker, studying the street with the keenest attention. His eyesight concentrated on the shadows, defining the edges of the buildings and fire escapes, looking for the crouched shape of a man trying to hide. When he walked between a set of parked cars, he dropped on his belly and looked under them.

He played this game for a full minute before seeing Waters hiding behind a trash bin.

Adam raised the gun.

"I haven't done anything," Waters pleaded. "Oh, God, don't kill me."

Adam threw him against a car. He punched wildly at Waters, and Waters offered no resistance. Perhaps Waters knew he was dead. If there had been a chance to escape, he had lost it. Instead, he was limp, letting Adam strike freely at his face.

"Where's my daughter?" Adam shouted. "What did you do with her?"

"Leave me alone," Waters said. He tried covering his head and Adam shoved him back to the pavement.

"Tell me where she is or I swear to God—"

"I don't know what you're talking about," Waters shouted.

Adam put a headlock on his victim and dragged him to a street lamp.

"I want you to see my face," Adam told him. "You're going to see who kills you."

"No," Waters kept begging. "Please don't kill me. . . ."

Adam pushed Waters under the street lamp, and Waters sobbed loudly, his eyes squinted tightly, as if blindness would save him.

"Look at me," Adam ordered.

Waters refused, and Adam cocked the gun. What difference did it make if Waters saw him or not? The important thing was he died.

"No, no, no . . ."

Adam pushed the nose of the gun under Waters' chin, and now Waters was drowning in tears. Adam concentrated, knowing the moment had come and there were no more excuses. Pull the trigger, he told himself. Do it for Sherry.

It was all he needed to finish the execution.

But then he stopped, staring hard at Waters.

"No, no, no . . ." Waters moaned.

Adam pulled the gun back and stood up, his eyes wide with terror. Waters still rested under the lamp, his own eyes tightly shut.

Adam ran away, disappearing down the street.

Five minutes passed before Waters opened his eyes. When he did, there wasn't any sight of his tormentor. He was free to stand up, brush himself off, and walk away, undisturbed. Waters did all these things, except instead of walking he ran.

In truth, there was no reason to run. Adam had given up the chase.

He had finally managed to shake free of his stupor long enough to truly look at the man's face.

The man was not Waters.

Chapter 18

He had almost killed the wrong man.

If not for the streetlight, he would have killed him. An absolute stranger, whom Adam had mistaken for Waters.

"Almost murdered the wrong fucking man," he said aloud. Then, into a mirror, "You would have done it, too. You fucking lunatic. You goddamn crazy son-of-a-bitch, you would have done it."

Yes, Adam knew the truth. He would have killed him. Not only that; there hadn't been the slightest resemblance between the person Adam nearly killed and Waters. Even at a glance, the man had a two-week-old beard. Adam had seen Waters shaving less than five hours earlier.

So what did it mean? Had Adam followed Waters to the bar, then lost sight of him and followed the trail of the wrong man? Or had Adam hallucinated, putting Waters' face on to someone who had the misfortune of leaving the hotel at the wrong time?

Or was the reverse true; did he have Waters begging for mercy, but then hallucinated someone else's face?

There was a knock on the door. Or was there? Nothing was certain anymore. Adam had taken too many pills, and for all he knew, half his world was phantoms. He had locked himself in his room for a day and night, giving up, ready to succumb completely to his imagination. The proof was on the bed — his supply of pills spread haphazardly on the folds of his blankets. A used syringe lay in a nearby wastebasket.

Adam wanted to die trying it all.

"Fucking lunatic," he said again, his voice almost a whisper. He covered his face and leaned forward, stumbling to his feet, turning slowly in a full circle, thinking now of the gun. It was somewhere in the room, and it was the obvious solution. Put the weapon to his own head. There wouldn't be any mistake doing that. Not like he made on the street, or when he walked out on Sherry, or when he gave illegal drugs to patients, or when he poisoned Casey's life, or . . .

Adam tripped. He rested briefly on his knees, then, instead of getting up, crawled forward, past the bed, certain he had left the gun on the bureau. But it wasn't there. He pulled open the top drawer, found it empty, threw it across the room, tried the second, threw it also, tried the third. . . .

He stopped and slid his hands along his back pockets.

There it was; on him the whole time.

He touched the gun, knowing he should use it, only wondering if he deserved such a quick death. That wasn't how he had destroyed everyone else, was it? Those who live by the gun, die by the gun. And those who live by drugs . . .

Adam crawled back on the bed, the gun forgotten, now wishing to hell he could overdose.

It was the only thing left for him to do. He couldn't even drive — just barely managing to find his way back to his own motel, then, in a last effort at thought, making it to his room, carrying his attaché case inside, and locking the door. Entering the room without any intention of again leaving, convinced his mind had at last failed him, and with it any chance of catching Sherry's kidnapper.

Christ; how could Adam finish the chase when he couldn't tell if the people he saw were real or dreams?

It was fitting, at least. For all his talk, he probably didn't have the courage to kill. He was a hack pharmacologist, not a cop. In the end, Waters and he were both cowards; both no good. Well, maybe Waters had escaped, but at least one of them wouldn't.

"Cleaning service," a maid called. Or did she?

"Go away," Adam shouted back. So what if it was a hallucination?

He had started the festivities with a taste of morphine sulfate. It seemed only right, after how he had fucked up the population of Manchester. A normal addict would have laid against a pillow, closed his eyes, and enjoyed the pleasure.

Instead, Adam spread his pills, pretending to be a master chef working in a kitchen overflowing with choice culinary treats. What combination would bring his mind to a new high? How much could he take before his heart failed or his blood became too toxic, dropping him into a coma?

He had stayed with the opiates for half a day before moving to his stimulants. It was like being whipped up the track of a roller coaster. Methylphenidate, pemoline, phenmetrazine, and of course, amphetamine. This brought Adam's first bout of stomach convulsions, and he vomited into the wastebasket. When he survived it meant he had enough life left to taste more pills. He moved on to his favorite, the hallucinogens.

"Hello?"

It was Casey's voice. Adam sat on the edge of his bed, the phone to his ear, not saying a word.

"Is anyone there?" Casey asked.

No one, Adam thought. He simply called to hear her a last time, then hung up.

Sorry, Sherry, he thought. Failed again. Couldn't be a father, couldn't save you, couldn't —

"Christ," Adam groaned, cradling his head, a kick of pain numbing his thoughts. This had to be death. The hurt was too awful. He fell on the floor, curled in a tight ball, the room flashing in a strobe of colors. He covered his eyes and tried to free his soul from his body. When a minute passed, and the pain began subsiding, he dared to uncover his eyes. He found the room pulsing, as if it all survived on his heart beat. Everything was liquid, from the table to the bed to the walls. And he was still alive.

"Why can't I die?" he cried, his tears making the world more fluid. Maybe this was his punishment: to become the ultimate junkie—able to live entirely on drugs; a man who could never overdose, because his body knew no limits. If so, it would be hell, and Adam deserved no less. He had abandoned everybody, including the children of Birchmere. . . . How quickly he had forgotten them, and after a week of standing guard. Now there was no one to protect the town. It would just be Waters, Birchmere, the children. . . .

"Amanda."

He crawled back on the bed. The loose pills pressed into his back, holding onto him like ticks.

"Amanda."

He was again repeating himself, but this time he talked more softly, more gently. Instead of himself, he was thinking of a vision—a young girl, as vulnerable as his own daughter. And every time he said her name, it was like tapping the brakes to a car. It slowed Adam down, calmed him, made him think of the little girl that seemed so like Sherry. He said it again and again, until she was his sole obsession. Then, after she consumed his heart, the only thing that mattered was seeing her one more time.

"Amanda"—his voice becoming firm—"Amanda . . ."

And he resolved to do it.

He would see Amanda just to let her know how special she was, and that he loved her, and that she had to be careful, because there were people out there who could hurt her.

He would go, just to tell her all the things he should have told Sherry. . . .

Yes, he thought. Absolutely.

But it was another hour before he found the strength and stomach to leave the bed; then, he took the time to clean after himself. He wanted to erase any traces of his existence. If all went well, he would see the girl, then his next stop would be a forgotten side road where he would park and fire one shot with his gun; this one through his own head. He didn't want the maid discovering a roomful of drugs and phoning the police about some notorious drug dealer; better the police found the drugs with Adam, out of anyone's reach.

He brushed the pills into the attaché case and had the good sense to take the syringe out of the wastebasket, wrap it in toilet paper, and throw it in the hall trash chute. With his pills collected and his bag stuffed with clothes, Adam left the motel room. He showed the courtesy of stopping at the main office to pay his remaining bill and return the room key, but Adam made an odd discovery. He had presumed the time was about noon. Now he realized it was eleven at night and the office was closed. He had lost all sense of time. A moment ago, it had been morning, and the maid had asked to clean his room; now, the day had disappeared, and it was almost midnight.

Adam pushed the key through a mail slot, along with enough cash to pay his bill. It left him with just pocket change, but that hardly mattered. There was still enough gas in the car to reach town and then he'd only need another gallon or two. He sat in the front seat, gripping the steering wheel and . . .

And, shit, everything lost hold. The wheel, the road . . . It only lasted a moment, but for that short time, the world was again water and Adam could barely hold his stomach. If he had been driving . . . If he'd been on the road . . .

Control, he thought. Take control.

He waited until the world settled and turned onto the highway.

He never considered that the hour was too late for visiting a family he barely knew, let alone a small girl. He was having a hard enough time just finding Birchmere. When he recognized the right road, however, it took no time at all identifying the home; the familiar line of ranch houses all had their lights on.

There was also a police car in the Ballinger driveway.

Adam drove past the house and parked in the nearby woods. He walked back, following the far side of the road so that he would be lost to the darkness. When he reached the driveway, he walked on to the front yard, stopping when he had a view into the kitchen.

There was Amanda's mother, seated by the same table where she had talked with Adam. Now she was there while a neighbor played host, offering coffee, doing her best to calm the mother's nerves and relieve the tired terror in her face. Opposite them, a policeman took notes, while another officer held a family photograph. Yet a third officer was on the telephone and thumbing through a phone book.

All the time Amanda's mother talked, she held tightly onto her youngest son. The boy sat on her left leg, puzzled by the attention of the crowd. The woman's right leg was also extended, used to the presence of her daughter. Tonight, it was bare.

Adam managed to duck back into the shadows as one of the neighbors appeared at the front door. The neighbor called out, thinking he had seen someone, thinking perhaps Amanda had found her way back home.

But Amanda was gone, and so was Adam.

Chapter 19

"You can always come back here," Murray had told him. "You got a business here."

The thought came from nowhere, just like a dozen others. Adam couldn't have seen more of his life rushing before him if he had been dying. He blamed the memories on his drugs. At the same time, the memories kept him alert.

"I love you, sweetheart." When was the last time he had said that to Sherry? He'd tell her soon. He'd find Amanda, and he'd find Sherry. He'd find them because he was the only one who could. He understood the kidnapper—probably always had. How else could he know the kidnapper had gone to Birchmere? Why else had he been drawn to Amanda? When you look in a mirror, you always see your reflection. Well, he would look again. And this time, when he found it . . .

He leaned back in the car seat, disoriented. The engine was off and the overhead light was on, but for a moment, it was as if the world was utterly dark. Blacking out? Now?

Adam rubbed his eyes and used the light to stare at an open map.

Amanda had been kidnapped; Adam knew that, without talking to her mother or the police. Adam was seeing his own tragedy relived, but there was an important difference—this time, he was prepared. He had even suspected Amanda would be the victim. Perhaps that was why he had seen so much of Sherry in the girl. For a change, Adam's judgment hadn't failed; he had correctly spotted the danger and done his best to prepare for the inevitable attack. At least he had until the wasted day in the motel.

But there was no time for guilt; he only had to make certain his body could last. To help, he had an amphetamine ready. He also had a nitro capsule in his shirt pocket, in the event his heart collapsed from the self-abuse.

Back to the highway, Adam thought, remembering the kidnapper's earlier path. A northern route. And here, in the mountains, there weren't many side roads Waters could travel.

"Forget the highway," Adam imagined Casey saying, as always, the voice of reason. "Find a phone and call the police." She sounded so real, he feared the hallucinations were returning.

But there was no point to calling the police. After hovering near the school yard, spying on the children, and then suddenly disappearing, Adam would be a key suspect, presuming the police were at the point of having suspects. They probably still thought Amanda was at a friend's house or hiding from home.

Of course, once he did convince the police to chase Waters—*if* he convinced them—there would be plenty of clues to follow. Waters had a rented car, which meant he had a driver's license and a credit card. Upon returning home, they could nab him at his house or office.

But that would be too late for the girls. Besides,

after the kidnapping spree Waters had enjoyed, Adam doubted Waters ever intended to return anywhere.

The police were of no use. Yet Adam wasn't sure he could do better.

Such a goddamn big state. Still, not that many turn-offs. And he had a good idea of Waters' direction. Adam could follow the main highway, checking the exits and the nearby motels.

"Just do it," he told himself. "Stop being so fucking afraid."

But first, he stopped at an all-night gas station, buying gas with a credit card and using his change to call Waters' hotel.

"Is Mr. Waters in his room?" Adam asked.

"He's checked out," the clerk answered.

"Did he leave a forwarding address?"

"No, sir; he didn't."

Adam hung up, satisfied Waters had indeed left town. The next thing to do was phone the major car rentals. Since Adam knew the make of the car, as well as the license number, he had no trouble passing himself off as Waters and pretending there was confusion on the rental terms. He asked the operator for details on the contract and learned Waters planned to drop the car off in Burlington, Vermont. With this information, Adam returned to his map. Of course, there was no guarantee Waters ever planned to return the car, but Burlington was only slightly off the path Adam had already mentally sketched. He marked the map with a pen, drove back on the road, and headed northwest on Route 89.

Having a direction didn't make finding Waters much easier — Adam would have to stop at every exit, search the local motels, then continue on his route. Nonetheless, he began his mission with a kind of tireless dedication that he hadn't experienced since his first few days searching for Sherry. Of course earlier he had supported himself with drugs—not just to keep awake, but for his sanity. Now Adam was past narcotics. While he had the amphetamine ready, he knew that another dose of anything stood a good chance of killing him. This time, he would have to swim or drown on his own adrenaline.

But Adam swore that he wouldn't let Waters escape. And if only he could succeed on a promise, then the chase would already be finished. But the longer Adam traveled, the less promising his search seemed. His one companion on the trip—a distant Portland radio station—became lost to static at three in the morning. Worse, his car was again running low, and since leaving the main highway, he hadn't seen an open station. This meant he had to be more selective when choosing exits to search for motels, and every time he decided to pass an exit, he wondered if this was the one mistake which would let Waters get away.

By five in the morning, he had purposely passed a number of small towns, and his doubts became more serious. When he entered the town of Webster, he was truly sensing failure. Four roads converged on the town, including two alternate routes to Burlington. Along with the difficulty in choosing the right route, Webster was deceptively large. During the winter, it transformed into a ski resort; consequently, Adam not only had his usual road motels, but dozens of hotels and lodges tucked inside the mountain valley.

Adam stopped the car. He had reached the town's center and faced a rotary that circled about a World War One mortar cannon. Near him was a grocery store and a pharmacy, both closed, just like a dozen other stores. In different circumstances, he would have stared at the pharmacy and wondered what supplies he could steal from its shelves.

Now there was a more critical problem. Adam didn't know which way to drive. The car idled for fifteen minutes, Adam not bothering to pull off the road. He wondered what the hell to do, feeling the street again turning liquid, terrified for his girls. Sherry, Amanda . . . Which way did you go? Left? Right? Straight?

Then, suddenly, Adam wasn't alone.

He was so absorbed in thought, trying to beat the odds on a long-shot guess, that he missed the approaching patrol car. It was a town deputy, and he pulled alongside Adam, rolled down a side window, and flashed a light on Adam's face.

"Need help?" the deputy asked.

"Looking for a place to sleep," Adam answered, squinting against the light.

"No place open this early," the deputy said. "Might try Sleepy Hollow. They open by six."

"Maybe I'll just drive to Burlington," Adam said.

"The Hollow's just a half mile south. Might even be someone awake."

"Thanks, but I'll go to Burlington," Adam said.

"Just don't want any accidents," the deputy said. "I'd sure feel better if you pulled off the road."

When the deputy refused to leave, Adam understood he was being politely ordered off the road, and he followed the deputy's instructions to the motel. It was worth a check, anyway. The motel was built for the skiing season and was large. This meant that during the off season anyone staying in the motel might have a room without coming close to a prying neighbor. If Waters was looking for a safe place to stop, this would be perfect.

Still, Adam was surprised when he found the car.

He was also unprepared. Despite his exhaustive search, he hadn't considered what to do when the search ended. Take the gun into the room and fire, he

254

supposed. But the simplicity of the idea was defeated by its lack of design and Adam's fear. A long minute passed before Adam realized his headlights were not only focused on Waters' car, but shining on the window of what Adam presumed to be his motel room.

Adam turned off his lights and cut the engine. If the street had appeared fluid a moment earlier, now the whole world wavered. Adam sat in the car, struggling to win control over himself, finally giving up and taking the extra amphetamine. "Fuckers," he muttered, making sure the gun was in his pocket. He closed the case and left his car.

In another ten minutes, the faint spray of orange light would silhouette the eastern mountains. But at the moment, the sky was pitch black, and the sole light came from security lamps that hung along the walkway. Adam walked quietly to the motel bedroom and tried looking through the front window, only the curtain was drawn. He could see little, even though he could hear the whisper of a television set. A light against the curtain flickered in vague synchronization with the noise, and Adam guessed that the television was the only light in the bedroom.

Adam left the window and walked far enough away to think without fear of being caught.

He still needed a plan. Should he knock on the door? Maybe try firing through the window? He could always try the police, but now that he had found Waters, he didn't want to leave the motel; not for a minute. Another possibility was to wait him out. But that seemed to give Waters too much power, and besides, what was he doing to Amanda?

He decided to check the back of the motel.

The rear of the motel faced a swimming pool and deck. Each room had its own back door and small, fogged window for the bathroom. Room numbers were posted on all the doors, and when Adam located the right room, he tested the knob. Not surprisingly, it was locked. He was ready to try the front again when he gave the bathroom window a second look.

It wasn't locked.

Still, it wouldn't open easily. The pane had been sealed shut with paint. If he tried pushing too hard, the noise would warn Waters.

He tried anyway, wedging a key into a corner of the window and pulling at it as if the key were a crowbar. The paint cracked along one edge of the sill.

Adam listened for any movement inside the room. Satisfied, he wedged his key into the opposite side of the window. The paint again cracked, and when Waters still didn't appear, he pocketed the key and jammed his fingers under the window, pushing up.

The window screeched open.

This time Waters came to life, and the bathroom light flicked on. Adam, still outside the motel room, kept absolutely still. He didn't dare duck away or reach for his gun, for fear of having the window slam down. He could only hold his breath, knowing the one thing hiding him from Waters' view was a small cloth curtain. Waters searched the shower, the closet. . . .

Finally, the light flicked off and Waters left the bathroom.

Adam remained motionless.

A mistake, he thought. He was drifting way out of his league. Anyone who kidnapped children was a psychopath.

Shut up and do it, he told himself.

Adam moved one hand down to his pocket for the gun, then did his best to slide silently into the room. It was no easy trick; Adam had little strength, and the drugs and driving had done hell to his concentration. Fortunately, Waters was just as exhausted. Adam saw this after positioning himself by the open door. Waters sat at the foot of the television, stripped to his underwear, his knees pressed to his chin. Next to him was an open bottle of Scotch whiskey and the empty cans of a six-pack. On his lap was a kitchen knife.

Behind him, on the bed, was Amanda.

The girl's feet were tied together and knotted to one end of the bed, her hands tied to a headboard. A single sheet kept her from getting cold. A gag crossed her mouth, and her eyes had the closed, restful look of someone who had died. For a moment, Adam thought Waters had killed her. But finally the bed sheet moved, and Adam realized she was only sleeping.

"Going north," Waters said to himself. He rocked forward, barely able to keep his balance from the liquor. His eyes focused on the television, but they showed the empty gaze of someone whose mind had long ago drifted elsewhere. "Montreal," he said. "North." He almost sang the words. "North. Across the border." He reached behind him and touched one of the girl's feet. "You're gonna like it," he told her. His fingers caressed her skin, and his eyes fixed on her the way he had stared at the television.

Or did they?

Waters blinked, and his eyes bleached white, the pupils disappearing beneath a clean, milky surface. He blinked again, and they changed to the black eyes of an animal. A last time, and they were again human, but he looked different. Waters was no longer in the room. Now, it was Adam and Sherry.

Adam fought the hallucination. He aimed the gun at Waters' head, pulling back the hammer. The hammer clicked into position.

Waters' hand stopped moving. He cocked his head, then turned, seeing Adam for the first time. His complete surprise became terror as he saw the raised gun.

He screamed and covered his face.

Adam pulled the trigger.

The hammer gave another dull click.

A misfire.

Waters sensed a second chance, and he grabbed his kitchen knife and leaped onto the bed. Before Adam could again pull the trigger, Waters had wrapped himself about Amanda, with the knife across her throat.

"Drop the gun," Waters ordered. Amanda, wide awake, looked at Adam. Adam kept the gun raised, uncertain what to do. "What? You think I won't cut her throat?" Adam lowered his gun, but it wasn't good enough. "*Drop* it." Amanda tried screaming, but the gag muffled her voice. The knife pressed against her skin. "Do it *now.*"

Adam obeyed, throwing the gun on the floor and slumping against the bathroom door.

At first, Waters didn't move. He didn't know what to do. If killing a man had been new to Adam, disarming another man was also new to Waters. "Move against the wall and sit on the floor," Waters finally said.

There was no need to repeat the order. They both knew Waters had gained complete control of the situation. Adam obeyed, and Waters used his knife to cut the rope that tied Amanda's wrists.

"Don't you dare move," Waters warned Adam, but the warning could have been for Amanda as well, because they both obeyed it. When her hands were free, Waters pulled her to the bottom of the bed, freed her feet, then dragged her to the floor. With his eyes fixed on Adam, he reached forward and took the gun.

"Okay," Waters said. His voice relaxed, but his eyes kept their intensity. He examined the gun. "What's the matter? Didn't it work right?"

Adam didn't answer. Waters slid his hand against a

wall switch and turned on an overhead light. All three of them winced.

"You're the guy in the hotel," Waters said. He sat on the edge of the bed, Amanda at his feet, the gun pointed at Adam.

Adam wasn't sure how to answer. Waters talked as if someone had invaded his privacy. "You kidnapped my daughter."

Waters seemed to look embarrassed. He glanced down at Amanda, all too aware that the girl was naked and he was in his underwear. To calm his nerves, he grabbed for the Scotch. "She's yours?" Waters asked.

"Sherry Druit's my daughter," Adam said.

Waters looked more uncomfortable. "Who?"

"I suppose you wouldn't know the name," Adam said. "Why bother with the names."

Waters shook his head. "I still don't know what you're talking about. I told you that at the hotel."

"You're lying."

"You should have left me alone."

"I should have killed you," Adam said.

The remark pushed Waters, and he pulled the trigger. This time, the gun worked perfectly. The hammer fell, the gunpowder exploded. The bullet grazed Adam's neck, and Adam fell back with the punch. Amanda screamed and tried running for the door, but Waters threw her back against the bed. He warned her to shut up, then turned his attention on Adam. Adam thought briefly of playing dead, but Waters kicked him and threatened to fire again if he didn't sit up. Adam obeyed, the blood flowing freely from his wound.

Waters turned off the television and positioned himself by the front window. The sun was rising, and a porch light had turned on at the main office. Another fifteen minutes and it would be impossible to sneak out of the room.

He looked back at Adam and found him smiling.

"What? You think this is funny?"

Adam started laughing. He laughed at his own failure and bad luck. Still, he caught himself, worried that the girl would also give up. Christ, Adam was pitiful. Here they were, on the verge of death, and he worried about being the wrong influence. No matter what he had been in the past, he was determined to die a father.

Waters studied Adam with a new intensity. Adam did the same to Waters. The drugs and the closeness to death had made him more sure of himself . . . more at ease with the certainty of losing; more relaxed, as if his life finally made sense.

Waters, unnerved, finally broke the silence. He shook off Adam's trance and again looked out the window. "That your car?"

Adam didn't answer; the question was too obvious. Instead, he remembered his wound. He pressed his shirt sleeve against the hole in his neck.

Waters accepted the silence as agreement. "Okay, we're going to take your car," Waters said. "I won't shoot you again if you behave. Nothing's going to happen."

Adam looked at Waters as if he was the world's greatest fool.

"You better listen to me," Waters warned.

Adam again laughed. "Yeah? Or what?" He couldn't help himself. Waters was a joke, acting as if Adam didn't know that, sooner or later, Waters would kill him. But there was no advantage in again getting Waters angry. "Don't worry," Adam said, calming. "You got the girl, right? I can't do a thing with the girl here."

"Yeah," Waters agreed. "You wouldn't want her killed."

Adam looked at Amanda. "Let her dress," he said.

Waters didn't know how to react. He sneered as if Adam had made the most obvious suggestion in the world, then gave Amanda the dress Adam had seen in the hotel and told her to change.

Amanda took the dress, but refused to drop the bed sheet until Adam and Waters turned their heads.

"Dress, honey," Waters said.

Amanda, sobbing, dropped the sheet and began dressing. For a moment, Waters forgot the situation and approached the girl. "You look pretty, child," Waters whispered.

When Amanda finished dressing, he grabbed her wrist and ordered Adam to the door.

"We're going straight to your car," Waters said. "You get in the driver's seat, and we'll sit in the back."

Waters opened the door. Adam pressed a hand against his neck and left the motel room. He looked back, hoping Waters would follow him. Adam imagined that somewhere between the motel room and the car, he would get a chance to knock the gun from Waters' hand. Waters, however, waited at the door, Amanda against his chest and his free hand cradling the gun and the bottle of Scotch. When Adam looked back, Waters motioned him to bring the car to the door.

If only it had been an hour later; the front office would be open, and there would have been a real chance for someone to see them leaving the motel. Adam looked at the office's direction and could see a light, but there was no one in sight. He walked especially slowly, just to give someone time to see him.

He sat in the front seat and opened his overnight bag. Inside was a spare shirt. He tied the shirt about his neck to bandage his wound. Then he looked into his attaché case for a painkiller. He looked up only to

261

check on Waters, hoping Waters wasn't catching on to the stall. But Waters was more than impatient; he suspected a double cross and was dragging Amanda back into the motel room. Adam stopped stretching the time and turned the ignition. After roaring the engine—his one last effort for attention—he drove to the motel room and idled, waiting for Waters to appear. When Waters felt it was safe, he walked the girl quickly into the car, the two of them sliding together onto the backseat. Adam didn't have a chance of pulling away and leaving Waters at the motel.

Waters closed the side door quietly. "Keep looking forward," Waters said, watching Adam with the rearview. Waters was furious. He grabbed the shirt Adam had wrapped around his throat and twisted it. The knot choked Adam, and the pain from the wound was overwhelming. He raised his hands, clawing at the shirt, but Waters held tight.

"Listen to me," Waters said. "I know what you tried pulling. You do it again, and you're dead. Make any sudden turns, and you're dead. Hit the accelerator, or slam the brakes, and you're dead. You do what I say and drive like your ass and hers depend on it. Okay?"

When Waters released him and told him to drive, he couldn't manage it. Waters tapped the back of Adam's head with the bottle of Scotch. "This will kill the pain," Waters said.

Adam obeyed, taking a small sip, then returning the bottle. "Now get going," Waters said. Adam shifted and drove out of the parking lot. "Make a right through town, then head north."

Adam drove as he had been ordered, trying hard to be the perfect chauffeur. Waters sensed his triumph and relaxed enough to take another swallow of Scotch. He slouched forward, dropping the bottle on the front seat.

"So you got your own daughter, do you?" Waters asked. "What's she like? Pretty?"

Adam glanced in the mirror, praying to catch sight of the deputy.

"I asked is she pretty?" Waters insisted.

"You should know," Adam said.

Waters tapped the gun butt against Adam's head. "Stop saying that," said Waters. "You're like a broken record, you know that? So tell me about her."

Adam hesitated, then said, "She's pretty." Waters grinned, leaning back in his seat, staring at his own prize. Amanda had curled against the far door.

"What's she like?" Waters asked.

Adam looked again in the mirror, and then to his sides. They went over a bump on the road, and his attaché case bounced against the bottle of Scotch.

"She would be seven," Adam said. "Beautiful brown hair. Her mother's eyes." He dropped his right hand off the steering wheel and rested it on his lap. Waters didn't move or care, his thoughts on the girl. "I didn't see her much over the last year."

"Sweet girl, huh?" Waters asked.

"That's right," Adam said. He slid his hand over the open attaché case, feeling for his last vial of sufentanil. He found the tip of it, but the vial was buried under the loose pills. There was no way of taking the vial without making noise.

"I like sweet things, too," Waters said.

Adam saw a small pothole on the road, and he guided the car over it. The car heaved up and down.

"Hey," Waters said. "Watch your driving." But it wasn't a serious complaint.

Adam had the vial in his hand. He slipped off the plastic cap with his thumb, then used his forefinger to grab the neck of the Scotch bottle. In one motion, he poured the medicine into the bottle.

"So what's she *like,*" Waters insisted. "What's she *really* like."

Adam studied him in the rearview mirror. For an answer, he lifted the Scotch bottle and offered it back to Waters.

"You first," Waters said graciously. "Might as well enjoy it. It's gonna be your last."

"I'm not thirsty," Adam said.

It wasn't the answer Waters wanted, and he again choked Adam. Adam struggled to keep the car on the road.

"Don't fucking lord over me," Waters said. "I've seen you looking at her."

He let go of the shirt and forced the bottle on Adam. Adam held the bottle, lifted it to his lips, and pretended to drink. The act didn't fool Waters, and Waters used one hand to hold Adam's nose and the other to force the liquor into him. The liquor poured over Adam's shirt and down his throat.

Waters fell back in the seat, satisfied. "There," Waters said. "Makes you feel like a man, doesn't it? Makes you want to do things."

Now it was Waters' turn to drink, and he did so. On one try, he swallowed almost a quarter of the bottle.

"How about you, honey? Old enough to drink?"

Amanda didn't answer. Waters offered her the bottle.

"She's too young," Adam said.

"And what are you, her escort?" Waters asked him. He laughed, suddenly feeling better than he had in ages. Adam knew the feeling; had seen it before and was almost feeling it himself. Except Adam knew the next stage—the pain in the chest, and then the suffocation. "How'd you find me anyway?"

Adam glanced in the mirror.

"I asked a question," Waters said.

"I've been on you from the start," Adam said.

"From the start of what?" Waters said. "You're crazy, that's what you are. I bet if this girl wasn't in the car, you'd run us off a cliff."

"Maybe," Adam said.

"You're a crazy, dead son-of-a-bitch."

"You and me both."

"You and me nothing," Waters said. "I'm not like you."

Adam didn't answer.

"You hear me?" Waters said.

"I heard you but I know better," Adam said.

Then he felt the first pains. Waters saw him wince and thought this was another trick. He reached for Adam's bandage, but Adam swerved the car into the gutter, throwing Waters against the side door.

"What the fuck are you doing?" Waters shouted. "Drive *straight* or I'll kill her."

"I'm trying," Adam managed to say, but the pain was too much. Waters shouted as the car again skipped off the road. He lifted the gun, ready to keep his promise, but suddenly the gun wasn't so important. Something else mattered; a terrible pain, twisting through his chest. He breathed quickly, holding onto the seat, tossing side to side as Adam drove completely off the road and scratched against a guard rail.

"What's happening?" Waters cried. "Jesus, what's going on?"

The car crashed into a telephone pole, and Waters cleared the front seat, falling near Adam's feet. Adam looked down at his kidnapper, in too much pain either to take the gun or to feign a fight. They were both dead, anyway. What would be the point of fighting?

"Oh my God," Waters gasped. "Get me a doctor. Get me—" He winced, losing all his air.

Adam opened his side door and fell out of the car.

He looked down the road and could see Amanda running away.

Waters struggled after him, the gun still in his hands, apparently set on revenge. Adam crawled farther away, wanting only to die in peace or at least keep Waters occupied until someone made sure the girl was safe from the bullets. Death, Adam knew, was certain. The one drug that could cure him was in the attaché case, and Waters was lying on top of it, using the edge of the front seat as a rest for the gun. Waters fired a useless shot, then jackknifed out of the car.

"You bastard," Waters moaned.

Adam pulled himself off the road and onto a sidewalk. He looked up and saw the base of a cannon. To his left was the town center, with its closed shops and restaurants.

Adam struggled to stand straight, then leaned in the direction of the pharmacy. His weight carried him across the street.

"Bastard," Waters shouted a last time, firing and striking Adam in the back. The force of the bullet carried Adam the last remaining feet, and he smashed through the pharmacy's shop window.

A burglar alarm rang and Adam rested, too dazed for motion, the paralysis setting in. Soon he would stop breathing.

With a final effort, he slid across the floor and broken glass to the back counter. Above his head was the sign PRESCRIPTIONS. He pulled himself on top of a stool and collapsed across the counter. His blood smeared the clean surface, and the professional in him sank into another hallucination. He dreamed he was in his old pharmacy in Calverton. There was Murray, at the front, making sure the kids didn't steal too many magazines. And here he was in the back, working on a special order. A rush job. Intravenous dosage of cyclobenzaprine hydrochloride. Or chlorzoxazone. Any curariform drug to relax the muscle spasms. But where was it? Someone had moved the bottles. He stared at the aisles, tilting his head to the side, trying to make sense of the pharmacist's shop. He leaned away from the counter and fell to the floor.

There was the bottle. All the way on the top. A hundred miles away.

Then the bottle disappeared behind the massive shape of the deputy.

"I'm a pharmacologist," Adam told the man, looking in the direction of the bottle. "I've been poisoned. I need medication. Naloxone." The deputy followed his eyes and took the bottle off the shelf. "Injection," Adam managed.

"What?" the deputy asked. "Stick you with a needle?"

Adam didn't answer. He was unconscious.

Chapter 20

Casey sat in the hospital waiting room, her hands on a folded newspaper. It was a Burlington paper, and it featured yet another article on Adam's rescue of Amanda Ballinger. A sidebar focused on Sherry's disappearance and the long, crazy path Adam had followed, all the time convinced that he was only a step away from finding his daughter. It ended with a picture of Sherry, asking readers if they could identify her.

The paper was a morning edition and had been published hours after the police had discovered Sherry's body.

Sherry was dead. She had been found in a patch of woods ten miles from the gas station where she had disappeared.

Ten miles southwest of the station — opposite to the direction Adam had traveled.

Casey heard the news at five in the morning. A police sergeant had called while she was at a motel near Adam's hospital. No more than a sentence was passed between them, and then Casey dropped the phone, unable to speak. Phillip finished the phone call. Among the facts was that it didn't appear

Sherry had been molested, nor were there any bruises on her body, aside from a mark at the back of the head. While an autopsy still had to be performed, the police suspected Sherry's killer had struck her once on the back of the skull. "It would have been quick and painless," the sergeant said.

Phillip listened, one moment thinking of Sherry, the next of that bastard Waters. Then he thought of Adam, still lying in his hospital bed. The irony was horrible. "Any clues about who did it?" he managed to ask.

"It's too early to say," the sergeant answered, beginning a three-minute speech about what the police had already done and planned to do. The sergeant obviously felt more comfortable talking about the investigation than the condition of the girl's body. That was all right; so did Phillip.

Back in the hotel, Casey dressed in black. Phillip had tried convincing her not to visit the hospital—at least not that day—but Casey insisted. Adam had gone through hell. By all rights, he should be dead, except the deputy had somehow managed to follow Adam's instructions. As for the dosage, the officer took no chances, simply filling the syringe and choosing a vein.

When the sheriff found out what the deputy had done, he suspended the man and waited for a lawsuit. But the drug, along with the deputy's mouth-to-mouth resuscitation, saved Adam's life. In the end, the deputy would get his job back, along with a special commendation. As for Adam, he was given a private room at the hospital, where he had now spent ten days recuperating, the first three in a comatose sleep.

The newspapers followed his recovery. What they

didn't report was the narcotics found in Adam's blood and urine. The doctors kept this detail to themselves. They had, however, told Casey that many of the drugs found in Adam's car had in fact been used by Adam. "What a surprise," she answered bitterly. She just didn't know why the drugs hadn't killed him.

So Casey visited him, because she did love him, and he needed her care. Foremost, Adam needed to be pulled out of his own drama. Sherry was dead. If there had ever been a chance of rescuing her, it was gone. Now, it was time to bury their daughter, along with the torment.

Casey and Phillip followed a nurse to the corner room—the best in the hospital, the doctors had told her—where they found Adam resting in bed, his head deep in a soft pillow and an arm extended for an IV. Casey went to his side and touched his forehead. Phillip stood by the door, watching.

"Do you feel like talking?" Casey asked Adam.

Adam had the blanket pulled to his chin, as if fighting a terrible chill.

"It's all right," Casey told him.

Adam looked at Casey, but she couldn't tell whether he recognized her. Adam wasn't just recovering from gunshot wounds; his body was coming clean, hopefully for good. Casey remembered how painful the transformation had been after her addiction. She could only begin to comprehend what Adam was feeling, or the delusions that played in his imagination.

"He'll be okay," Phillip felt obliged to say.

Casey reached forward to run her fingers gently through Adam's hair, but Adam jerked away. Casey settled back in her chair, leaving him alone.

"Calm down," Casey whispered to Adam.

At first, her words seemed to relax him, but he was only reacting to the pain of his healing wounds. He took a deep breath, let his fingers slip off the blanket, and pushed his head deeper into the pillow.

Casey sat still, quietly watching him until Phillip touched her shoulder.

"We should let him sleep," Phillip suggested.

Casey stared at Adam a moment longer, then agreed. She touched Adam's arm and bent forward, kissing his cheek. When Casey's hair brushed his face, his fingers lifted so they could stray through it.

"He didn't do it."

Casey stopped moving, not certain what Adam had said. Phillip heard him, too, and moved closer to the bed.

Adam's eyes were closed. Casey couldn't tell if Adam knew what he had said or to whom he talked.

"I don't think he was the one who kidnapped Sherry," Adam said.

Phillip leaned over Casey and whispered, "He's talking about Waters."

Casey kissed Adam's hand.

"I've thought about it," Adam mumbled. "At the time, I thought he was lying, but he didn't know her. Didn't know her name, what she looked like."

He winced, again grabbed by pain, and when he opened his eyes, they were raw from tears. Still, he seemed to recognize Casey.

"I think I was the one who kidnapped Sherry."

"You wouldn't do that."

"Who knows what the hell I'd do?"

"You wouldn't *do* that," she insisted. "You loved her too much."

Adam shook his head — sweating, delirious. "Lis-

271

ten to you. Do you know what that means? Do you know what it means to love someone too much?"

Casey didn't want to hear, but Adam grabbed her wrist.

"You know who else loved 'too much'?"

Adam struggled to free his thought.

"Waters," he finally said.

"That's not true," Casey said.

Adam shook his head, unable or unwilling to hear her. "That's why I could find him," he said. "Sherry, Amanda . . . I knew what he would do, where he'd go."

"You never hurt Sherry, Adam," Casey said. "The drugs only confused you. I know you. I know her."

Adam stopped talking, and Casey thought he had fainted; but when she moved, his eyes again opened.

"Sherry," he said to no one. "Christ, what happened to her?"

Chapter 21

She was buried five days later. A week afterward, Adam visited the grave.

He went there alone. Casey offered to accompany him, but he had his own peace. He stood before the grave, dressed in the same business suit he had worn to purchase his gun. In his hand was a gift for his daughter: a small hand mirror, similar to the one she had kept in her purse. But this was for an older girl. A teenage one, on the verge of womanhood.

He put it beside a wreath of flowers.

He sat on the grass and talked for an hour. There was a lot for Adam to explain; a lot of love to give that he hadn't shown when Sherry lived. He tried making up for it now, knowing he couldn't, but hoping Sherry at the very least felt his love and mourning.

Then he kissed the ground and left. Phillip had invited him back to their house after his visit to the cemetery. At the time, Adam had accepted, but he had never intended to return. Adam had seen himself in the mirror. The only color in his face came from the veins which bulged across his scalp. Otherwise, he looked, and felt, like death.

The doctors said he'd feel better with a good diet and exercise. Adam couldn't imagine it. At least there would be no more work at the pharmacy. Despite his unwanted fame, Adam's pharmacist's license had been permanently revoked, and the liability insurer had been stuck with a quarter million out-of-court payment. Things might have been different if Adam had testified, but now it made no difference.

No; whatever Adam's past, it had nothing to do with his future. There was just a question of tying up a few loose ends in Calverton and then taking to the road. He drove back to the turnpike and followed the same route Sherry and Casey had taken the weekend of her disappearance. He made only one detour—to see the woods where Sherry's body had been found. He stared at the area from the road, seeing nothing unusual. But now, it was a kind of shrine to his daughter. A place that brought a special horrible intimacy.

God, how he hoped the grass and the trees had been gentle with her.

By midafternoon, he was at Murray's store.

The neighborhood hadn't changed, or if it had, not for the better. The street was noisy, and the rush hour traffic was just beginning to build with the usual rush of commuters. Adam did notice one thing: Murray still had Sherry's picture at the front window. Beneath the poster was a potted plant, along with a news clip of her death.

Adam walked in the store.

Murray was ringing the cash register, busy with customers during the peak of afternoon business. He glanced at the open front door and saw Adam.

"Oh my God . . ."

Murray left his post to clasp Adam's hands. Adam smiled.

"Better finish your business," Adam said.

"Get yourself a beer," Murray said. "It's in the back, where you used to store some of those prescriptions."

Murray returned to the cash register and rushed through his customers. Adam, meanwhile, went back to his old post behind the prescription counter. Most of the drugs were gone; put in storage, until the pharmacy could again be opened for business. Now there wasn't a chance of Adam's opening the shop. He went to the refrigerator, chose a soft drink over a beer, and sat on his old stool. He stared out the side window, remembering the lunch hours he had spent experimenting with his supply, relaxed in drug heaven. Perhaps it was the aftereffects of his last experience with narcotics, or maybe he truly was changing; either way, the thought of experimenting with anything—even the thought of taking an aspirin—was nauseating.

"How are you doing?" Murray called back.

Adam returned to the cash register so Murray could keep an eye on the customers, but the store had been emptied. At the height of the business hour, Murray had closed shop.

"You should have a kid helping you out," Adam said.

"I do all right," Murray answered. "How about you?"

"I'm all right," Adam said.

Murray knew otherwise. It wasn't just the news stories or Sherry's death; he could see for himself.

275

Still, he didn't say anything—just nodding his head and grabbing Adam by the shoulders.

"You're looking great," Murray said.

"Thanks for putting her picture by the window."

"I wish it had helped," Murray said. He showed a look of terrible defeat. It expressed Adam's feelings better than he could do it himself.

"I can't practice anymore. I guess you heard that," Adam said.

"I heard something," Murray said. "Who cares? You didn't want to stay buried in that garbage anyway, did you?"

"No," Adam said. "I don't think so."

Murray studied him. "You thought about what to do?"

"I've been thinking," Adam said.

"And?"

"I've got some ideas."

"You could stay here, you know. This place isn't that bad. You got a future here."

Adam looked at Murray as if they both knew better.

"Okay," Murray said. "Maybe you don't want to be stuck behind a cash register with me. But in Calverton, a guy like you—"

"I've got plans," Adam said.

"Plans?" Murray said. "What plans?"

Instead of answering, Adam shook Murray's hand and walked to the front door. Murray didn't know what to make of the situation.

"Where are you going?"

"I'll be in touch," Adam said, not even close to meaning it.

Murray stared at him, incredulous. "What's your

hurry?" he shouted. "Christ, Adam; you got a *home* here. Doesn't that mean anything?"

But Adam left the store. He took a deep breath, then headed around the corner to Yu Ling's shop. It was the last stop he had to make before leaving Calverton.

Yu Ling was in the same position Adam had last seen him—at the rear of his fruit and vegetable market, sitting on a crate, enjoying one of his specially mixed herbal teas. The store also looked the same, with one exception: a teenager was near the cash register, labeling heads of lettuce and giving Adam the cold, suspicious look the boy reserved for strangers.

"Hello, Yu Ling," Adam said. Yu Ling looked up slowly, his age weighing heavily upon him. A moment passed before he recognized Adam, but when he did, a smile came to his face. He tried talking to Adam, and as usual, Adam had no idea what Yu Ling said. But there was something wrong with the way Yu Ling talked. His speech slurred, and Adam doubted that even if he understood Chinese, he could understand what Yu Ling said.

Then the whole picture came to view. Adam had spent so much time suffering under his own misery, he had lost the ability to see it in other people. He saw the deepening wrinkles in Yu Ling's face, the yellowing skin, his bloodshot eyes, the caked dirt that infected his thinning hair. Yu Ling's eyes were especially revealing. They had always been filled with insight and interest; now his eyes were wet and soft, as if they had lost all substance. Adam had seen the same look when he had worked in the hospital. It came from the use of antipsychotic and antianxiety drugs. Prazepam, Adam guessed. Sixty milligrams a day. Physical dependence in a matter of weeks. Prolonged misuse, and you'd see fatigue, dizziness, confusion.

He looked to the side and saw the bottle of pills, just to the side of Yu Ling's teacup.

Yu Ling nodded genially while Adam examined the bottle for a prescription label. There was none. It was a small container, without any instructions or identifying label. Adam recognized the drug by studying one of the tablets. Meprobamate — similar to prazepam.

"Who gave you this?" Adam asked.

Yu Ling didn't attempt an answer. Instead, he patted Adam's hand, then firmly took the bottle back into his possession. Once he had his pills, he sank back on the fruit crate and closed his eyes.

Adam returned to the front of the store.

"Where's Michael?" Adam asked the new boy.

The boy studied Adam, not at all certain Adam was worth answering. At the same time, Adam knew Michael's name, so there was a connection to the store.

"Mike comes by now and then," the boy said. "I fill in while he takes care of other business."

"What business is that?" Adam asked.

"You'll have to ask him," the boy said.

Adam glared at the teenager, then left the store to sit on a nearby stoop. He wouldn't leave his post until he found out for certain what he already suspected.

Forty minutes later, Michael arrived.

Adam couldn't miss him. He arrived on a motor-

278

cycle—a roaring, gleaming bike that announced it-self a block before it could be seen. It was about as cheap a thrill as anyone could buy. Michael ran it up the sidewalk and parked against a meter. Over his shoulder was a canvas satchel. Adam guessed it could hold more narcotics than his own attaché case.

"Michael?" Adam shouted.

Michael cut off the engine and faced his mentor. His eyes were hidden behind a pair of mirror sun-glasses, and the rest of him was protected by a creased brown leather jacket and new designer jeans.

"Mr. Druit." Michael smiled back. "Heard about your daughter. That's tough."

Adam stared into the sunglasses, hoping to meet Michael's eyes. "I saw your father." Then he paused, waiting for an explanation, still treating Michael as a grocery clerk.

"Bet you didn't have much to talk about," Michael joked.

"He's on meprobamate, and he doesn't have a pre-scription," Adam said. "Did you give it to him?"

Michael thought a moment, wondering if Adam was worth a lie. "Sure I did."

Adam had expected the answer, but not the cocki-ness.

"How did you get supplied?" Adam asked.

"No problem," Michael said. "Just talked to your boss and got the name of your sales rep. Very friendly man, especially if you pay up front. Didn't ask for a license or anything. But, hey, you already know that."

"You used my name?"

"Just the first call," Michael said. "I thought it might help, but I was wrong. People in the pharmaceutical profession don't seem to think much of you, Mr. Druit. Why is that?"

Adam looked toward Yu Ling and said, "He's addicted, you know. If your father keeps this up, he'll be dead in a month."

"Dad's never been happier," Michael said.

"You're turning him into a junkie."

"You're a fine one to talk about junkies," Michael said. "Keeping your old friend on the hook."

Michael meant Ben. "How is he?" Adam asked.

"How do you think? When you left he was a brickhead. You think he kept to his daily dosage? You really think you could treat a shit like that as if he was stopping by the pharmacy for a daily medication?"

Adam listened, overwhelmed by all that had happened. "How is he?" he whispered.

"You can't make a charity case out of an addict," Michael said.

"What *happened?*"

"Ben ran out of money," Michael said.

"What does that mean?"

"It means I cut him off."

Adam didn't believe it. "Ben couldn't last a day without something. You're crazy to be telling me this."

"No I'm not." Michael grinned. "What are you going to do, tell the police? I don't care how big a hero you are; you had that asshole doped up before I ever touched him." Michael relaxed. "Who gives a crap anyway. What about you? You sticking around town?"

Adam was uncertain whether to answer, but finally shook his head. Michael grinned again, amused by anything Adam said.

"Actually, I know," Michael admitted. "You're turning into a regular manhunter, huh?" He moved closer. "I got a friend with the police. Said you'd been down there asking questions about your daughter again. Said you were thinking of looking for the guy who did her. Sounds like you're making this thing a regular profession."

Adam grabbed at Michael, but Michael stepped back.

"You're crazy to waste your time," Michael said. "That guy's long gone."

Adam didn't answer. There was no point. Michael was talking *at* him, not *to* him.

"Do something that makes sense," Michael said. "I mean, you couldn't find your daughter the first time. What makes you think you can find the guy who snuffed her? How long's it been. Two months? More?" Michael looked smug. "I took a psych class once. You know what you've got, Mr. Druit? You've got an obsessive personality. First the drugs, then your kid, now this. My dad isn't the only one who could use a tranquilizer."

Adam had had enough. Quietly, he said, "Whatever connections you had . . . Whatever suppliers you were using have just shut down."

"Forget it," Michael said. "I'm one of their best customers."

"Not anymore," Adam said.

Michael shrugged. "All right; so I'll make my own connections. If I were you, I'd worry more about burning my own bridges. You think you can do anything dry?" he said. "You look at yourself in the mirror lately? Bet you can't even find your

281

nose, let alone a kidnapper."

"I'm phoning the police and I'm phoning the hospital about your father."

"Do whatever the hell you want. Makes no difference to anyone. Never did." He turned and walked into the fruit market. Adam could see Michael and the other boy talking and laughing at him. Adam was leaving when Michael pressed his face against the store window.

"Hey!" he shouted, tapping the glass. "Hey, Mr. Druit; maybe you'd like some meprobamate too?"

They were still laughing when Adam returned to his car.

Chapter 22

It was odd being clean.

It was an empty feeling, as if he had been robbed of blood—not enough to kill, but enough to steal his energy. Nor could his mind handle quite as many thoughts as it used to, nor was his imagination as vivid. He felt smaller, weaker, vulnerable. . . .

He felt like a father who had forever lost his daughter.

Adam sat in his car, staring off toward a municipal park, watching a crowd of children run about a playground. He sat there, watching, while his hands rested on a pile of unfolded maps. He had taken them out to read . . . to do his deductions, to start thinking about his plan of action, to help him choose a direction. That had also been the reason for visiting the library. Focus. A chance to get control of his thoughts and make up for lost time.

Except it was so hard to think. . . .

His thoughts drifted back on Michael Ling. Michael had been right. Adam could cut Michael's connections—Adam *would*—but it was Adam who needed them most. Before so much had made sense, and all of the tracking came so easily. Now he went through the books, and stared at the maps, and tried thinking about Sherry's killer, and tried imagining what had gone through the man's head what . . . the killer had felt when he took her life, and where he would have gone, and what he would have done next. . . .

But all Adam could do was sit in the car and stare out the window, watching the children in the playground.

And they were so beautiful.

He wiped his face and started driving again, not stopping until he found a vacant parking lot. Then he slammed the brake hard, slapping the steering wheel with his hands, finally rolling forward, tight in a ball, screaming in the fold of his lap.

Sherry. He had loved her so hard, and then he had lost direction. He had let his emotions confuse and leak. Somewhere, sometime, he had made a mistake by mixing his worlds—one world, deep in the human soul, which spent its time calculating, imagining, haunting, experimenting . . . testing love and hate and sensuality, crossing and cutting until nothing mattered or made sense—and one that lived firmly on the earth . . . the one in which Adam loved and cared. The one where life belonged.

But it also meant so little. Because now that he was ready to love his daughter, there was nothing. Sherry was gone, just as Waters was gone.

Michael was right; it was all gone.

It was over, he thought. It was really over.

The only thing left was him—an obsessive without an obsession.

Adam again began driving, finally pulling onto a side street and parking before a corner store. PHARMACY, read the sign. On the window was an ad for discounted goods. HALF PRICE TOILET PAPER, it said. THIRTY PERCENT OFF PRESCRIPTION GENERICS.

Adam walked inside and found the booth in a rear alcove. He lifted the receiver, dropped in his change, and dialed. Within seconds, Casey answered.

"It's me," Adam said.

"Adam, where are you calling from?"

"I'm not sure. I think Connecticut."

Casey sounded tired; as tired as he. "How are you doing?" she asked.

"Not too good," Adam said.

"You're not high, are you?"

"No," he said. "I'm not high."

There was a moment of quiet, then Casey said, "It's hard." Then, guessing his thoughts, she added, "She loved you very much."

Adam listened. He tried focusing on her voice, on the telephone call, on anything that he could grasp and take hold of.

"Relax," Casey said.

Adam did.

"You're pressing yourself too hard," she said. "It'll all come together, Adam. Just give it time."

"Casey," he said, "this isn't making sense to me. I'm trying to figure out what to do, but it's like—"

"I know what it's like," she said. "I know what it's *all* like."

285

"I've got these road maps and these roads and—"

"You don't know what to do," she repeated.

"I need a direction," he said.

Casey listened. Adam waited. There was an answer; Adam knew she had one. It wasn't about Sherry, either. It was about him. About his own life.

"Do you want to come back to New York?" she asked.

"No."

"Do you want to stay there?"

"No."

"All right," she said. "Then don't. Get in the car and drive south."

"But I—"

"Come to New York and then keep on driving. Or drive north to Maine, or head west. Or head northwest. It doesn't make a difference. Do you understand?" Then, carefully, saying, "Just get yourself in motion."

Adam listened.

"That's what I did," she said. "After you left and I was alone with her and she was getting clean . . . The only thing that mattered was moving. I drove for a week, and every hour spent in the car was an hour spent out of reach from everything. The problems, the drugs, you, Phil . . ."

"But I still want to help her, Casey," Adam said. "I want to—"

"You've got to start with yourself," Casey said. "You're rehabbing. Can't you understand that?"

Adam couldn't answer. He hung up and walked slowly through the aisles, his eye on the selection of drugs, his mind on Sherry. When he was back in his

286

car, he stared at the pharmacy, thinking of New York but also of one last idea.

Maybe, he thought, he didn't have to give up.

Maybe he just needed a little help.

The drugs. They had made it possible to track Waters. They had kept him awake, alive—stimulated his thoughts, pushed him in every possible way.

The drugs had given him an edge, and wasn't that what he lacked now? The intensity. The full force of his mind and body. The killer instinct.

Yes, the drugs could give it all back to him. Especially the last one—the killer instinct . . .

Oh, *Christ,* the killer instinct.

Without another thought, he shifted gears and turned back on the road. He headed south, toward New York, still uncertain whether to see Casey, knowing that it didn't matter. The important thing was driving. Casey had said so. Blending back in the world, merging into the traffic until, like the hundreds of cars up and down the highway, he was again part of the mass that slid slowly and steadily over the horizon. So he did. Moving, steering, controlling . . .

Controlling.

It was a new idea, being in control. Relaxing. For the first time in a year, he started feeling the pain disappear. And as he concentrated harder, it slipped farther away.

Find the rhythm, he thought. Feel your heartbeat. Feel *Sherry's.* Match them. Keep them alive. Keep them going.

He leaned back, resting his head, his eyes locked on the car in front of him.

Yes, his mind whispered—the word itself calm-

287

ing, feeling his body settle into the seat. Find the beat and keep it, deep inside. Live off it.

The thought gripped him.

And finally, somewhere within the traffic, Adam also disappeared.

Dear Reader,

Pinnacle Books welcomes your comments about this book or any other Pinnacle book you have read recently. Please address your comments to:

Pinnacle Books, Dept. WM
475 Park Avenue South
New York, NY 10016

Thank you for your interest.

Sincerely,
The Editorial Department
Pinnacle Books